Warriors of the Code
(The Founders 4)

by

Robert Vaughan

Print Edition
© Copyright 2017 Robert Vaughan (as revised)

Wolfpack Publishing
P.O. Box 620427
Las Vegas, NV 89162

All rights reserved. No part of this book may be reproduced by any means without the prior written consent of the publisher, other than brief quotes for reviews.

ISBN: 978-1-62918-810-2

This book is dedicated to Richard Gallen, modern day warrior of the code. The battles aren't as bloody, but it still pays to have a good man on your side.

Robert Vaughan

Chapter One

THE BOY COULD see him from quite a distance. Heat waves shimmering up from the sun-baked earth gave the rider a surrealistic appearance, bending the light in such a way that sometimes the rider was visible and sometimes he wasn't. The boy wasn't even sure that there really was a rider. If there was, was he human?—or an Angel of the Lord, come to take him to join his mother and father?

The boy was leaning against a broken wagon wheel, and he looked around at the burned wagon, and at the scalped bodies of his mother and father. A few of the arrows the Indians had shot at them were still protruding from their bodies.

There was very little left of the wagon's contents. The Indians had taken all the clothes, household goods, food and water. They hadn't found the little pouch, though. It contained all the money from the sale of their farm in Illinois, and it was to have been the -start of their new life in Oregon. The boy's father had managed to hide it just as the attack began.

The rider reached the wagon and swung down from his horse. He carried a canteen over to the boy. The boy watched him, almost without interest, but when he felt the cool water at his lips, he began to drink, thirstily.

It had been a long time since he had water, not since before the Indians attacked. He couldn't remember now whether that had been today, yesterday, or the day before.

"Whoa, now," the rider said gently, pulling the canteen back. "Take it easy, boy, you mustn't drink it too fast. It'll make you sick."

The rider wet his handkerchief, then began rubbing it lightly on the boy's head.

"You took a pretty good bump on the head," he said. "They must have thought you were dead. You're lucky, they generally prize blond scalps like yours. I guess they thought you were too young."

The water seemed to bring back the boy's awareness, and with it came the realization that both his parents had been brutally killed. Tears began to slide out of his eyes.

"Your folks?" the rider asked gently.

The boy nodded.

"I don't understand it. Most of the Indians around here are friendly right now. This must have been a bunch of renegades."

"There was a white man with them," the boy said, speaking his first words.

"What? A white man? Are you sure?"

The boy thought of the big red-headed man who had cursed when they found no money. He had been the one who stopped the Indians from scalping him—not out of compassion for the boy, but because he was angry and frustrated; and anxious to move on.

"Yes," the boy said. "I'm sure."

"That explains it, then," the man said. "There's nothing worse than a white man who has gone bad and thrown his lot in with the Indians." The man looked over at the bodies of the boy's parents. "You stay here. I'll bury them for you."

"I want to help," the boy said, stirring himself to rise.

The rider smiled at him. "Good for you, lad," he said. "In the years to come it'll be a comfort to you to know that you did what you could for them." He looked toward the wagon and saw the bottom half of a shovel, the handle having been burned away. "You can use that. I've got a small spade on my saddle."

They worked quietly and efficiently for the next several minutes, digging only one grave, but making it large enough for his mother and father. They lowered his parents into the hole, then shoveled the dirt back over them.

"You want me to say a few words over them?" The boy nodded.

The rider walked back to his horse and opened a saddlebag. The boy watched as he took out a small leather-bound book and returned to the gravesite. With his own survival now taken care of, and with the business of burying his parents out of the way, the boy now examined his benefactor closely.

He saw a tall, powerfully built man, clean-shaven, with dark hair. The boy wasn't old enough himself to shave yet, but he knew the trouble it took to shave every morning, and he thought the rider must be a particularly vain man to go to such trouble on a daily basis, especially when on the range like this. The man was also wearing a suit, rather than the tough denim trousers and flannel shirts which were the common uniform of the man on the plains. The boy thought that a little unusual, as well.

"What are their names?" the man asked, interrupting the boy's musing.

"What?"

"If I'm going to say a few words, I need to know their names."

"Oh. My mom's name is Edna. My pa is George. George Ford."

The older man cleared his throat, then began to read:

"I am the resurrection and the life, saith the Lord; he that believeth in me, though he were dead, yet shall he live; and whosoever liveth and believeth in me shall never die.

"Oh God, whose mercies cannot be numbered: Accept our prayers on behalf of thy servants George and Edna Ford, and grant them an entrance into the land of light and joy, in the fellowship of thy saints; through Jesus Christ thy Son our Lord, who liveth and reigneth with thee and the Holy Spirit, one God, now and forever. Amen."

"Amen," the boy said.

The rider closed his book and looked down at the mound of dirt for a long moment, then he looked over at the boy and smiled, and stuck out his hand.

"I'm C.V. Battenburg," he said. "How are you called?"

"Grady. Grady Ford," the boy said, shaking the offered hand.

"Grady Ford . . . that's a fine name for a man," C. V. said. "Well, climb up on back of my horse, Grady Ford. We can ride double."

Grady started toward the horse, then he remembered the hidden pouch of money. It was under a loose board in the front of the wagon, a part which hadn't been damaged by the fire. He started toward it.

"What're you going after?"

Grady looked back toward C. V. The man had saved his life, helped bury his parents, even read prayers over their graves. But a sudden cautiousness made him hesitate to tell C.V. of the money. What if all the help this man had given him had only been a ruse to see if there was anything of value left? He felt almost ashamed of himself for being suspicious, but he thought it would be better to be safe than sorry.

"Some letters," Grady said. "I want to keep them."

"All right."

Grady moved the board to one side and picked up the small leather pouch. He could feel the wad of bills inside. He had overheard his mother and father talking about it, and he knew they had five hundred dollars left over after buying the wagon and supplies.

Grady slipped the pouch down in his waistband, then

walked back over to the horse. C.V. was already mounted, and he offered his hand to help Grady climb up.

Rabbit roasted on a spit while C.V. and Grady drank coffee. Grady hadn't been a coffee drinker before, and it tasted a little bitter to him, but he was determined to acquire a taste for it. C.V. chuckled.

"I take it you aren't much of a coffee drinker."

"I like it just fine," Grady said.

C.V. slurped his own coffee through extended lips and studied Grady over the rim of his cup. "How old are you, Grady?"

"I'm twelve," Grady answered.

"Have you got relatives back in Illinois that you want to go to?"

"No," Grady said. "All my mom's folks live in England. I don't know any of them. I don't even know their names. My pa had a brother, but he was killed in the War."

"Any close friends or neighbors?"

"Pa was feudin' with the neighbors over property lines," Grady said. "It got to be pretty bad. I think that might be one of the reasons we was movin'."

"Were moving," C.V. corrected.

"What?"

"The correct grammar is *'were* moving,' not *'was* moving.' Since it takes no more effort to use proper English, you may as well use it."

Grady chuckled. "You sound like a school teacher."

"I have taught school," C.V. said. "But now I'm an attorney."

"A what?"

"A barrister, a counselor, a member of the bar."

"A bartender?"

C.V. laughed, "I'm a lawyer," he said.

"A lawyer? Why didn't you say so?"

"I did."

"I don't like lawyers," Grady said.

"Oh?" C.V. stuck his knife in the rabbit to test it. "I believe this is about ready," he said. "You think you could eat some of it?"

"I think I could eat all of it," Grady said enthusiastically.

"Don't be greedy."

Grady blushed. "I'm sorry," he said. "I didn't mean I would eat all of it. I was just...."

C. V. chuckled as he cut the rabbit in two. He put the biggest portion on a tin plate and handed it to Grady.

"I was just teasing. I know what you meant," he said. He took a bite, then dabbed at the juices. Grady was much less careful, and much hungrier. He tore at his rabbit, pulling big pieces away and chewing ravenously.

"Is it good?"

"You bet," Grady said. "I mean, yes, sir!"

"Tell me, Grady, why don't you like lawyers?"

"Pa says—" Grady started, then paused, remembering his father was dead. "That is, Pa said lawyers cheated him once. Ma wanted him to see a lawyer about the property lines back home in Illinois, but Pa wouldn't do it. He never liked lawyers, and I never did either."

"I've no doubt that your father was cheated, but he shouldn't have let that one incident prejudice him against the entire profession. Tell me, are there other professions you don't like? What about doctors? Do you have anything against doctors?"

"No, I got nothin' against 'em. I ain't never . . ." Grady stopped and corrected himself. "I have never used one."

"Very good," C.V. said, noting that Grady had tried to improve his grammar. "But back to our discussion. Do you think every doctor, everywhere, is totally honest? Or, do you think that, somewhere, there might be a dishonest doctor?"

"I'm sure there's a dishonest doctor somewhere," Grady agreed.

"Then do you think all doctors should be judged by that one dishonest character?"

"No."

"Why not?"

"'Cause that wouldn't be fair."

C.V. smiled. "Precisely my point, Grady. If you don't judge all doctors by one dishonest doctor, then why should you judge all lawyers by one dishonest lawyer?"

"Bein' a doctor and bein' a lawyer ain't . . . isn't the same thing," Grady said. "Doctors help people."

"So do lawyers."

"Not like doctors."

"Being a lawyer is a very noble calling, Grady. The thing that differentiates man from the beasts is the law. And without lawyers to represent the common man, law would be an exclusive tool of the government!"

"Yeah, well, I still don't like 'em," Grady said. "I like you all right though," he added quickly.

"Well, so much for my brilliant defense of the profession," C.V. laughed. He finished his meal, then cleaned his plate with sand. "Grady, what do you have in mind to do?" he asked.

"I ... I don't know exactly," Grady said. He was reflective for a moment. "I guess I haven't really thought about it."

"I'm going to Coulterville to try a case. We'll be there before noon tomorrow. There'll be a judge there, I'll get him to decide your case."

"What do you mean, decide my case?"

"Decide what to do with you," C.V. said.

"Oh." Grady was quiet for a long moment. "Mr. Battenburg, will he put me in an orphanage?"

"He may," C.V. said. "There's an orphanage in Coulterville."

"I don't want to go to an orphanage."

"Why not? There will be people there to look after you. You'll be fed arid clothed, and you'll go to school," C.V. said, trying to paint as attractive a picture as he could.

"I don't need to be looked after. I can feed and clothe myself."

"Grady, I don't know how much money there is in that pouch you've got stuck down in your waistband, but I'd be willing to bet that it isn't enough to take care of you until you are old enough to get work."

Grady gasped and felt the pouch.

"You were right not to tell me about it," C.V. said. "I'll give you credit for that. But this should prove something to you, I hope. If I were the type of person who would rob you, I could have already done it. So even your attempts at secrecy weren't enough. No, you'd be better off going to an orphanage." C.V. pulled a blanket from his saddleroll and tossed it over to Grady. "Here," he said. "Wrap up in this and get some sleep. It's been a bad day for you, but you'll see things more clearly tomorrow."

Black thunderclouds rumbled ominously in the northwest all the next morning, but they held off long enough for Grady and C.V. to reach their destination.

Coulterville was laid out like the letter X, with the railroad and Front Street forming one leg of the X, and Main Street forming the other leg. Main Street continued on as a wagon trail running in a generally north and south direction out of town.

Grady looked at this town which was to be his home while he was in the orphanage. It seemed to consist mainly of bars and saloons. He counted nine before they got to the center of town, and that was just on this street. He was sure there were at least that many on the other street.

Coulterville was busy. There was a lot of wagon and buggy traffic, and dozens and dozens of people walking along the plank walks which lined both sides of the street. Every so often there were boards stretched all the way across the dirt streets to allow people a way to cross when the roads were full of mud. This was the first town Grady had seen since his family left Kansas City more than two months earlier. Despite the unhappy circumstances under which he was seeing it, he found it exciting.

C.V. stopped in front of the Morning Star Hotel.

"Why don't you take Buck down to the livery and get a stable for him?" C.V. said. "Tell them to feed him oats and rub him down. Then come on back to the hotel here. I'll be up in my room."

"Where will your room be?"

"I don't know yet, I haven't registered. You can check with the desk, they'll tell you."

"What's the desk?"

By now C.V. had slipped down from the horse and Grady had moved up to the saddle. C-V. looked at him and smiled.

"Are you serious?"

"I've . . . I've never been in a hotel before," Grady admitted.

"Believe me, from the condition of some of the ones I've been in, you haven't missed much," C.V. said. He removed his saddlebags and hung them over his shoulder, then pointed through the door. "Look, when you come back, just go inside here. There will be a man behind a counter. Ask him what room number C.V. Battenburg is registered in, and he'll tell you."

"All right," Grady said.

Grady rode Buck down to the far end of the street to the livery barn, then he turned the horse over to the attendant, a boy not much older than himself.

"This your horse?" the boy asked.

"It belongs to a friend."

"I ain't seen you around here."

"I've never been here."

"You 'n your folks gonna live here?"

"I ... I don't have any folks."

"You an orphan?"

"Yes."

Warriors of the Code

"I'm only half an orphan. I got a ma. She ain't much, she works down at the Crystal Palace 'n she's drunk more'n she ain't. But she keeps me from havin' to live on The Hill. Any ma's all right if it keeps you offen The Hill."

"What's The Hill?"

"You kiddin'? You an orphan 'n you ain't never heard of The Hill? It's the orphanage. It's run by ol' man Slayton. Ebenezer Slayton. They say he's the meanest son-of-a-bitch ever lived. He works the orphans till they're 'bout ready to drop, 'n he beats 'em when he don't think they're workin' hard enough. Just you wait. If you're a orphan like you say you are 'n you're movin' here, you'll find out soon enough."

Grady turned and started back to the hotel.

The thunderclouds finally delivered on their promise, and the rain started coming down in sheets. Grady dashed across the street and up onto the wooden sidewalk. Many of the stores had roofs that overhung the sidewalk, so, though the dirt street was already turning into a river of mud, Grady was able to return to the hotel without suffering too much from the weather.

He stomped his feet just outside the door to make certain he had no mud on his shoes, then he went into the hotel.

The hotel lobby seemed huge to him. There were a dozen or more chairs and sofas scattered about, several potted plants, mirrors on the walls, and a grand, elegant staircase rising to the second floor. Grady looked around for a moment, taking in all the images of this, his first time in a hotel, then he saw a counter and a man behind the counter, looking at him.

"May I help you, sir?" the man behind the counter asked.

It was the first time anyone had ever addressed Grady as 'sir,' and he smiled.

"I'm looking for Mr. C.V. Battenburg."

"He's in room 212," the man said.

"Where's that?"

"Well, if it's 212, it must be on the second floor," the man said in exasperation.

"Oh."

The man sighed, and pointed to the stairs. "Go up these stairs," he said. "It's the first room on the left."

"Thank you."

Grady climbed the stairs, then when he saw the door he opened it and went inside. Instantly he heard a metallic click, and he turned to see C.V. holding a cocked pistol leveled toward him. Grady gasped in surprise and took half a step back.

"Boy, don't frighten me like that," C.V. said, sighing in relief. He released the hammer and lowered the pistol. "Most people knock before they come into someone's room."

"You told me to come up," Grady said.

"So I did," C.V. said. "So I did."

C.V. was just in the act of changing clothes. He had already put on another pair of trousers, but he was bare from his waist up.

"I had some bathwater brought up," C.V. said. "I've already taken my bath. You take yours, then we'll go downstairs to the restaurant and eat our lunch. I'll bet you've never eaten in a restaurant either, have you?" He tied his tie, then reached for his jacket.

"No, I haven't," Grady admitted. "But listen, I don't need a bath. It hasn't been that long since I had one."

C.V. smiled at him. "It's been long enough," he said. He pointed to the tub. "Take a bath. I'll be back in a little while." C.V. started for the door.

"Mr. Battenburg?"

"Yes."

"Are you going to check on the orphanage?"

"Maybe."

"I already did," Grady said.

C.V. stood there with his hand on the door frame.

"What did you find out?"

"They got one," Grady said.

"Yes, well, go ahead and take your bath. I'll be back after a while."

After C.V. left, Grady began to get undressed for his bath. He held the pouch of money for a moment, trying to decide what to do with it, then he saw the bed. He hid the pouch under the mattress, then slipped down into the still warm water.

"Don't forget to wash behind your ears. Grady," his mom's voice came back to him.

"I won't. Mom."

Grady used the time alone not only to take a bath, but to have the first and good cry he had allowed himself since the massacre. Finally, when he was all clean, inside and out, he climbed out of the tub, dried himself off, and put his clothes back on. A moment later, C.V. came back.

"You look a little better," C.V. said. "Smell better too. It's too bad you don't have a change of clothes to put on."

"This is all I have."

"You need to spend some of that money to buy yourself some more clothes," C.V. said. "And a horse."

"A horse?"

"We can't go on riding double forever. I don't think Buck would like that."

"Riding double? What do you mean? I thought you were going to leave me at the orphanage."

"Yes, well, I checked up on that, and it didn't seem like all that good of an idea to me. I know you don't like lawyers, but if you think you could stand being around one, I thought you might like to ride with me. What do you say?"

"Oh, thank you Mr. Battenburg!"

C.V. held up his hand and said, smiling at the boy, "If we're going to be partners, I think you should call me C.V., don't you?"

Grady grinned broadly.

"Yes, C.V., I think so too," he said.

Chapter Two

A LONG LAYER of blue tobacco smoke hung just beneath the ceiling of the Bull's Head Saloon. Normally there were as many as five or six poker games going on at the same time, but now there was only one. All the other games had stopped and the other players, the bar girls, and even the casual drinkers, had been drawn to the action at the remaining game table.

C.V. had three piles of poker chips stacked in front of him, representing over fifteen hundred dollars in cash. He pulled out a long, thin cigar and lit it, then examined the man across the table from him. The man had just taken a seat at the table, attracted by the size of the stakes.

"I'm Martin Kyle," the man said. "Have you ever heard of me?"

"No," C.V. answered easily. "Should I have?" The one who had introduced himself as Martin

Kyle smiled easily. "Not necessarily," he said. "But you'll know me after tonight." He pulled two large stacks of money from his jacket pocket. "Do you have chips for this much?"

"No," C.V. said. "But the cashier does."

"I'll be right back," Kyle said. "Hold a seat open for me."

C.V. took a drink of his beer while he waited for Kyle to return with the money. He and Grady had come to Dodge City two days ago to file a lawsuit on behalf of a cattleman from Texas. The cattleman had accepted a bank draft for his cattle, but the draft hadn't been honored by the bank. The case was still in the preliminary stages, thus giving C.V. the opportunity to play what he thought would be a relaxing game of cards. He had, however, experienced a phenomenal run of luck. Now that luck was going to be sorely tested.

"Were you kidding?" someone asked C.V. while Kyle was gone to buy his chips. "You mean you really haven't heard of Martin Kyle?"

"No," C.V. replied.

"You've heard of Angus Martin, haven't you? Angus Martin is about the wealthiest man in Kansas."

"Yes, I have heard of Mr. Martin," C.V. said. In fact, Angus Martin was the cattle buyer against whom C.V. was filing suit.

"Well, Martin Kyle is Angus Martin's grandson. That's where he gets the name Martin."

"I see," C.V. said. "Then he should be able to afford the game, shouldn't he?"

Martin returned a moment later with his hat full of chips. He dumped them on the table in front of him, then looked at C.V.

"No limit?"

"That's fine by me," C.V. agreed.

There were two others at the table, and both of them finished their drink with a gulp, then got up.

"I guess it's just you and me, lawyer," Martin said, smiling.

C.V. raised his eyebrow. "You know me?"

"I know you and that young dog you got workin' for you have come to town to try and steal some money from my grandpa," Martin said. He smiled broadly. "That's why I'm goin' to enjoy this. You come to town to steal from my grandpa, only I'm goin' to take your money instead."

C.V. tasted the beer, made a face, and put the glass

aside.

"My beer's grown stale. Could I have another?" he asked one of the pretty bar girls who stood near by.

"Certainly, lover," the girl purred, and she stepped over to the bar to get him another.

"I suppose you'd like a new deck of cards?"

"You're damned right I would," Martin said. Martin smiled. "Not that I'm accusin' you of anything you understand. "

"I understand," C.V. replied.

One of the other girls standing nearby handed C.V. a new deck of cards, and he broke the seal, then dumped them on the table. They were clean and stiff and shining. He pulled out the joker, then began shuffling the deck. The stiff, new pasteboards clicked sharply. His hands moved swiftly, folding the cards in and out, until the law of random numbers became king of the table. He shoved the deck across the table.

"Cut?"

Martin cut the deck, then pushed them back. He kept his eyes glued on C.V.'s hands.

"Five card stud?" C.V. asked.

"That'll be fine," Martin answered.

Martin won five hundred dollars on the first hand, and a couple of hands later was ahead by a little over a thousand dollars. C.V. was ready to concede that his string of luck had run out. At that he was still almost a hundred dollars above what he started with. He finished his beer.

"Well," he said easily. "I guess you've fulfilled your ambition. You've taken money from me. Now, I suppose, I shall have to get it back from your grandfather. I'm going to quit while I have something left."

"Come on, lawyer," Martin goaded. "You've got almost five hundred dollars on the table, what do you say we play one hand of showdown for it?"

C.V. sighed. "All right," he said. He dealt five cards to

each of them, and took the pot with a pair of twos.

Martin laughed. "Not exactly a smashing hand, is it? How about another hand for a thousand?"

C.V. won that hand with a Jack high.

"Want another one?" C,V. asked.

"Yes, for two thousand dollars," Martin said. He smiled. "You can't possibly win three in a row."

C.V. did win with a pair of tens, and Martin threw his cards on the table in disgust. He slid the rest of his money to the center of the table. "I've got another thousand here," he said.

"High card." C.V. covered his bet, then fanned the cards out.

"You draw first," Martin said.

C.V. started to reach for a card, but just as he touched it, Martin stopped him. "No, I changed my mind," Martin said. "I'll draw first." Martin smiled triumphantly, and flipped over the card C.V. was about to draw. It was a three of hearts.

"What the . . ." Martin shouted in anger. "You cheated me, you son-of-a-bitch! You knew I was going to do that, so you reached for a low card!"

"Friend, how was I supposed to know that was a low card?" C.V. asked. "The cards were face down on the table."

Martin drew a pistol and leveled it at C.V, "Draw your gun, shyster," he said. "No one cheats me and gets away with it."

"I'm not armed," C.V. said easily.

"It don't make any difference. We hang card cheats here in Dodge, I'll just shoot you 'n save the citizens the cost of a hangman."

There was a cold, ominous click of metal, then the barrel of a .45 pushed against the back of Martin's head.

"Put your gun down."

"What?" Martin asked in a frightened voice. He lowered his pistol, and tried to look around but the gun barrel prevented him from turning his head. Beads of perspiration suddenly popped out on his upper lip. "What are you gettin' mixed up in this for? This ain't none of your concern."

"Let's just say I'm a defender of the language," the voice said. "Your improper use of grammar has forced me to this drastic action."

"What?" Martin asked nervously. "Who the hell are you?"

"I'm the young dog who's working for C.V. Battenburg. Put your pistol on the table, please." Gingerly, very, very gingerly, Martin lay his pistol down. C.V. picked it up, emptied all the cartridges, then put it back down.

"Grady, I'm going to cash in the chips," he said. "Then I propose that we take our dinner at the finest restaurant in town."

"Good idea," Grady said. He let the hammer back down on his pistol, and returned it to his holster. Martin turned around to see who had accosted him. He saw a strongly built youth of sixteen or seventeen, with sun bleached blond hair and bright blue eyes.

"Why you're . . . you're just a kid!" he sputtered. "You're going to get yourself into trouble playing a man's game. I should've taken you."

"Oh, don't make the mistake of underestimating my partner," C.V. said. "He's quite capable of taking care of himself. Shall we go, Grady?" Grady and C.V. left the saloon, with C.V. poking bills into every pocket. He handed a packet of money to Grady. "Be a good lad and keep up with this for me, would you? I'm running out of places to keep my money."

"I can't believe we're walking down Front Street in Dodge City, in the middle of the night, carrying this much money. How much did you win in there?"

"Something over five thousand dollars, I think," C.V. said.

Grady whistled softly. "That's more than you can make in a year of handling legal cases. Listen, have you ever thought of ..."

"Forget it," C.V. said easily. "I did it once."

"You did what? You don't even know what I was going to

say."

"You were going to ask if I ever considered being a professional gambler."

"Yes, I was. What do you mean you did it once? You never told me that story."

C.V. chuckled. "Boy, we've only been together for four years, and most of that time I've been trying to give you an education. There hasn't been time for me to tell you all the details of my boring life."

"I don't know all the details of your life, C.V., but I'd be willing to bet they aren't boring." Grady had heard only bits and pieces of C.V.'s life over the last four years. The stories were rationed out to him, and each one was a gem, disclosing a new and fascinating facet of this man who was his mentor and friend. And yet, for all the stories C.V. had told, Grady believed that the real C.V. had only been hinted at. C.V. carried, deep inside him, some terrible, crushing secret. Whether Grady would ever learn that secret, he didn't know, but he did know enough not to ask. If C.V. ever wanted to unburden himself, Grady would be ready. But he would never push his friend into telling more than he wanted to tell.

"C.V., do you think I ought to go back east for a year or so? Maybe attend a University?"

"And what University would that be?" C.V. replied. "Harvard? William and Mary? Yale?"

"They're all pretty nice schools," Grady said.

"They are at that;" C.V. said. "But, my boy, the most brilliant scholar in the history of civilization was Plato, and Plato had but one teacher ... Socrates. Socrates believed that the best University was a log, with . . ."

"I know," Grady said, laughing. He had heard it many times before. "A log with the teacher sitting on one end and the pupil sitting on the other."

"And it becomes even more effective when it is difficult to tell the teacher from the pupil," C.V. went on.

"We'll never reach that point," Grady laughed. "There's

nothing I could ever teach you."

"Don't be so sure of that," C.V. said. "I've already learned a great deal from you."

"You've learned from me? What have you learned from me?"

"Courage, for one thing."

"Courage? Why, C.V., you're the bravest man I've ever known! I remember the way you faced down that killer in Abilene. He took three shots at you, but you just stood there, cool and collected, taking aim as if you were shooting at bottles. And when that bullet went through the sleeve of your coat, it didn't even phase you! You just went and hit him right between the eyes!"

"That wasn't courage, boy, that was survival, pure and simple," C.V. said. "No, Grady, you have shown me real courage. Ever since your parents were murdered you have gone about the business of living without self-pity, and without looking back. It took a lot of courage for a twelve-year-old boy to be able to do that."

Grady was embarrassed by C.V.'s unabashed accolades, and he coughed to cover his embarrassment; then he remembered why he had returned to the saloon in the first place.

"Oh, I located Judge Reardon and I got him to give us a court order to examine Angus Martin's bank account."

"And?"

"He has ten times the amount of money to cover the draft."

"Did you present the draft?"

"Yes, but he has a stop payment order in effect which has locked his account."

"Then we'll just have to take him to court and unlock it, won't we?"

They turned into Miguel's, a restaurant everyone agreed was the best in Dodge City. Unlike the unpainted board floors of most of the buildings in the city, Miguel's boasted a sparkling clean, white- tiled floor. There were decorative hat stands scattered about the room, and gleaming brass gas chandeliers. They were shown to their table by a waiter, then given a menu.

"Is your seafood fresh?" Grady asked.

"Oh, yes, extremely fresh," the waiter replied proudly. "It comes up from Galveston by train, packed in ice."

"Very well, I think I'll have the Pompano *en papillote*."

"And I'll have the same," C.V. said, handing his menu back to the waiter. C.V. chuckled.

"What is it?" Grady asked.

"While you were ordering Pompano *en papillote,* I was thinking about the first time you ever ate a meal in a restaurant. Remember? I had to force you to take a bath first. And when we got there, you didn't have the slightest idea of what to do. Now you sit here like a drawingroom dandy from New Orleans, ordering Pompano *en papillote."*

"It was in Coulterville," Grady said. "I remember. I thought you were going to leave me at the orphanage there."

"At the time I thought that was the best thing for you," C.V. said. "Until I met the son-of-a- bitch who ran the place. I hadn't talked to him for two minutes when I knew there was no way I could leave you there. Another minute and I was trying to figure out how to get everyone else sprung!"

"I didn't realize then what a Don Quixote you were," Grady said.

"Listen, if there were no Don Quixotes in the world, we'd be overrun with windmills," C.V. said with a grin.

"I wasn't going to stay there, you know," Grady said. "Even if you left me."

"You weren't?"

"Not at all. I was going to wait until you left, then I was going to slip away. As I look back on it, I realize it was a rather foolish idea, but that was what I had in mind."

"Not so foolish," C.V. said. "Had you left, you would have made it just fine. Of course, I would have been without a law partner. And the people in this country are sorely in need of lawyers."

"'Tis true, they are a lawless brood; But rough in form, nor mild in mood," Grady said.

"And every creed, and every race; With them hath found—may find a place," C.V. continued. "Lord Byron. Very good, Grady."

Grady laughed. "I wonder how many other people have learned Byron in between shooting lessons," he mused.

"Culture preserves the soul, my boy," C.V. said. "But a quick draw and straight shooting is often required to preserve the body. You do well to learn both disciplines, along with your pursuit of an education in law."

"C.V., who did you study law with?" Grady asked.

"I've never told you, have I?"

"No," Grady said. "You haven't forgotten his name, have you?"

"Hardly, my boy," C.V. said. "Hardly."

Their meal was brought then. The waiter cut open the paper sacks in which the fish had been cooked, along with a wine-based shrimp sauce, and the aromatic steam escaped. C.V. inhaled the aroma, nodded his acceptance to the waiter, then began to eat.

"As a matter of fact, I remember him quite well," C.V. went on after the waiter had left. "I was nineteen when he took me under his wing. It was eighteen years ago, in the spring of 1854, when I first began to read the law."

"Where is he now?" Grady asked.

"He's dead."

"Oh," Grady said quietly. "I'm sorry."

"So is the whole world," C.V. said simply. "His name was Abraham Lincoln."

Grady gasped, and looked across the table at C.V.

"You . . . you read law with Abraham Lincoln?" he asked.

"For two years," C.V. said.

"What was he like? I mean, he's probably the single most important person of this century, and you knew him!"

"He was a very friendly sort," C.V. said. "He had an exceptionally quick wit, and a tremendous sense of humor, but you know . . ." C.V. paused, reflectively, then went on. "There was a sense of sadness about him. In the midst of the funniest joke and the heartiest laugh, you could still see it in his eyes. It's as if he always knew what fate had in store for him."

"You mean the assassination?"

"No," C.V. said. "Not that. I don't think Abe ever really gave two hoots about his own life. I think the sadness was much greater than that. I think he was aware, even then, that the destinies and the lives of millions of people would be in his hands."

"Did you ever see him after he became President?"

"Once," C.V. said. "During the Civil War I was a Major in the same Regiment in which Lincoln had served during the Blackhawk War. After Lee surrendered, our Regiment returned to Washington for the Victory Parade. We arrived there on Good Friday morning, April 14th. The President was to review our parade the next morning, but when he learned I was a member of the Regiment, he sent for me, and asked me to call on him that very day."

Grady knew that his food was getting cold and his drink tepid, but he didn't care. One of the most fascinating things of his association with C.V. had been C.V.'s prowess as a raconteur. Whether C.V. acquired that talent from having argued cases in the courtroom, or whether he was good at arguing courtroom cases because of his skill as a raconteur, Grady didn't know. He did know that C.V. had the power to make his stories come alive, and as C.V. went on with his tale, Grady could almost believe that he was there, a third party at the meeting between the President of the United States and the man who had once been his student. He could see Lincoln's six-foot four-inch frame, his thin face, and his bristling chin whiskers as clearly as if the man were standing before him.

"Nine years had passed since last we met," C.V. went on. "But his smile, his sense of humor, his essence as a human being came through at once. While we were together that afternoon he wasn't the President. He was the lawyer who used to read the newspapers aloud back in Springfield, Illinois, much to the chagrin of Bill Herndon, his partner, I might add," C.V. chuckled. "And for a few moments there, I actually believe the terrible, terrible burdens of his office weren't on his shoulders. We spoke of old happenings as freshly as if it had been the day before. He was going out that night, and he invited me to come along."

"And did you go?"

"No," C.V. said quietly.

"Why not?"

"I don't know. I suddenly looked around the room and realized that I was in the White House, talking to the President of the United States of America. Suddenly he wasn't my old friend and teacher any more. He was a giant, a legend, a god if you will. Who was I to associate with the likes of Abraham Lincoln? I begged off—I don't know, I made some excuse. I learned later that a Major Rathbone accompanied him that night. Maybe if I had gone, things would have turned out differently. I might have been able to prevent it from happening."

"April 14th!" Grady said. "Of course! I didn't think about it when you mentioned the date, but that was the day—"

"He was killed," C.V. finished for him. He sighed. "The whole world knows the story. He was watching a play when Booth opened the door to his box and stepped inside. Rathbone, who was supposed to act as the President's bodyguard, was absorbed in the play, and he didn't see Booth. If I had been there, I would have seen him, I know I would. The man to whom I owed so much asked for my help and I turned him down."

"You turned him down, yes," Grady said. "But not for some self-serving reason. You shouldn't feel guilty about that."

C.V. smiled sadly. "Oh, I know that, Grady. I've told

myself all the reasons why I shouldn't feel guilty. But I do. And it was that sense of guilt which drove me to . . ." he stopped, then shrugged his shoulders. " . . . uh, leave the legal profession and try other ways to earn a living."

"Meaning gambling?"

"Among other things," C.V. said. He smiled broadly, and the somber mood which had temporarily descended over them was broken. "You should have seen me," he said. "I was a Mississippi Riverboat gambler, and you never saw a more finely turned-out dandy. And the ladies, Grady," C.V. said. He kissed the ends of his fingers then opened his hand. "Oh, did I have my share of the ladies. But of course, you're much too young to appreciate that," he teased.

"You might be surprised," Grady countered.

The courtroom was filled the next day as C.V. argued the case of his client, Jack Longworth, a cattleman from Texas, against Angus Martin. Grady sat at the table with C.V. and helped him with his notes and preparations. At first he feared the crowd would be hostile. He was surprised to see, however, that they weren't hostile at all, but seemed supportive of C.V.'s client. He commented on it.

"It's simple," C.V. said. "Dodge City came into existence as the trail end of the Texas herds. Most of the businesses in town depend upon that fact, and if someone does something that might cause the cattlemen to drive their herds somewhere else, it hurts everyone. Besides, I have a feeling that old Angus Martin has run roughshod around here for so long now that more than one person is ready to see him receive his due."

Martin's lawyer presented his case, submitting documents which disputed the dates in question, the number of cows received, the name of the consignee, the railroad shipping number by which the cows left Dodge City, and half a dozen other papers, none of which had any bearing on the real issue, which was that Angus Martin had stopped payment on his draft, and thus hadn't paid for the cattle.

C.V. was able to counter most of the so-called 'evidence'

of Martin's innocence, though the shipping document number on his client's claim did differ with the actual shipping document number. Finally it was time for C.V.'s closing argument. He walked over to the jury box and smiled pleasantly at the men who had drawn the duty.

"Gentlemen, I'm going to tax your imagination for a few moments. This isn't a tactic I can use with just any jury, because it's a tactic which depends upon not only the integrity of the jurors, but the intelligence as well. I have researched each of you, and I feel this court is blessed with a jury of exceptionally intelligent composition."

The jurors looked at each other and nodded smugly. Grady smiled. The old C.V. magic was already working. C.V. went on with his argument.

"Gentlemen, imagine if you will, a fine, elegant brick building." He held his hands in the shape of bricks to help with the imagery. "Each brick is sturdy and perfectly made, and they are piled one on top of the other until the four walls go up and a roof goes across the top so that we have a big, modem two-story building."

C.V. paused to allow his word picture to sink in.

"Let's say that this brick building is built right here on Front Street, a landmark to the fair community of Dodge City. People will come from miles around to look at it, and to marvel at the beautiful lines of the building."

He paused again, and as Grady looked into the faces of the jurors, he could see that every man in the juror box had the image of a brick building in his mind.

"Oh," C.V. said softly. "What a magnificent building this is. What a beautiful architectural design. It is the showpiece of the entire state of Kansas." He ended with a dramatic inflection of his voice, then he was silent and for a long moment the only sound to be heard was the ticking of the big wall clock, and a peal of laughter from some children at play in the next block.

"But no one will dare to set foot inside the building," C.V.

said softly.

The jurors all looked at C.V. in surprise and Grady felt a little thrill that C.V. could play them so masterfully.

"No one will dare set foot inside the building," C.V. went on, raising the inflection of his voice, "because the bricks have no mortar, arid the slightest wind, the least rumble of the earth under a passing train, and down the building will come!" C.V. literally shouted the last line, and as he did so he made a gesture with his hands, demonstrating the collapse of a building. He waited a moment for his imagery to sink in, then he went on with his presentation.

"Such is the importance of mortar, that the finest brick, the most skillful design means nothing if there is no mortar to hold the bricks together. Trust, gentlemen of the jury," he said quietly, "is the mortar of civilization. When mankind lived in the caves, there was no trust. It was dog eat dog, kill or be killed, survival of the fittest. It was a society more terrible than the most savage Indian tribe ever to inhabit this continent. Imagine, if you can, what it must have been like to live in such a society. What if you had to be able to run like a deer and fight like a mountain lion every day, just to survive? How would you fare in such a world?"

A few of the jurors seemed to sit up straighter, and Grady watched them as they surreptitiously eyed their neighbors, and he saw them blanch at the prospect of having to live in such a world as C.V. was describing.

"Fortunately," C.V. said, changing his tone from ominous to hopeful, "we don't live in such a world. We live among civilized people, where trust...." He paused and held his finger up. "Where trust, gentlemen, accounts from more than strength, speed, or even skill with a six-gun. Trust must be maintained, and we, as civilized members of our society, must, as our bounden duty, see to it that the trust which holds everything together isn't weakened. When a man issues a bank draft for a certain amount of money, he is saying to you, 'Here, here is my word, my bond with you and with the trust of our society, which promises that you will receive the money I owe you.' Angus Martin issued such a bank draft. He made such a promise. And now I ask you, as watchmen of our society, as keepers of our faith, to see to it that the sacred ideal of trust is not betrayed. Find for the plaintiff."

As C.V. turned away from the jury box the men and women in the audience rose to their feet in applause. Grady, smiling broadly, stood with them and added his own applause.

It hardly seemed possible that he had once told C.V. he didn't like lawyers. At this moment he could think of no more noble calling in all the world, and he longed for the day when he would pass the bar and be able to defend honor as C.V. had just done.

Chapter Three

GRADY HAD CARRIED the heavy saddle for nearly two miles, and when he reached the railroad track he dropped it with a sigh of relief. He climbed the small grade and stood in the middle of the track, scratching the beard he had recently affected, and looked back toward the west into the sinking sun.

Grady was twenty-five years old. It had been thirteen years since C.V. Brattenburg found him, more dead than alive, by the burned out remains of his parents' wagon. In that time C.V. Brattenburg had been his surrogate father, his teacher, and his friend. And now C.V. Brattenburg was his legal partner, because Grady had realized his ambition to pass the bar and was now a full partner in the law firm of Brattenburg and Ford.

After years of wandering around the West like an itinerant preacher, C.V. Brattenburg finally decided to settle in one place, and he chose Dodge City.

"Mind you," he cautioned, "this settlement is only temporary. After too long a time I start getting itchy feet, and, like Daniel Boone, I need to get out and find some elbow room."

Despite C.V.'s protestations, however, Dodge City had been good to the law firm of Battenburg and Ford, and they were now so firmly established that a citizen's committee had recently approached C.V. to suggest that he run for Congress. C.V. had thanked them very much, walked them to the door, then spent the rest of the day getting drunk.

"If you ever think I'm seriously considering a life in politics, please shoot me and put me out of my misery," C.V. said in a drunken plea that very night.

C.V. was 46 years old, and though that was a long way shy of being old and infirm, Grady took most of the jobs which required the most stamina. One such job was the job he had just finished. The firm was representing a farmer way up in Finney Country, on the other side of the Pawnee River, and Grady rode up there to get some papers signed. On the way back to Dodge City his horse stepped into a gopher hole and went down. Reluctantly, but without a choice, Grady had to destroy him. He was better than forty miles away from town when it happened, but only a few miles from the railroad. He could only hope that the train from Garden City would stop for him.

Now Grady knelt by the track and put his ear to one of the iron ribbons. He could hear the faint humming of the track which told him that the train was just over the curve of the horizon. He knew he was lucky, because had he missed it, there wasn't another one due until the next morning.

He looked around until he found a couple of branches which were just about the right size. He wrapped sage grass around the end of the branches when he saw the first wisp of smoke from the train. He watched as the train approached. He knew that it was running at thirty miles an hour, but the vast openness of the plain gave the illusion of slowness to its approach. Against the gold and red vault of the late afternoon sky, the train appeared little larger than a crawling insect.

Grady lit the sage grass and the torch began smoking. He stepped up to the side of the track and watched as the train grew nearer. He could hear the chugging of the engine as it labored, pulling the train across the vast, open prairie, and he started waving the smoking torch back and forth in signal to the engineer.

A moment after he began waving the torch the engineer blew his whistle and Grady knew he had been spotted. He ground out the fire on the end of his torch, then walked back down and picked up his saddle and gear. He climbed back up and waited as the train approached. He knew now that the engineer had not only seen him, but planned to stop, for he heard the steam valve close as the engineer braked his train.

As the engine drew very close, Grady was able to put into perspective just how vast this country was, for the train which had resembled an insect but moments before was now a behemoth, lurching toward him. It ground to a chugging, squealing, squeaking halt, puffing black smoke, wreathed in tendrils of white steam which purpled in the light of the setting sun as it drifted away.

A coal-blackened face appeared in the window of the engine cab, and the engineer grinned down at Grady. Grady knew now why the engineer had stopped with no hesitation. The engineer was Herman Spangler, a man C.V. and Grady had represented a year ago. Herman had celebrated a little too much one evening, and had gotten into a fight with half a dozen cowboys. Herman more than held his own with the cowboys, but the saloon had been badly broken up. The saloonkeeper tried to assess Herman with the total cost of damages, but Grady managed to convince the judge that all seven participants should be responsible in equal shares for the damage caused. Herman was still grateful to Grady for that.

"Why, if it isn't Mr. Ford," Herman said. "What happened? What are you doing out here all alone?"

"My horse broke his leg," Grady said. "I had to kill him."

"Poor creature," Herman said. "Well, we've got lots of room. Climb on and we're off."

"Thanks," Grady said. At about that time the conductor came walking up to the engine, looking importantly at his watch.

"Mr. Spangler, what is the meaning of this?" he asked.

"You have no authorization to make an unscheduled stop like this. It's disconcerting to the passengers, and you put us in danger of not making our schedule."

"Oh, it's disconcerting to the passengers, is it?" Herman called down. "Well you 'n the passengers ain't runnin' this train, I am. And if I want to stop 'n help out a friend in need, I'll do it. This here feller is Grady Ford. He's a lawyer, Mr. Evans, and I reckon you know how important lawyer fellers are. He'll be ridin' into to Dodge with us."

"I've no provisions for selling him a ticket here in the middle of nowhere," the conductor said.

A sudden jet of steam escaped from one of the engine relief valves, enveloping the conductor in its cloud.

"Beg your pardon 'bout that," Herman said easily. Grady smiled because he knew Herman had done it on purpose. "Now, you was sayin'?"

The conductor sighed and looked at Grady. "I suppose you can make some arrangements for payment in Dodge," he said.

"No payment needed. He's my guest," Herman said. "Now the two of you get on the train. I got time to make up."

The conductor went on back to the last car, but Grady went into the first one. He dropped his saddle in the vestibule, but because he thought it not wise to leave his rifle unattended, he slipped it out of the saddle holster and carried it with him as he went inside.

There were half a dozen people in the first car and they looked at him nervously. Grady saw that they were frightened and he was surprised by it, then he realized they might think he was a train robber.

"I'm sorry about making the train stop, folks," he said. "I'm a lawyer returning from a case up in Finney County. My horse went lame and I needed a ride back into town, that's all." He touched the brim of his hat, then sat down near a window as the train, with bumps and jerks, started rolling again. Soon they were back up to speed and Grady sat by the window watching the countryside roll by as the light dimmed, and finally changed to darkness. The conductor came through the car and lit the overhead gas lamps. Patches of yellow were projected from the windows of the train to the ground below.

"Excuse me," a woman's voice said. She had come to sit beside him, and Grady turned from the window to look at her.

She was an exceptionally beautiful woman, with hair so dark it was almost blue. Her eyes were big and brown, her complexion rather a golden olive. Her beauty was a mature beauty, like that of a rose in full bloom, and Grady judged her to be in her mid-thirties.

"Yes, ma'am," he said. "Is there something I can do for you?"

"You said you are a consejero? A lawyer?"

"Yes. The name is Grady Ford."

"My name is Bianca."

"Bianca? That's all?"

"That is all the name I shall use until my rightful claim is established. Not until I have my land and my title will I use more than Bianca."

"I see," Grady said. "Where are these lands?"

"They are on the Arizona-Mexico border," Bianca said. "I need the help of a lawyer to get what is rightfully mine."

"Well, uh, I'm flattered you would come to me, Miss Bianca," Grady said. "But have you considered using a lawyer in Phoenix or Tucson, or someplace closer to the land?"

"Senor Clanton is a big man in Arizona," Bianca said. "I'm afraid to use an Arizona lawyer."

"What about New Mexico, California or Colorado? They're much closer to the situation than anyone you would find up here."

"Perhaps that is true, Senor," Bianca said. She smiled. "But I have taken a job in Dodge City, so I will need a Dodge City lawyer."

Grady smiled at her. "I can't argue with that," he said. "What exactly is the nature of the problem?"

"Please, Senor," Bianca said. "I do not wish to speak of

this on a train. Perhaps it would be more suitable to come to your office?"

"Perhaps it would," Grady said. He pulled a card from his pocket and handed it to her. "My partner and I have an office over the bank. We'd be glad to talk to you."

Bianca took the card and smiled broadly. "Thank you,' Senor," she said. Strangely, Grady felt a twinge of excitement from the -brush of her long, cool fingers. Perhaps she was a bit older than he was, but still, he thought he'd never met a more exciting woman.

It was very dark by the time the train reached the station, but the station platform was so brightly lit by nearly a dozen gas lamps that it shined like a golden bubbly. Grady got off the train then walked up to the engine to thank the engineer. The engineer smiled and waved at him, then Grady started down the street toward the boarding house where he roomed. He found the boardinghouse to be quite satisfactory, but not so C.V., who lived in the hotel. C.V. claimed that living in a hotel didn't give him quite the sense of permanence that living in a boarding house did, and he refused to live there with Grady, even though he could have done so for half the money.

Before Grady went to his room however, he dropped his saddle off at the livery stable.

"Where's your horse, Grady?" the liveryman asked.

"He broke his leg in a gopher hole," Grady said grimly. He didn't have to say anything more, because the liveryman understood exactly what had happened to him.

"That's a shame," he said. "I know you set quite a store by that horse."

"He was good horse," Grady said.

A couple of people ran by in front of the livery stable.

"They're on the other side of the track!" one of them called.

"Ed was a fool to go after 'em alone," the other one hollered back.

Grady saw a crowd of people gathered around a small

shed on the other side of the track.

"What is it?" Grady asked. "What's going on?"

"There were a couple of drunken cowboys shooting up the place a few minutes ago, just before the train arrived," the liveryman said. They told some people in the saloon that if the Marshal come for 'em, they was gonna kill 'im."

Suddenly four or five gunshots erupted from the other side of the track, and Grady heard someone shout. He started toward the track on the run, then he saw young Ed Masterson coming toward him.

"Ed? Ed, what is it? What's going on?" Grady asked.

Grady saw a peculiar glowing, then he realized that it was a circle of fire. Ed's coat was burning.

"I'm killed, Grady," Ed said with a half-smile on his face. He suddenly fell face-down to the ground, and Grady ran over to him. He rolled the young marshal over and patted out the ring of fire on his jacket. That was when he realized what had caused the fire in the first place. Ed Masterson had been shot at point-blank range, and the powderblast from the revolver had set his jacket ablaze.

"There he goes, Sheriff!" a man's voice sounded from the dark on the other side of the tracks, and Grady, instinctively, drew his pistol and peered into the darkness.

A figure suddenly appeared on the railroad track, having run up the slight grade from the dark on the other side. He was tall and rangy, with a bushy, walrus-type mustache. He was wearing a high- crowned hat of the type favored by the range cowboys, and Grady saw a flash of light from one of the rowels on his spurs. The man was carrying a pistol and Grady saw him pointing it back toward the dark from which he had come. The gun in the man's hand boomed three times, and in the light of the muzzle-flash, Grady could see the almost demonic features of his face.

His three shots were returned by three more shots from the darkness, so quickly that had it not been for the sharp definition of sound Grady would have thought them echoes.

The three shots which were fired from the darkness found their mark, for the gunman on the track suddenly threw up his gun, then fell backwards, sliding headfirst down the railroad embankment on the near side. Grady ran over to him, and he saw bubbles of blood coming from the man's mouth. His right arm was also covered with blood. He was trying hard to breathe, and Grady heard a sucking sound in his chest. He knew then that at least one bullet had penetrated his lungs.

"Is the son-of-a-bitch dead?" a voice asked calmly from the track. Grady looked up to see Bat Masterson standing there with his gun in one hand and his cane in the other.

"He will be shortly," Grady said.

"Where's Ed," Bat said, looking around. "I saw him coming this way. I don't know, I think he may have been hit."

"He's over there, Bat," Grady said, pointing to Ed's still form.

"What?" Bat gasped. "No, he wasn't hit that badly! He couldn't have been!" Bat ran toward his brother's body, then dropped to his knees beside him. By that time more than two dozen people had climbed the railroad embankment from the dark on the other side.

"There he is," someone said, pointing to the dead cowboy at Grady's feet. "Bat got both of them, slick as a whistle."

"This'n ain't dead yet," someone else said.

"He's about to be."

By now nearly a hundred people were gathered around the two bodies. Grady gathered from the conversation that there was another body lying on the other side of the track, as well. Several more people were running toward the commotion from town, and Grady could hear the clomp of boots on boards as many ran down the wooden sidewalks, drawn to the excitement.

Grady looked toward Bat and saw him squatted beside his brother, holding his hand over his eyes. His pearl-handled, silver-plated gun was lying in the dirt beside him, totally forgotten in his sorrow. A doctor was checking for Ed's pulse.

"I'm sorry, Bat," Grady heard the doctor say quietly. There were even more people coming to the scene now, and Grady felt the urge to leave, to disassociate himself with the morbid curiosity which was now running so rampant.

Grady had planned to go straight to his room, but now he decided he would stop by the Lady Gay Saloon and have a beer instead. He felt unique. He was the only one walking toward town, whereas he passed dozens of people coming away from town, drawn toward the scene of the shooting.

"What is it?"

"What happened down there?"

"Has there been a killing?"

The questions were shouted by passersby, but Grady made no effort to answer them.

The Lady Gay Saloon was midway down the street on the left. It was easy to find, because of all the golden patches of light which lay in the street, the brightest patch spilled from the door and through the windows of the Lady Gay. Grady pushed through the swinging doors and walked inside.

It was quiet inside. The piano player was sitting with his back to his instrument, drinking a beer, looking out over the nearly empty saloon. The bartender was wiping the bar with a towel, and a couple of the bar girls were sitting at the table where a single customer sat. The customer was C.V.

"Grady," C.V. said, smiling. "Come and join us. These two young ladies are new to our city. I'm doing my civic duty by welcoming them. What was all the commotion?"

"A gunfight down by the switching shack," Grady said. "Ed Masterson was just killed."

"Oh, that's really a shame," C.V. said. "He was a very courageous young man. I've often worried about his being a city marshal though. He seemed too easygoing, too gentle a person for such a job. Does Bat know about it yet?"

"Yes," Grady said. "Bat killed the two men who did it."

"Was it a fair fight?"

"I don't know about the first one," he said. "I saw the

second man killed. He was standing on the track, shooting at Bat, when Bat shot him."

"You saw Bat as well?"

"No, but—"

"Grady, you of all people know the importance of precise information," C.V. scolded gently. "Tell exactly what you saw, nothing more, nothing less."

Grady smiled. He was a grown man now, and a full partner in the law firm with C.V. and yet the education went on. In this case it wasn't learning something new, it was merely underscoring that which he already knew.

"Excuse me. Your Honor," he teased. "I didn't know we were in court. What I saw was a man, dressed in the manner of a cowboy, run up onto the railroad track. He came from the darkness on the south side of the track. When he reached the track he stopped, turned around, and fired three shots back in the direction from which he ran. I heard three answering shots, then I saw the man fall, sliding headfirst down the grade on the north side of the tracks. I went to see how he was, and while I was bent over him, Bat Masterson appeared at the top of the grade and asked if he was dead."

"That's good," C.V. said. "And it's very good for Bat. Deger is Deputy Marshal, he's sure to be marshal now, and he and Bat don't get along. I wouldn't be surprised if Bat didn't run into a little difficulty over this."

"There were a lot of witnesses," Grady said.

"That's bad. The more witnesses, the less certain we will be of the facts. One clear story by one honest witness is much better than two dozen stories by as many witnesses, each one adding embellishments to make more important his perspective."

"I see what you mean," Grady said. "And sometimes those embellishments can be tailormade to satisfy vested interests."

"Precisely," C.V. said. "And as you know our friend Bat Masterson is not without his detractors in our fair city. I think they may find in this tragic incident an opportunity to cause some trouble."

"You think they'll take the case to court?" Grady asked.

"I'd say the chances are very good that they would, yes," C.V. said. "If so, we'll make the services of Battenburg and Ford available to him. Provided, of course, you concur."

"Oh, I concur, I concur," Grady said.

"I swear, you two are the funniest talkin' men I ever did hear," one of the two girls said. "I never heard such big words in a real sentence before."

"Darlin', you stick around that young man and he'll teach you all sorts of things you never knew," C.V. said with a ribald smile. "Grady, you haven't had the privilege of meeting our town's newest citizens, have you?"

"I'm afraid I haven't had the pleasure, no," Grady said.

"Then allow me to introduce them," C.V. said. "The young brunette here is Kate. Isn't she lovely?" Kate, who was by far the most attractive of the two, beamed under C.V.'s praise.

"Kate allows as how she is nearly a virgin, since she will only go to bed with gentlemen for whom she feels a particular affinity."

"What does that mean?" Kate asked.

"People you like," Grady said easily.

Kate put her hand on Grady's and squeezed it lightly. For a moment Grady recalled the beautiful Bianca from the train, and he felt a slight tingling of sexual desire. He looked at Kate. She was a soiled dove, true enough, but she couldn't have been in the business very long for she hadn't yet taken on that dissipated look which was so common to women of her profession. The other woman did have that look.

"Molly, our redheaded friend, on the other hand, is considerably more democratic than her younger sister."

"We ain't sisters," Molly said quickly.

"I meant the term figuratively, my dear," C.V. said easily. "Molly, you see, believes devoutly in the Biblical commission to 'Love thy neighbor,' and she does her best to accommodate as many of her neighbors as she can. She has even been known to share a bed with a buffalo hunter. Or is it a buffalo?"

Molly laughed good naturedly. "You're really a pistol, you know that, C.V.?"-

"So I've been told," C.V. replied. "At any rate, I'm about ready to call it a night." He stood up and Grady looked at him, amazed by the fact that he had not aged appreciatively in all the time he had known him. C.V. looked right now exactly as he had looked on the day he rode into Grady's life. Though Grady knew he was forty-six he didn't look a day over thirty.

"Good night, C. V.," Grady said.

"Oh, do you have those papers? I'm going to stop by the office, I'll take them along with me."

"Yes, thank you," Grady said. He pulled an envelope from the inside pocket of his jacket. The papers in the envelope were the reason for his trip in the first place. "That'll save me a walk over there."

C.V. took the envelope, then walked away, leaving Grady with the two women. A few of the customers who had left earlier to see about all the excitement now returned. Molly, seeing that Kate had the inside track with Grady, left the table and walked over to mingle with the returning customers.

"What your friend said about me is true," Kate said. "I will only go to bed with people I like."

"I see," Grady said.

"I have a room upstairs," she said. "You could come up, if you like."

"Yes," Grady said. The sexual appetite was now stimulated to the point that he felt more than appetite. He felt a genuine need.

"It's the third door on the right," she said. "You go on up and wait for me there. I'll get us a bottle."

Grady got up and walked to the back of the room, then

started up the stairs. By now, several more of the saloon's customers had returned and snatches of their conversation reached him. They were all talking about the shooting. Grady thought of the corpses of the three young men who were now lying in the morgue just down the street. They would never again be with a woman. The thought made him feel a little uneasy, so he pushed it aside and hurried on up to Kate's room to wait for her. As he waited, he recalled his very first experience with a woman, and he smiled.

He was eighteen, and he and C.V. had gone to New Orleans. While there, C.V. informed him that it was time his education be expanded to include the pleasures of a woman.

"And the place to get that education is at Madame Gameau's Brothel," C.V. said.

"Brothel? Isn't that just a whorehouse?"

"Grady, my boy," C.V. said, "is Beethoven's Ninth just a song? Have faith in me. Would I entrust your education to a common prostitute in a whorehouse? No, sir. You are going to be educated by an uncommon courtesan in the finest brothel in all of New Orleans, and that means the finest in the country."

They rented a Hansom Cab for the drive over, and when they got there Grady thought there must be some mistake. This place looked like an elegant mansion, with a wide, porticoed porch, and a uniformed doorman to greet them. The illusion was carried even further inside, by the large, marble foyer, the pedestaled statuary, and the oil paintings on the walls. A magnificent staircase rose in a graceful curve to the landing on the second floor, while a gigantic crystal chandelier hung from the high ceiling at the end of a long brass chain which dangled down through the curve of the stairs.

An elegantly dressed, very handsome woman of perhaps forty met them.

"C.V.," she said, smiling broadly, and extending her hand. "It's been a long time. What has it been, two years?"

Grady smiled. They had been in New Orleans two years

ago, but C.V. had made no mention of this place then.

"Yes," C.V. said. "About two years, I believe." He cleared his throat. "Madame Gameau, allow me to introduce my friend, Grady Ford."

"*Enchante*, Mr. Ford," Madame Gameau said, extending her hand. "Welcome."

"*Merci beaucoup,* madame," Grady said. He took Madame Gameau's hand and kissed it.

"Oh, C.V., your young friend is so gallant and charming. What a delight to have him visit us here. Thank you for bringing him."

"He's, uh, a little new at this," C.V. said.

"You mean he's never been to a brothel before?"

"He's even greener than that, I'm afraid," C.V. said.

Madame Gameau smiled knowingly. "I understand," she said. "You come with me, Mr. Ford. I'll be most selective for you. C.V., you'll' be all right until I return?"

"I'll be fine," C.V. said, smiling at Grady like a proud father.

Grady followed Madame Gameau up the rose carpeted stairs, then down the hallway. She opened a door and beckoned him to go inside.

"Go right on in, Mr. Ford," she said. "Someone will be with you shortly."

Grady went inside and looked around. The room was quite large. In the middle of the room, on a raised platform, was a huge bed, covered with a deep-blue silk spread. The walls were wainscoated with white painted wood on the bottom half and covered with red, flocked wallpaper above. C.V. was never known to be tight with his money, and since Grady had been with him they had stayed in some very nice hotels, but no hotel suite had ever matched this one in his experience.

A moment later the door opened, and a young woman moved through the door in an effortless glide. Her skin was alabaster, and her eyes were a deep, cool green. Her hair was long, thick and jet black, her lips a shining red.

"Mr. Ford, my name is Tamara. Madame Gameau asked me to call on you. I hope you find me satisfactory."

Tamara's voice fell on Grady's ears like the tinkling of wind chimes. He was thunderstruck. He had never seen anyone so beautiful, or heard a voice so soft.

"Yes, of course," Grady mumbled. "You're beautiful!"

Tamara smiled, then walked over to the bed and turned down the covers. She turned her back to Grady then, and began undressing.

Grady watched, spellbound, as the smooth skin of the girl's shoulders was exposed, then on down her back to her legs until she was completely nude. Then she raised the comer of the sheet and managed to slip into the bed without letting Grady see more than her back.

"Mr. Ford," she said softly. "If you'll pull out the top drawer of that dresser, you'll find a robe. Please step into the dressing room and remove your clothes."

Grady wanted to answer but his tongue was thick and his mouth dry. He took the robe and left without a word. When he came back she folded the sheet back to invite him into bed with her. He started to get in with the robe still on, and she laughed, a musical, tinkling laugh.

"Are you going to wear your robe to bed?" she asked.

"No," he said feeling quite foolish. "No, I guess not."

Grady took off the robe, then slid in under the sheets. She reached over to touch him and her hand felt like fire and ice, contained in the same entity.

Tamara was no older than Grady in years, but in experience she was the handmaiden of Eros. Under her skillful guidance Grady explored all the mysteries, and experienced all the pleasures available for a healthy, curious, eighteen-year-old. He had walked into Madame Gameau's a boy. He left, the next morning, a man.

Kate opened the door and slipped inside. The noise of the customers downstairs swelled up and down as the door opened and closed. Kate put a bottle and two glasses on the table.

"I thought you might want this," she said.
Grady smiled and reached for her.
"Later," he said.
Happily, Kate went to him.

Chapter Four

C.V. WAS EATING breakfast in the hotel dining room. The cheese and mushroom omelet had been excellent, though he found the bacon a bit overcrisp. He was just about to start on a second cup of coffee when he saw Wyatt Earp standing in the doorway, looking around the room. C.V. raised his hand and Wyatt crossed the room to his table. "Have a seat, Wyatt. Had your breakfast?"

"I ate with Bat," Wyatt said. "Deger put him in jail last night."

C.V. dabbed at his mouth with the napkin, then pushed his plate aside. He sighed.

"I was afraid of that," he said.

"Deger claims Bat had no right to interfere in the case. He claims Ed had the situation well in hand till Bat came along. He claims nothin' would have happened if Bat hadn't opened fire first."

"In effect, he's accusing Bat of causing his own brother's death," C.V. said.

"That's about the size, of it," Wyatt said. "With Ed gone and Deger Chief Deputy, that makes him top dog now. I turned in my badge this mornin'. I don't want any part of that son-of-a-bitch Deger."

"You know what that means, Wyatt," C.V. said. "That means Deger will pack the office with his own cronies. He'll be running Dodge City."

"Yeah, I know," Wyatt said. "That's why I'm pullin' up stakes. I'm leaving Dodge, C.V."

"Where are you going?"

"Tombstone. It's in Arizona Territory."

"Yeah, I've heard of it. It's a pretty wild town from what I've heard."

"I suppose it is," Wyatt said. "But my brother James owns the Oriental Saloon there. He claims it's the nicest place in town. He's got me a position as marshal there, and he's selling me an interest in the saloon. I'd say that sounds a little like opportunity knocking, wouldn't you?"

C.V. chuckled. "In other words, you intend to see to it that drunken and disgruntled cowboys leave your establishment alone, is that it?"

"That's about the size of it," Wyatt said. "My brother Virgil's been in Prescott for six months now, prospecting, and my brother Morgan has said he intends to join us both in Tombstone. What about you? If ever there was a place that needed a law office, I'd say it was Tombstone."

"I must confess it does sound tempting," C.V. said. "If for no other reason than I'm beginning to get itchy feet. But what of Bat?"

"Oh, yeah," Wyatt said. "He wants you 'n Grady to represent him. Can you get him off?"

"We'll do what we can," C.V. said.

"That ain't good enough, C.V.," Wyatt said. "You've got to get him off scott-free. Otherwise, I'm gonna have to kill Deger and get Bat out myself."

"You shouldn't tell me things like that, Wyatt," C.V. cautioned. "I'm an officer of the court."

"You're also my friend," Wyatt said.

"That's true, but still—"

"I know you set a lot of store by doing things legal," Wyatt said. "So I'm gonna give you your chance to get him off before I do anything. Maybe you don't understand what it's like to see an injustice done, and have a fire burning in your gut to take the law into your own hands, just to make things right. But when I see people like Deger who are protected by the law, then I get mad."

"I do understand," C.V. said. "Believe me, I do understand."

"How can you understand? You've always done things by the book."

"Wyatt?" someone called from the door of the dining room. C.V. looked up to see who had called Wyatt, and he recognized Chalk Beeson, Wyatt's partner in the Long Branch Saloon. While Ed Masterson was City Marshal of Dodge City, Wyatt had managed to enjoy the same sort of set-up he was going to in Tombstone. He was a deputy city marshal, and a partner in a saloon. His position on the police force ensured an orderly place of business. But Wyatt's patron on the force had been Ed Masterson. Wyatt's bitterest enemy was Larry Deger. They were more than just rivals on the police force. They were business rivals as well, for Larry Deger had the same setup in the Alhambra Saloon that Wyatt had in the Long Branch.

"Excuse me, C.V." Wyatt said. "Beeson and I have some business. I'm selling him my interest in the Long Branch before I leave."

"When will you be leaving?" C.V. asked.

"When justice is done for Bat Masterson," Wyatt said. "Whether by you, or by me."

C.V. drank his coffee slowly and watched as Wyatt left the dining room with Chalk Beeson. Wyatt had told C.V. that he didn't understand what it felt like to have a fire burning in his gut to right an injustice. C.V. was a lawyer, trained in the profession and dedicated to the principle that the rule of law must take precedence, first, last, and always. No one could imagine that a man of such idealism would have ever violated the codes which guided his life. But there had been a time . . .

once.

On the morning of April 15th, 1865, two thousand soldiers formed the military posse which galloped out of Washington in pursuit of John Wilkes Booth. C.V. Battenburg was one of those two thousand men, and, as he rode, his eyes were often blinded by tears. He felt a much greater loss than anyone else in the posse, not only because Abraham Lincoln had once been his friend and teacher, but also because he had refused Lincoln's personal invitation to attend the play with him on the night before. Had he accepted, he believed the President would still be alive. Now, all that remained for him to do was to help bring the President's killer to justice. It seemed too little too late.

The detachment of soldiers to which C.V. had attached himself located John Wilkes Booth and his accomplice, David Herold, in a tobacco barn near Port Royal, Virginia. They surrounded the barn.

"What do you think, Major?" Lieutenant Doherty asked.

"This is your command, Lieutenant," C.V. had replied. "I just came along as a volunteer."

The young lieutenant rubbed his chin. The two most wanted criminals in the history of the United States were now less than fifty feet away, trapped inside a tobacco barn.

"Secretary Stanton wants them alive," Lieutenant Doherty said.

C.V. stepped away from the lieutenant and looked at him, and at the resolute expressions on the faces of the soldiers who made up this detachment. In the trees behind him he could hear the constant croaking of frogs, the chirping of crickets, and the soft warbling of whippoorwills. One of the horses blew, nervously, and stomped its feet. C.V. went over to the animal and tried to calm him down, but the horse continued to prance about nervously.

A very tall, bearded soldier came over and took the horse's halter. The horse calmed. The soldier, who was a sergeant, patted the horse on the nose and spoke soothingly to it. He

Warriors of the Code

looked at C.V.

"Major, they tell me you knew ol' Abe," the sergeant said.

"Yes, Sergeant, I did know him," C.V. said.

"You're probably a mite more upset than the rest of us, then," he said. He continued to stroke the horse's nose. "Not to say that the rest of us ain't upset ourselves."

"Lincoln's death was a loss to all of us," C.V. said.

"Yes, sir, I reckon it was." The sergeant smiled and put out his hand. "My name's Corbett. Boston Corbett."

"You seem to have a way with horses. Sergeant Corbett," C.V. said.

"I'm from Texas," Corbett explained. "I reckon we're sorta raised knowin' horses down there." C.V. looked at the sergeant in surprise. "You're from Texas, but you fought for the North?"

"I fought for the Union," Sergeant Corbett said. "Seems to me the Union is for anyone who believes in it, be he from the North or the South."

"You've got a point there," C.V. said.

"I'm comin' out!" a voice shouted from inside the barn. A pair of hands were thrust through the barn door and two soldiers quickly manacled the prisoner, then led him away and tied him to a tree.

"That ain't Booth," Sergeant Corbett said. "That ain't the one who killed Lincoln."

"Who are you men?" the prisoner shouted. "Why have you hounded us like this? We're innocent of any crime! We didn't do anything!"

The prisoner continued on with a constant stream of almost incoherent protestations of innocence, but the soldiers paid no attention to him. The big fish, John Wilkes Booth, was still inside the barn.

Lieutenant Doherty made a straw torch, then tossed it into a pile of hay just inside the door of the barn. He was going to force Booth to come outside.

C.V. felt a white, churning heat, boiling up inside him, and he knew what he had to do.

"C.V.? C.V., where were you? You seemed about a million miles away just now."

Grady sat down opposite C.V. in the same chair occupied by Wyatt Earp a few minutes earlier. Or had it been only a few moments? C.V. had been so lost in thought that he had no idea how much time had passed. He got some indication, though, when he discovered that his coffee had grown cold.

"I was just thinking about something, that's all," C.V. said. He smiled. "How was your evening?"

"It was well spent, thank you," Grady said. His breakfast was put before him and he thanked the waiter. "I went down to the jail this morning to see Bat. He wants us to represent him."

"Yes, Wyatt was in here earlier and he told me as much. How is Bat? Is he very highly agitated?"

"No, he seems pretty calm," Grady said. He spread jam on a biscuit and took a big bite. "You know what he told me he'd like to do when all this is over?"

"What's that?"

"He'd like to go back east somewhere and work for a newspaper. He wants to be a journalist."

"He wants to leave Dodge?"

"Yes."

"So does Wyatt."

"I know. His brothers have already left."

"Perhaps there's a lesson to be learned there," C.V. suggested.

"What do you mean? What are you talking about?"

"I'm talking about leaving Dodge City," C.V. said.

"Now? Before the trial?"

"No, of course not. But once we've defended Bat, I'd like to propose that we move the firm somewhere else."

"Do you have any place in mind?"

"Perhaps Tombstone," C.V. suggested.

"Tombstone, Arizona . . . that reminds me. C.V., last night

I met the most breathtakingly beautiful woman I have ever seen in my life."

"Oh, come now," C.V. said. "The young lady was attractive, but I'd scarcely say she deserved accolades on that order."

"What? Oh, no. no. I'm not talking about Kate. I'm talking about Bianca."

"Bianca? Who is Bianca?"

"She's the woman I'm talking about," Grady explained. "I met her on the train. She wants us to do some legal work for her. C.V., wait until you see her. She'll absolutely take your breath away."

C.V. chuckled. "I can hardly wait. I haven't seen you this taken with a woman since your first visit td Madame Gameau's establishment in New Orleans."

Grady blushed, and C.V. chuckled again.

"Now I know why you decided to grow that beard," he said. "You've never learned to control your blushing."

"There's really no comparing Bianca to one of the women who work for Madame Gameau," Grady said. "And I'm quite sure she would resent such a comparison."

"Hold on, hold on there," C.V. said, holding out his hands. "You've no need to defend the lady's honor with me, Grady. I meant nothing by my remark."

"I know," Grady said. "It's just that, well, **I** .... "

"I know, you were stricken with her. That's understandable. Well, you turn your boyish charm loose on her and I'll wager she'll soon be returning your affections."

"I doubt it," Grady said. "She's a lot older than me."

"Oh?"

"Yeah, she's probably almost as old as you are.

"Heavens; she must be ancient!" C.V. grinned. He stood up. "I've got a few things to do over at the office. You see Judge Head and get Bat out on bail, then the two of you stop by and we'll start working on our defense."

"All right," Grady said, buttering his third biscuit.

C.V. stepped out onto the porch of the hotel. A kiosk sat in the middle of the dirt street right in front of the hotel. A sign on top of the kiosk read, "The carrying of firearms strictly prohibited, Ed Masterson, City Marshal. Below that sign a would- be entrepreneur had put up an advertising board. "Try Prickty Ash Bitters" the board read.

This was Front Street. He looked at the line of buildings across the street. Directly opposite was a place called Beatty Kelly's. It was a barber shop where one could also get a bath. Next to it was the Long Branch Saloon, next to that another barbershop, then another saloon, then a drygoods store, then another saloon. Down at the end of the street was the cemetery, called 'Boot Hill' because so many of the occupants of the cemetery had died with their boots still on. The idea of calling a cemetery 'Boot Hill' spread to other towns throughout the West, but it was Dodge City which first coined the name.

C.V. walked across the street on the plank walkway, stepping over a freshly deposited 'horse- apple' to avoid mussing his boots. He climbed up the stairs alongside the bank then opened the door and went into the law office. He raised the window to catch the morning breeze, then tore a sheet off the calendar to mark the passage of another day. The picture on the calendar was of a train crossing a high trestle over a deep mountain pass. The tops of the mountains were covered with snow, while the lower elevations were studded with Ponderosa pine trees. It was a night scene and the moon shined a vivid yellow from a starry, midnight sky. The train's headlamp sent a long, yellow beam stabbing ahead while every window in every passenger car glowed brightly. Sometimes when C.V. got tired of the view of the manure-spotted, dirty street outside his window, and of the weatherbeaten buildings across the way, he would stare for long moments at the picture of the train. During those moments he could almost project himself into the picture.

For some reason he found himself studying the picture this morning. He could almost feel the cool, mountain air, smell the pines, and hear the lonesome whistle.

"Excuse me, Senor. I hope I'm not disturbing you."

"The voice was soft, and well modulated. It was a woman's voice, and it reminded C.V. of a rushing brook. He turned around to stare into the large brown eyes of a devastatingly beautiful woman. She was so beautiful that, for a moment, she took his breath away. He knew without asking who she was.

"Miss Bianca, what can I do for you?" C.V. asked.

Now it was the woman's turn to gasp, and a quick flash of fire lit her eyes. C.V. could see that his calling her by name had startled her, and he smiled. "My young partner is rarely at a loss for words," he explained. "And though I recognized you from his description, even his glowing words were insufficient."

Bianca smiled.

"Thank you," she said. "I am most flattered by your remarks, and by the remarks of Senor Ford, your . . ." she smiled and raised one eyebrow, "young friend, as you call him."

"A boy," C.V. said. "A mere youth who has grown a beard because it amuses him. Please, Senorita, have a seat."

"It is Senora," Bianca said.

"Oh." C.V. said the word quietly, as if crestfallen.

"I'm a widow," she added.

"Oh," C.V. said again, smiling brightly. He sat down opposite her. "Tell me, Senora, what brings you to a lawyer?"

"I prefer to be called just Bianca," the darkeyed beauty said. She sighed. "I come here because I need help. I have tried to study the law so that I could help myself, but I am not so foolish as to think I can do it alone. Indeed, the territorial courts of Arizona may not even allow me to present my case."

"Arizona?"

"Yes," Bianca said. She tossed her head back, flipping a small strand of hair back into place. In a way it reminded C.V. of a beautiful horse tossing his head. There was the same sort of wild beauty to this woman, and he discovered that he was having a difficult time concentrating on what she was saying, because he was so. intrigued by the woman herself.

"My late husband was Don Esteban Lopez de Santa Anna."

"Santa Anna? The Santa Anna?"

"Yes," Bianca answered easily. My husband was the grandson of the Presidente."

C.V. gave a low whistle.

"I realize that my husband's grandfather is not one who is considered a hero to Americans. But that was many years ago, and my husband had nothing to do with any of that."

"It would take an evil-minded person to hold someone accountable for the sins of his grandfather," C.V. said. "But I gather that isn't your problem."

"No," Bianca said. She opened her reticule and removed a parchment. "I have here a land grant, transferring several thousand acres of land to my husband's family," she said. "This land grant was made in 1745, but, following the Mexican War, then the Gadsden Purchase, when the territory of Arizona became a part of the United States, the United States agreed to recognize all private land owners' rights to the land they then held. Here was the decision," she said, and she handed a piece of paper onto which had been copied the decision and the date of the decision.

"I see," C.V. said.

Bianca sighed.

"My husband raised cattle, Senor. He was a very good cattleman, and he had success where others failed. Then an American rancher, a man named Clanton, became jealous. He wanted my husband's land, and he devised a clever trick to steal it."

"How?"

"He went to Phoenix and he paid the taxes on my husband's ranch. When he paid the taxes, the title of the ranch passed to him. The sheriff, a man named Behan, came to see my husband. He told him that our land was no longer our own. He ordered us off, he wouldn't even let us take our belongings. My husband grew very angry and . . . " Bianca began to cry and she fished through her purse for a handkerchief. She found one, then dabbed at the tears. "He tried to reach for a gun which was near by, but Sheriff Behan pulled his own pistol and shot my husband dead."

"I don't like to say this. Bianca, but under the circumstances, Sheriff Behan could make a case for self defense. And, if your husband didn't pay his taxes . . . "

"But he did pay them," Bianca said. "He paid them and I have the receipts right here." She showed him the papers which she had so carefully preserved. "Do you see? Here it tells when the taxes were due, and here, when they were paid. Clanton had no right to pay the taxes on our ranch. The government had no right to give him the title."

C.V. looked through the papers without speaking.

"Senor Battenburg." Bianca said, "I want you to help me get my land back."

C.V. ran his hand through his hair. It appeared that Bianca had a very good case for the recovery of her property, and a substantial amount in damages. But this was a case which would have to be worked in Arizona, not Kansas.

"Bianca, why do you come here with this?" he asked. "Why don't you pursue this case in Arizona?"

"It is as I told your friend on the train last night," Bianca said. "I don't trust the lawyers in Arizona. And, I have a job here, in Dodge City."

"You have a job?"

"Yes. In Arizona I met a man named Virgil Earp. He told me his brother owned a place here, a restaurant, and that he would hire me to run it for him."

"You're talking about Wyatt Earp," C.V. said, stroking his chin. "It seems to me I do remember Wyatt speaking about opening a restaurant in the Long Branch. But that was before last night."

"Last night? What happened last night?"

"The City Marshal, a good friend of Wyatt's— mine too, as a matter of fact—was killed. The Marshal's brother killed the two men who did it, and now he's being held in jail. Wyatt is so disgusted with it all that he plans to leave Dodge. He's selling his interest in the Long Branch this morning."

"Oh," Bianca said. She leaned back in her seat and her face grew white. "Oh, my. I'm here without any means of support."

"That isn't necessarily so," C. V. said. "I think you have a very good case here. And if you recover your property, and damages, you'll come out of this with quite a tidy sum."

"I am mostly interested in recovering the land," Bianca said.

"Yes, but Mr. Clanton has had illegal use of your land. He owes you damages and we'll get it from him."

"We? You mean you will take the case?"

"Yes."

"Oh, Senor, that's wonderful!" Bianca said excitedly, then, just as suddenly as she had grown excited, her excitement cooled. "Oh, but I have no idea how I can pay you now. I had hoped to be able to earn enough by working for Mr. Earp to keep myself, and pay your fees."

"As far as my fees are concerned. I'll collect them from the damages we win," C.V. said. "And as far as earning your keep, well, how would you like to work for the firm of Battenburg and Ford?"

"Work for you? How? What would I do?"

"You say you have been reading the law?"

"Yes."

"Then you can clerk for us. There are many jobs which require both a knowledge of the law and neat penmanship. Grady and I are sufficient with the former, but sadly lacking in the latter. You could keep records, record deeds, that sort of thing. If you would like such a job, that is."

"Yes!" Bianca said. "Yes, I would very much like such a job. Thank you, Senor . . . "

C.V. held up his finger and wagged it back and forth to stop her.

"No. If we are going to work together, and if I am going to call you Bianca, then I insist that you call me C.V."

"C.V.? But aren't those just letters? Don't you have a name?"

C.V. chuckled. "If I ever did have a name my parents must have forgotten it before I grew up. I never heard them call me anything but C.V., and that's how my birth was recorded in the family Bible."

"C.V. ... I like it." Bianca said with a smile. "It is distinguished."

There was the sound of footfalls on the stairs, and men's voices in conversation. The door was pushed open, and Grady and Bat Masterson came inside.

"I got Bat out of jail, C.V., but we're going to have to work fast, the circuit judge is—" Grady saw Bianca and stopped in mid-sentence. He smiled, almost sheepishly, it seemed. "Good morning," he said. He looked at C.V.

"She's the one I . . ."

"Yes," C.V. said. "I know. Go on, you were saying something about the circuit judge?"

"That can wait until you've taken care of Miss Bianca."

"Bianca is all taken care of,' ' C.V. said. "We've just hired her."

"What? Hired her? To do what?" Grady sputtered.

"She's going to be our legal clerk. She's studied the law; she'll be quite good at it." C.V. saw that Grady was looking at Bianca in shock. "Grady," he went on. "Surely you wouldn't have us turn such a lovely creature out into the street?"

"No," Grady said, turning to the woman. "But I thought you told me you had some sort of problem with your land, down in Arizona."

"Yes," Bianca said. "I do."

"And we're going to take the case," C.V. said. "As soon as we have Bat free of this trumped-up charge, you and I are going to Tombstone. Isn't it great how it's all working out? We had planned to go there anyway, and now our first case has already presented itself."

"We hadn't planned to go there," Grady said. "You planned to go there."

"Well, so I did," C.V. replied. "Well, what do you say, Grady? You are a full partner in this firm. Shall we go to Tombstone and rescue this fair damsel in distress? Or shall we stay here in Dodge City and do daily battle with the likes of Mr. Larry Deger?"

Grady shook his head slowly, and smiled in resignation.

"If I said no, you would go anyway, wouldn't you?"

"If not to Tombstone, then somewhere else," C.V. admitted. "I told you, lad. I'm getting awfully itchy in the feet."

Grady sighed; then, laughing, gave in. "All right," he said. "The law firm of Battenburg and Ford will soon be doing business in Tombstone, Arizona Territory. But not until we've defended Bat."

"Of course not," C.V. said. "Now, you were saying about the circuit judge?"

"Oh, yes, he's due in this afternoon. They want to try the case tomorrow."

"Good, good, the quicker we come to trial, the better. Right now the incident is still fresh enough in everyone's mind that Bat is being talked about around town as a hero, while Mr. Walker and Mr. Wagner are being regarded as drunken no-account cowboys who terrorized the town and murdered the very likeable Ed Masterson; If we wait too long, however, they'll become poor cowboys who were victimized by Bat's fast guns. That's why I say the quicker we can come to trial, the better off we'll be."

"I'm sure you're right," Grady said.

"Of course I'm right. Now, Grady, you circulate around town, buy a few drinks, listen in on a few conversations, add a comment here and there if you have to, but make sure Bat stays the hero."

"All right," Grady said.

"Bat, in the meantime, you tell me everything that happened. Don't leave out a thing. Bianca, you take notes."

Chapter Five

JUDGE PHINEAS T. SHELBY was sent to Dodge City to preside over Bat Masterson's trial. The case had created a great deal of excitement around town, so much so that the courthouse was unable to hold everyone who wanted to attend. Because of that, Judge Shelby decided to hold court in the Comique Theater, where the comedian, Eddie Foy, was now appearing nightly. The opening session of Bat Masterson's trial drew more onlookers than did any of Eddie Foy's performances.

Judge Shelby was a no-nonsense judge, a former Texas Ranger who held court with a lawbook on one side of his bench and a six-shooter on the other. In a case he was hearing once, someone slipped the defendant a pistol. The defendant suddenly jumped up on the table and began blazing away at Judge Shelby. While the jury and the lawyers dived for cover under the tables and behind chairs, Judge Shelby coolly picked up his pistol and returned fire, blasting the defendant off the table. He allowed a doctor to treat the defendant's wounds before he continued the trial. The defendant was found guilty and sentenced to hang, but he died of his wounds two days later, a full day before he was scheduled to go to the gallows.

The Judge's bench, the jury box, and the tables for the

prosecutor and the defense were set up on the stage. At one table sat the prosecutor and Marshal Deger. At the other table was C.V. Battenburg and Bat Masterson. Bianca was also there, her presence granted by the Judge when C.V. explained that she was his law clerk. Grady wasn't present.

The gallery sat in the audience. Perhaps it was the theatrical atmosphere which caused them to applaud when Judge Shelby made his appearance. Judge Shelby rapped his gavel hard on the bench to restore order.

"This isn't a musical revue," he said gruffly. "We may be in a theater, but my very presence makes this a court of law. You will behave as such, or I shall have the bailiff throw you all out." Shelby was a tall, rangy man with skin like leather. His eyes seemed almost lazy behind half-drooping lids, but they missed nothing. He pulled his pistol out and lay it on the bench, then cleared his throat.

"Mr. Masterson, before we start this trial, I want to say a few words to you."

C.V. poked Bat in the side, and Bat stood up. "Yes, sir?"

"Mr. Masterson, the law our founding fathers put together has been working very well back East. It's had a bit more difficulty this side of the Mississippi, but there are some of us who intend to make certain that it does work. You, sir, were charged with just such a responsibility. If I find you guilty of misusing your authority as a law officer to gun down these two fellows . . . " Judge Shelby looked at a sheet of paper on his desk. "Wagner and Walker," he went on, "I intend to sentence you to hang. Is that clear?"

"Yes, Your Honor."

"And you, Marshal Deger. If Sheriff Masterson is found innocent of these charges you have brought against him, then I can only conclude that you brought the charges not out of a desire to see justice done, but for some personal reason. If that is the case, I shall deal harshly with you as well. Is that understood?"

"Yes, Your Honor," Marshal Deger answered.

"Very well," Judge Shelby said. He banged his gavel sharply. "Let this trial begin."

As C.V. had suspected, the prosecutor, a lawyer from Hayes City hired by Marshal Deger. began bringing on a chorus line of cowboys, all of whom testified as to the sterling behavior of the two dead men.

"They was good men, both of 'em," the foreman of the Lazy J said. The Lazy J was the ranch where Wagner and Walker worked. "I call 'em men, but they wasn't much more'n boys, really. I know they was always wantin' to buy somethin' to send back to their mamas."

"How long did they work for you," Mr. Anderson?"

"About six months," Anderson said.

"Did they ever get into fights with any of the other hands?"

"No, not a bit of it."

"Were they particularly adept with their guns?"

Anderson laughed. "I recall as to one afternoon when a group of the men was sportin' out in the barn lot. Wagner pulled his pistol from his holster tryin' to do a quick draw, 'n he damn near shot offen his own foot."

The gallery laughed out loud.

"So you wouldn't say that Mr. Wagner, or Mr. Walker, were either one a match for Bat Masterson, a man known all over the West for the quickness of his draw and the accuracy of his shooting?"

"Are you kiddin'? Mister, they couldn't both of 'em together have faced down a man like Bat Masterson, let alone one of 'em."

"Well, we have proof of that, don't we?" the prosecutor said.

"What do you mean?" Anderson asked. "They're both dead, Bat Masterson is alive." The prosecutor stood quietly for a long moment to let the impact of his words sink in. then he turned toward C.V.

"Your witness," he said.

Grady hurried from the telegraph office to the Comique Theater. He had told C.V. he was going to work on a hunch. He had telegraphed sheriffs and marshals within a five hundred mile radius of Dodge City, asking for any information on Casper Wagner and Charlie Walker. Now he had that response.

Grady arrived at the theater as C.V. was questioning Mr. Anderson, the first witness. He hurried over to the defense table and sat down between Bianca and Bat. He smiled at Bat. "How's it going?" Grady asked.

"I don't know," Bat mumbled. "To hear that fellow on the stand talk, I just killed a Baptist minister and a Methodist Sunday School teacher."

"Not quite," Grady said, smiling broadly. He showed Bat the answer to his telegram.

"It says here they're wanted dead or alive," Bat said. "But that's out of Arkansas."

"It's out of Arkansas, yes," Grady said. "But it's Judge Parker's warrant."

"Judge Parker? Hanging Judge Parker?"

"Yes," Grady said. "And he's a Federal Judge, .so his warrant is good anywhere in the United States, and the last time I checked, that still included Dodge City."

Judge Shelby suddenly banged his gavel in agitation."

"If the gentlemen at the defendant's table have something so important to discuss that they must interrupt this court, may I suggest that they share it with the bench?"

Grady was a little embarrassed at being publicly chastised, and he stood up and cleared his throat.

"Please the Court, Your Honor, may I speak with my partner?"

"By all means," Judge Shelby said in obvious exasperation. "Send him a telegram if you must. But please get on with it and allow the trial to continue."

C.V. walked over to the table, smiling at Grady's discomfort.

"What is it, Grady? What do you have?"

"I told you I had a hunch," Grady said. "The hunch paid off." He showed C.V. the telegram. C.V. read it, then turned to the bench.

"Your Honor, with your permission, I would like to yield to my colleague at this point."

"What? C.V., no!" Grady said in a near-whisper. "I've never represented anyone who was being tried for murder before. This is too important, you handle it."

"Bat, what do you think?" C.V. asked. "You're the one with the most at stake. You think Grady can handle it?"

"I've got complete confidence in him," Bat said easily.

Grady looked over at Bianca and saw that she, too, was smiling at him, so he cleared his throat, then stood up.

"Your Honor, I see by the notes our law clerk took, that the two dead men, Wagner and Walker, have been presented to the Court as fine, upstanding citizens."

"I thought they were running for Congress," C.V. said, and everyone laughed.

"I know Mr. Anderson," Grady said, looking at the ranch foreman. "I know he is a decent man, and I'm certain that he described Wagner and Walker as he knew them. Perhaps they managed to fool Mr. Anderson into thinking they were honest, hard-working cowboys, who only came into town to have a good time. But the facts speak differently."

"What facts?" Judge Shelby asked.

"Your Honor, I have in my hand a telegram, a reply from Judge Isaac Parker of Fort Smith, Arkansas. I believe you once worked for the Honorable Judge Parker?"

"I did," Shelby said, reaching for the telegram. "As you can see, Your Honor, they were not quite the innocents Mr. Anderson thought them to be."

"Objection. Whatever their past, it has no bearing on the matter at hand," the Hayes City lawyer- cum-prosecutor said quickly.

"In this case, I believe it does," Grady said. "As you can

see, Mr. Wagner and Mr. Walker are known to have robbed a bank in Guthrie, Oklahoma Territory. There they killed two unarmed bank tellers."

There were several exclamations of surprise from the gallery.

"Judge Parker issued a warrant for their arrest. It is a dead-or-alive warrant," Grady said. "The truth is, Judge, that even if there was no case for self-defense, which we say there is, then the homicide would still be justifiable. Sheriff Masterson was discharging his duty. I request that this case be dismissed."

"Hold on here! Masterson didn't know they were wanted men," Marshal Deger said.

"Nevertheless, the fact remains that they were wanted men," Judge Shelby said. He looked over at the jurybox. "Gentlemen of the jury, you are dismissed." He picked up the gavel and banged it down sharply. "This case is dismissed, and court is adjourned."

A rousing cheer went up from those in the gallery, and Bat reached out, happily, to shake C.V.'s hand.

"Don't shake my hand," C.V. said. He beamed at his younger protege. "There's the man who got you off the hook."

"You would have gotten him off anyway." Grady said, modestly. "It was a clear case of self-defense and everyone knew it."

"Maybe," C.V. said. "But when walking a path of peril, one should always take the path of least resistance. Your hunch paid off and our client is freed."

"Congratulations, Bat," Wyatt said, hopping up onto the stage then. "If I ever get into trouble, I want you guys in my corner," he added, looking at C.V. and Grady. He touched the brim of his hat toward Bianca. "Now, what say we all go over to the Long Branch for a drink?"

C.V. looked at Bianca. "Provided we drink in your private dining room," he said. "I would like our new assistant to join us."

"Sure," Wyatt said easily. "Why not? It's my last day here anyway. Tomorrow I'm headin' for Tombstone. This can be a celebration and goodbye, all at the same time."

"I judged some down in Texas," Judge Shelby was saying. Judge Shelby, C.V., Grady, Bianca, Wyatt, Bat, and Chalk Beeson, Wyatt's one-time partner in the Long Branch, were all sitting around a long table in a back room of the Long Branch. The table was set with the remains of their dinner, and half a dozen bottles of wine had already been consumed. They were swapping yarns now, and Judge Shelby, the stern disciplinarian of the courtroom, was now one of the celebrants at the dinner.

"You were a judge down there? I thought you were just a lawman," Wyatt said.

"In those days you sometimes had to be lawman and judge. And sometimes even jury. The country I worked was pretty desolate." Shelby chuckled. "I remember one time empanelling a jury to try a horse thief. I noticed one of the jurors wasn't wearin' a jacket and I figured that was an affront to my court. I pointed my finger at him and in the sternest voice I could muster, I ordered him to go home and get a jacket on, then come back so we could continue with the trial."

Judge Shelby took a cigar out of his inside jacket pocket, silently asked Bianca for permission to smoke and when she granted it he bit the end off and lit it, continuing his story between puffs.

"Well sir," he went on, "the feller left my court and I called a recess so we could wait for him. That was about ten o'clock in the mornin'." Shelby took several more puffs so as to drag the story out. "Noontime come and the feller wasn't back, so we broke for lunch. We waited all afternoon and he didn't come then either." He took a few more puffs then examined the end of his cigar. "He didn't show up the next day neither. Then, on the third day, just as I was gettin' ready to swear in a new juror, in he come, wearin' a black frock coat you would'a thought he'd had dinner with the Governor in. 'Is this here coat good enough, Your Honor?' he asked, as he took his seat in the jury box. 'Why, sure 'tis,' I answered. 'But where in tarnation have you been?' 'Your Honor,' says he, 'you told me to go home and get my coat. I live more'n eighty miles from here.'"

Everyone around the table laughed, and Judge Shelby held up his hand. "Wait," he said. "I asked the feller, I said, 'Whyn't you tell me how far away you lived?' And he said, 'Cause you never asked me.'"

"I'm right glad this trial came out the way it did," Wyatt said, pouring another round. "I wanted to leave here with a clean slate."

"Where are you going?" Shelby asked.

"Wyatt's going down to Tombstone," Bat said. "So are Battenburg and Ford," C.V. added.

"And you, Bat? Are you going to Tombstone as well?"

"No," Bat said. He swirled the wine around in his glass then took a swallow before he answered. "But I am leaving Dodge."

"And where might you be bound?"

"New York City."

"New York?" Judge Shelby said, surprised by Bat's statement. "What the hell is a man like you gonna do in New York?"

"Hang up my guns for one thing," Bat said.

"And take up journalism for another," C.V. said. He held up his glass. "Bat, I know you'll make a fine journalist."

"And you, madam," Judge Shelby said to Bianca. "You've been very quiet tonight. What are your plans? Will you be going to Tombstone or New York?"

Bianca smiled. "I'll be going to Tombstone," she said. "I have some unfinished business there."

"Tombstone's gain will be your loss, Chalk," Wyatt said, speaking to his ex-partner.

"What do you mean?"

"This is Bianca. Remember, I told you I had answered a

letter from a lady who wanted to run a restaurant in the back of the Long Branch?

"Yes."

"This was the lady."

"Really?" Chalk said, looking at Bianca. "Listen, you don't have to go back to Tombstone just because I bought Wyatt out," he said. "Whatever opportunity he offered you, I shall make as well."

"Sorry, Chalk, I've already hired her," C.V. spoke up quickly. "She's been reading Law, and I've hired her as a clerk for our firm."

"I've never known a lady to read Law before," Judge Shelby said. "Though I can think of no reason why she shouldn't. Are you thinkin' of takin' up the profession?"

"No, Your Honor," Bianca said. "I have a personal matter back in Arizona I want to take care of. I thought there might be some advantage in learning the Law."

"I don't know what your problem is. madam, but I hope it is favorably resolved," Judge Shelby said. He looked at C.V. and Grady. "And if these two gentlemen are allied with you, I would say you have an excellent chance of success. Young man, that was a very good move on your part today. There's no better way to stop a railroad job than to derail the train and that's just what you did."

"I'm glad you recognized it as a railroad job," Bat said. "To tell the truth, I was a little worried."

"If this had happened a year or so ago, under Judge Landis, you might have had cause for some worry," Judge Shelby said.

Chalk Beeson chuckled. "I remember Landis," he said. "He once hung half a dozen men at the same time."

"Yes." C.V. said dryly. "I remember that as well. I'd been assigned by the court to defend one of them."

"I don't remember that," Grady said.

"It was before you came along," C.V. said. He brushed his hand through his hair. "It wasn't one of my happier experiences," he went on.

"Was your man guilty?" Wyatt asked.

"I'm sure he was." C.V. said. "The court had half a dozen witnesses against him. He and a friend came into town and got drunk. They had a falling out over the favors of some girl down in the red light district. Ebersole, my client, went back for his gun, then returned to the house and killed his friend."

"Then I'd say hanging was a just punishment," Wyatt said. "Why do you say it wasn't one of your happier experiences?"

"Ebersole was entitled to a defense, the best defense I could give him. Yet Judge Landis had everything arranged so there would be no chance of a surprise. I could only talk to my client in the courtroom, I couldn't visit him in the jail. And while he was in jail, for the whole time, he was kept bound, hand and foot, and he had to wear a hood with thick pads over the eyes and ears so he could neither see nor hear. He may have been a murderer, but he was a still human being and he deserved humane, civilized treatment while he was in jail."

"Sounds to me like a violation of the Constitution—-it could have been considered cruel and unusual punishment," Judge Shelby suggested.

"I attempted just such a plea," C.V. said. "But Judge Landis threw the plea out."

"I didn't know anything about all that," Chalk said. "I just remember the day of the hanging. There must have been seven or eight thousand people here to watch it."

"That many people in Dodge at one time?" Grady said. "I can hardly imagine it."

"It was crowded, all right," Chalk said. "They built the scaffold right out in the middle of the street, well, about where that kiosk is now. It was a fine piece of workmanship, with posts and crossbeams made of eight-inch timbers. From the time word went out that there was to be six men hung at the same time, folks started pourin' into Dodge. For three days wagons came into town, to the point where they was parked double along both sides of the street and had completely filled the livery. So many folks come by train that the Santa Fe had to add extra cars. All the businesses in town closed down, the farmers and ranchers and their families let their land go, just so's they could see. On the day of the hangin' there was folks crowded in the street from one end to the other, packed in so solid a body couldn't get from one side of the street to the other even if he wanted to. There must've been five or six hundred of 'em on the roofs, though most of them was youngsters."

"Children?" Bianca gasped. "Children came to watch such a spectacle?"

"Yes, ma'am," Chalk said. "Of course, one thing you gotta remember is that this here was a legal hangin.' I believe it was the first legal hangin' ever to take place here. The only kind before that was lynchin's, so nobody wanted to miss a real, legal hangin.' Well, you seen it, didn't you, C.V.?"

"No," C.V. said. "I was too disgusted with Judge Landis' court to stay around. I left before the hanging." He looked at Grady. "That was just before you and I hooked up, Grady."

"You saw the hanging, didn't you, Chalk?" Bat asked.

"Yeah," Chalk said. Though he had been telling the story almost proudly, he paused now, and was silent for a moment, as if reflecting. "Yeah, I seen it," he went on. quieter than before. "It . . . it wasn't pretty. The Sheriff, a fella by the name of Mason, I believe it was . . . you remember him, Bat—he got hisself killed off in Wichita not too long after you come here."

"I remember him," Bat said.

"Anyway, Sheriff Mason read the six death sentences, then they let the condemned men speak their last words.

"I'll never forget what one of 'em said. He said, 'Boys, this is really gonna teach me a lesson,'" Chalk laughed, dryly. "It got a chuckle, even then. Another one, the fella you defended, C. V., said I'm 'bout as ready to get out of here as you folks are to see me go.' Anyway, after all that was said 'n done, the hangman pulled the lever that opened the trap. There was only one trap door for all of 'em, so they all went at the same time. Four of 'em looked like they died pretty quick, but a couple of 'em went real slow. They kept bendin' at the waist like as if they could take some of the weight off their necks. It took one of 'em near half an hour afore he quit twitchin.'"

Bianca shivered, and C.V. put his arm around her.

"Can't we find something else to talk about?" Grady asked, noticing Bianca's reaction.

"Sure," Bat said. "Chalk, why don't you play your fiddle for us? Wyatt, go on out front and send some of the ladies back here. We'll have a dance."

"I don't think so," Wyatt said, looking toward Bianca.

Bianca smiled and stood. "Please, gentlemen," she said. "Don't let me spoil the evening for you. I feel I may have eaten too much. I think I'll just get a little air if you don't mind."

"I'll go with you," C.V. said quickly. They left by the back door, then walked down the alley, away from the hotel. They passed by the rear of the Alhambra Saloon, and they heard a piano cranking away. A few moments later they passed a Chinese laundry, and they could hear the workers jabbering away in their strange, musical language. They heard a baby crying, then they were at the western end of the row of buildings, and nothing lay before them except wide open spaces. They stood there, looking at the track as it curved out to the west, it's twin steel ribbons gleaming softly in the moonlight.

Bianca sighed.

"What is it?" C.V. asked. "What's wrong?"

"C.V., when God created us, did he leave something out?" Bianca asked. "Is there some part of our heart missing which will allow man to be so cruel?"

"You're talking about the hanging?"

"Yes," Bianca said. "Well, not just the hanging. The killing, whether it is by a Judge or by another man."

"Bianca, have you ever seen how a forest fire is fought?"

"No," Bianca answered, puzzled by the question.

"When a fire begins in one part of the forest," C.V. said,

"It is sometimes necessary to start a fire in another part, so that the two fires burn together. When that happens there is nothing left to burn and the fire dies. You have to do that to save the rest of the forest, to fight fire with fire. Sometimes it's like that with men. The law has to take as hard a position as the criminals, or there Would never be any respect for the law."

"You have a great love for the law, don't you?" Bianca asked, looking up at C.V.

"Yes," C.V. said. "With law, we can touch the face of God. Without it, we are animals."

C.V. had been looking off into the distance as he made that remark. He believed that with all his heart and soul. Maybe it was the fact that he believed in it so strongly which made it so difficult for him to live with what he had done that night in Virginia. He blinked his eyes once to get the thought out of his mind, then he looked back at Bianca. She was looking up at him, her face radiantly beautiful in the moonlight. Then, as if moved by a force outside himself, he brought his lips to hers.

C.V. had known many women, but he had never known a woman quite like Bianca. Because of that his kiss was, at first, hesitant, and he was ready to back away at the first sign of resistance on her part. To his surprise, though, she didn't resist him. Instead her lips were soft, eager, receptive, and she put her arms around him and pulled herself against him.

C.V. could feel every curve of her womanly body as she clung to him, and he knew, also, that she was aware of the immodest pressure of his growing need for her. When he tried to pull away, Bianca plied herself to him even more tightly, not shying away from his condition. Finally they separated, and C.V. looked into her face.

"I . . . I'm sorry," he said. "I had no right to do that."

"C.V.," Bianca said in her exciting, husky voice. "I'm not a whore, but neither am I a young virgin, quivering in fear at the thought of a man's touch. I've been married before. I know the pleasures a man and woman can share, and . . . " she paused and looked into his eyes. Never had C.V. stared so deeply into another person's eyes, and never had he seen a soul as bared as the soul of this lovely creature with him. "I want us to share those pleasures," she went on. "I want to go to your room with you ... I want us to make love."

Chapter Six

WHEN THE SOLDIERS from Fort Hauchuca, Arizona, happened across Ed Schieffelin in the Dragoon Mountains of southeastern Arizona, he looked like the remaining survivor of some lost tribe of savages. His long, black hair was matted and stringy on his shoulders, his beard was a nest of crawling things, and his clothes were filthy, and patched with rabbit skin. The soldiers had to look a second time before they realized that he was a white man, a civilized member of their own society.

"What the hell are you doin' out here?" the sergeant in charge of the patrol asked.

"I'm prospectin'," Schieffelin answered.

"Prospectin'? Ha!" the sergeant laughed. "Prospectin' for what?"

"For whatever I can find," Schieffelin answered.

The sergeant laughed again. "Mister, I'll tell you what you're gonna find here. Your tombstone, that's what."

The soldiers rode on, leaving Ed Schieffelin to poke around the hills alone. A short time later he discovered silver-bearing ore, and not just in some small amount, but in huge veins which stretched for thousands of yards back into the

Warriors of the Code

mountains. A town soon sprung up on the desert bedrock around the silver hills, and Ed Schieffelin, remembering the sergeant's derisive comment, decided to call it Tombstone.

When Grady, C.V. and Bianca stepped off the train in Tombstone, they were looking at a town whose reputation as "hell's wide open playground" exceeded even that of Dodge City. If ever there was a place which needed the civilizing influence of law, it was Tombstone, Arizona Territory. C.V. and Bianca took a cab to the hotel to arrange for rooms for all of them. Grady volunteered to stay back and see to the luggage.

Grady's first impression of the town was one of incredible heat. It bore down on him like some great weight. He stood on the station platform while behind him vented steam from the train's escape valve sounded like some exhausted monster, gasping for breath in the terrible heat. Heat waves shimmered up from the streets and Grady wondered what kept the town from just melting.

He saw a black frying pan sitting on a stump as he walked toward the depot, and, curious about it, he walked over to pick it up. The handle of the skillet was as hot as if it had been sitting over an open fire, and with a sharp exclamation of pain he dropped the pan.

There were three or four of the town's citizens sitting on a baggage cart under the shade of the car shed's overhang. When they saw Grady's reaction, they all burst out in loud guffaws.

"Was the pan hot, mister?" one of them asked.

"Not really," Grady answered, managing a goodnatured grin despite his embarrassment.

"You shore put it down fast," one of the men said.

"Well, how long does it take to look at a frying pan?"

"How long does it take to look at a pan?" one of the men replied, and he and the others laughed loudly at Grady's rejoinder. "That's pretty good. We've got lots of folks with that skillet, but you been the best yet. Mister, you're all right in our book."

"Why do you keep this skillet sitting out here like this?" Grady asked.

"Well, since you been such a good sport about it. I'll tell you the truth," one of the men said. "We're trollin' for fools."

"What?"

"You got 'ny idea how hot a black iron skillet like that can get in this sun? Well, you do now, you picked it up. But there's lots of folks who are just as curious, 'n if you'll excuse me for sayin' so, just as much a fool as you were. They can't keep their hands offen it. They walk over 'n pick it up, 'n we get our little laugh. Like I say, we're trollin' for fools."

"Let me show you somethin', mister," one of the others said. He picked up an egg and brought it over to the pan, then broke it. The egg began to sizzle and turn white.

Grady chuckled. "There must not be a hell of a lot to do in Tombstone if you have to stay down here and do this," he said.

"Oh, I wouldn't say that. Problem is, Tombstone really only comes to life at night."

Grady went into the depot then, and made arrangements for the luggage to be sent over to the hotel. After that he walked up the wide, sun-baked street, hurrying from the shade of one adobe building to the next, taking every opportunity to get out of the sun. After a walk of no more than a few blocks he was drenched with sweat, and the cool interior of a saloon beckoned him. A sign outside the saloon promised ice-cold beer, and Grady thought nothing could be better than that. He pushed his way through the bat-wing doors and went inside. It was so dark that he had to stand there for a moment or two until his eyes adjusted. The bar was made of burnished mahogany with a highly polished brass footrail. Crisp, clean white towels hung from hooks on the customers' side of the bar, spaced every four feet. A mirror was behind the bar, flanked on each side by a small statue of a nude woman set back in a special niche. A row of whiskey bottles sat in front of the mirror, reflected in the glass so that the row of bottles

Warriors of the Code

seemed to be two deep. A bartender with slicked-back black hair and a handlebar moustache stood behind the bar, industriously polishing glasses.

"Is the beer really cold?" Grady asked.

The bartender looked up at him, but he didn't stop polishing the glasses.

"It's cooler than spit," he said, matter-of-factly.

"I'll have one."

The bartender drew a mug and set it in front of Grady. Grady blew away some of the foam, then took a deep, thirsty swallow. It was as cool and refreshing as a mountain stream, and he drank the whole mug without putting it down.

The bartender set another one in front of him and Grady picked it up and took another long drink before he turned and looked around the place. A card game was going on in the comer and he watched it for a few moments while he drank his beer.

Suddenly the back door opened and a tall, broad shouldered, bearded man, wearing a badge, stepped through the door. He pointed a gun toward the table.

"John Fairchild? I'm United States Marshal Boston Corbett, and I've come here to take you in."

"For God's sake, don't shoot, mister!" someone shouted. Three of the four card players jumped up from the table and moved back out of the way. The fourth player, the man Grady figured to be John Fairchild, remained seated. His hands were still on the table in front of him, the cards were still in his hand.

"It's taken a while, Fairchild, but I finally caught up with you."

"Aw, now, Marshal, you've gone 'n busted up a winnin' hand," Fairchild grumbled.

"Money won't be doin' you any good where you're goin'," the tall marshal said. "Stand up and face me, then, with your left hand, unbuckle your gunbelt, slow 'n easy."

Fairchild stood up and turned to face the marshal. For a moment it looked as if he had a notion to try him.

"I'd advise you not to try anythin' foolish," the marshal said. "Give yourself up peaceful, 'n you'll at least get your day in court."

"They was half a dozen witnesses seen me gun down that stage guard," Fairchild said. "What good's a day in court gonna do me?"

"Didn't say you'd get off," the marshal said. "I just said you'd have your day in court. Now, shuck out of that gun."

Grady watched the drama unfolding before him, thrust by fate into this ringside seat. Then he heard a sound, a soft squeaking sound as if weight were being put down on a loose board. He looked up to the top of the stairs and saw a man standing there, aiming a shotgun at the back of the United States Marshal.

"Marshal, look out!" Grady shouted. When he shouted his warning the man wielding the shotgun turned it toward Grady.

"You squealin' son-of-a-bitch!" he shouted. The shotgun boomed loudly.

Grady had no choice then. He dropped his beer and pulled his pistol, firing just as the man at the top of the stairs squeezed his own trigger. Grady had jumped away from the bar as he fired and it was a good thing, because the heavy charge of buckshot tore a large hole in the top and side of the bar right where Grady had been standing. Some of the shot hit the whiskey bottles and the mirror behind the bar, and pieces of glass flew everywhere. The mirror fell except for a few jagged shards which hung in place where the mirror was, reflecting twisting images of the dramatic scene before it.

Grady's shot had been more accurately placed, and the man with the shotgun dropped his weapon and grabbed his neck. He stood there, stupidly, for a moment, clutching his neck as blood spilled between his fingers. Then his eyes rolled up in his head and he fell, twisting around so that, on his back, head-first, he slid down the stairs, following his clattering shotgun. He lay motionless on the bottom step with open, but sightless eyes staring up toward the ceiling.

The sound of the two gunshots had riveted everyone's attention to that exchange, and while their attention was diverted from him, John Fairchild took the opportunity to go for his own gun. Grady was still looking on with sick disbelief at the man he had just killed when the bar was suddenly filled with the roar of another handgun as Fairchild shot at Marshal Corbett.

The marshal had made the mistake of looking at the man Grady shot, and it was nearly his last mistake. Fortunately for him, Fairchild's aim wasn't as good as Grady's had been, and the forty-four caliber bullet from his gun whistled through the crown of the marshal's hat, whipping it off his head but doing nothing more.

Marshal Corbett recovered quickly from his moment of distraction, whirling back toward Fairchild, returning his fire. His bullet struck Fairchild in the forehead, and the impact of it knocked Fairchild back on a nearby table. He lay belly up on the table with his head hanging down on the far side, while blood poured from the hole in his forehead to form a puddle below him. His gun fell from his lifeless hand and clattered to the floor. Marshal Corbett swung his pistol toward the three men who had been playing cards with Fairchild, thumbing back the hammer as he did so.

"Any of you men aimin' to take a hand in this?" he asked gruffly.

"Not me, Marshal," one of the men said, throwing up his arms.

"No, not me either," a second one shouted. He, like the other two men, threw up his hands.

"I never seen this here feller before a couple of days ago," the third one said. "I didn't even know he was a wanted man."

Gunsmoke from the four charges had merged to form a large, acrid-bitter cloud which drifted slowly toward the door. Beams of sunlight became visible as they stabbed through the cloud. Grady heard rapid footfalls on the wood walk outside, then someone stepped in through the swinging doors. He was carrying a pistol, but there was a flash of light from the star on his chest. Then Grady recognized him, and he smiled brightly.

"Wyatt?"

Wyatt Earp recognized Grady and he returned the smile and put his pistol back in his holster.

"Hello, Grady," he said.

"Wyatt, do you know this fella?" the tall marshal asked.

"I sure do. He and his partner are two of the finest lawyers you'll ever meet. I'll vouch for him, Boston, if need be."

Boston Corbett smiled and holstered his own gun. "Don't reckon I need anyone to speak for him," he said. "He just saved my life. Plugged this fella at the top of the stairs while he was drawin' down on me with a scattergun."

Wyatt walked over and looked at the two men. "Met both these men yesterday," he said. "They told me their names were Parker and Brown." - "That one over there on the table is John Fairchild. I shot him. The one your lawyer friend shot is called Avery Miller. You'll find paper on both of them."

Wyatt chuckled, and looked at Grady. "It didn't take you too long to get involved here, did it?"

"I guess not," Grady said. He felt a little queasy inside. "This is the first time I ever had to shoot a man."

"You did it right the first time," Wyatt said. "You killed him deader than a doornail."

"I didn't have time not to."

"You handle a gun pretty good for someone who's never had to use it," Boston said.

"I know how to use it," Grady said. "I've just never had to before. I prefer to let the law do my talking."

"That's good," Boston said. "When we get enough fellers like you out here, we won't need quite as many like me."

"I saw C.V. and Bianca down at the hotel a moment ago," Wyatt said to Grady. "They told me you were down at the depot taking care of the luggage. I came down to give

Warriors of the Code

you a hand. I was just outside when the shooting started."

"Did C.V. get us rooms?" Grady asked.

"Yes. Oh, and I haven't been wasting my time over the last month either. I got an office for you. It's a room up over my saloon, but you have an outside stairs. The sign is already up too." Marshal Corbett pointed at the two bodies. "Guess we better send the undertaker back for these two galoots."

"He'll hear about it soon enough," Wyatt said. "Come on, let's get over to the hotel."

"Why don't you come along. Marshal?" Grady asked. "I'd like you to meet my partner."

"All right. It's nice to know one good lawyer, it should be even better to know two."

The three men walked back out into the sunlight, and Grady had to squint his eyes to keep the painful sun out.

"They're at the Grand Hotel over on Allen," Wyatt said. "Actually, I think they're in The Grotto, which is the dining room just below the hotel. Say, that Bianca is a fine looking woman, isn't she?"

"Yes," Grady said.

"I think C.V. is taken with her, don't you?" Wyatt chuckled.

"He'd better never do anything to hurt her," Grady said with a bit more passion than he intended. He really didn't want anyone to know how he felt about Bianca.

Wyatt looked at him with surprise. "She's a mite old for you, isn't she boy?" Wyatt asked with surprising gentleness.

Grady grinned sheepishly. "Age is only a matter of the mind," he said.

They were walking on Fremont, and they turned to go down Fourth, which led to Allen Street, just one block away. Wyatt pointed to a livery stable.

"That's the O.K. Corral," he said. "You can buy a good horse there and keep him there too. Or you can rent one when you have a need for it."

"I'll drop in and take a look around later," Grady said.

They turned onto Allen Street and a moment later went inside the Grand Hotel. The Grotto was off the lobby to one side, and Grady heard C.V.'s laugh, as soon as they stepped inside.

"He's in there, all right," Grady said with a smile.

"Say, C.V. what is it about your young friend, here?" Wyatt asked when they stepped into the dining room. "He wasn't in town much more than an hour when he got involved in a shootout over at the Capitol Saloon."

"What?" C.V. asked, rising. "Grady, are you all right? What happened?"

"What happened is he saved my life," Boston said.

C.V. looked at the tall U.S. Marshal, then gasped and took a step backwards. "Sergeant Boston Corbett," he said, speaking the words almost as if in shock.

"Major Battenburg? Is it you?" the Marshal asked, just as surprised as C.V.

The two men shook hands heartily while the others looked on in surprise at their recognition.

"I gather that you two know each other?" Grady said.

"We met during the war," C.V. said.

"Well," Wyatt put in, smiling broadly. "Then that calls for a double celebration. One because my friends have joined me here in Tombstone, and another because two old war veterans have gotten together. How about champagne?"

More chairs were brought up to the table so that everyone could be accommodated, and a moment later they were happily drinking champagne.

As C.V. and Boston Corbett talked, Wyatt watched quietly, as if he were deep in thought. Then, suddenly, he snapped his fingers and pointed at the tall marshal.

"Now I remember where I've heard your name." he said. "You're the man who shot Booth."

"Booth?" Grady asked.

"John Wilkes Booth, the actor who killed President Lincoln. Boston Corbett is the man who shot him."

Boston looked down at his glass.

"I really don't like to talk about that," he said.

"Why not?" Wyatt asked. "Is it because you didn't face him down in the street with both guns blazing? Hell, Corbett, don't worry about that. You've proven your courage enough times, and that son of bitch deserved to die like a dog."

"I guess so," Boston said quietly.

"What happened?" Grady asked.

"Grady, he said he didn't want to talk about it, so why don't you just forget it?" C.V. said gruffly.

Grady was a little stung by the sharpness of C.V.'s remark. C.V. hadn't spoken to him in such a tone since Grady was very young, and he looked at him in surprise.

"C.V.," Bianca said, also surprised by the lawyer's uncharacteristic outburst.

C.V. sighed and ran his hand through his hair.

"I'm sorry, Grady," he said.

"No, it's my fault," Boston said quickly. "Look, there's not much to tell, really. I was a sergeant then, on one of the detachments which was sent after Booth. We found him in Virginia, hiding out in a barn, and Lieutenant Doherty, the officer in charge of the detail, set fire to the hay in the barn.

I was around to one side and I could see Booth through the cracks in the wall. Then I . . ."

"Boston," C.V. said, holding up his hand to interrupt him. "Let me."

"Major, you don't have to say—

"Please," C.V. interrupted again. "Let me tell the story."

C.V. drank the rest of his champagne, then looked around the table. In all the years Grady had known him, he had never seen an expression quite like that which was on his face now. It was an expression of pain. It was the manifestation of all the secret sorrow Grady had ever seen in his friend's face over all the years he had known him.

"I was on that detail too," C.V. said, brushing his hair

back nervously. "Grady, I've told you how Lincoln asked me to go to the theatre with him the night he was assassinated, and how I turned him down."

"Yes," Grady said.

"Well. I blamed myself for what happened. I was insensate and guilt-ridden, and I volunteered for the first detachment of soldiers I could find who were searching for Booth. That turned out to be Lieutenant Doherty's detail, the same detail to which Sergeant Corbett was assigned."

C.V. started to pour himself another glass of champagne, but he changed his mind and poured himself a glass of whiskey instead. He drank it, then wiped his mouth with the back of his hand.

"We searched for him for eleven days. Then, before daylight on the 26th of April, we found Booth and Herold in a tobacco barn on a farm belonging to a family named Garrett. The farm was near Port Royal, Virginia, and it was less then sixty miles from Washington. We surrounded the barn and Herold shouted out to us that he wanted to surrender. He came out and we tied him to a tree. Then, just as Boston said, Lieutenant Doherty set fire to the hay inside the barn, intending to smoke Booth out. I remember standing there in the dark, listening to the fire snap and pop, and hoping ... no, praying, that Booth would stay in there and die in the flames."

"If you were a major, why was the lieutenant in charge?" Wyatt asked.

"I wasn't attached to the division which made up the posse," C.V. said. "I was just a volunteer. I volunteered because I felt I had to do something. I had let Lincoln down, you see, and I had to make it up to him. Add to that the sorrow I felt, along with every other American, at losing our President, compounded by the fact that Lincoln was also my personal friend, my mentor, the man who introduced me to Law. Those were the thoughts going through my head as the barn burned. Then, I don't know, I can barely remember doing it, but I walked around to the side of the barn. I saw Boston standing there, looking through the cracks at the fire inside. He was holding his carbine down by his side. 'Can you see him?' I asked. He nodded yes, and I looked through at him. By now the fire was roaring, and smoke was pouring out of the loft window. But there, inside, silhouetted by the blazing fire, I saw Booth step close to the door. He was holding a carbine, leaning on a crutch and looking through the slats, as if trying to find a target. He was only holding the gun with one hand, and even had he found a target I doubt that, under the circumstances, he would have been able to make an accurate shot. Nevertheless, I ordered Sergeant Corbett to shoot him."

"I did, too," Boston said. "I didn't have to be told twice. I took one shot and hit him right in the back of the head."

C.V. continued the narrative. "As soon as Boston shot him, Lieutenant Doherty sent soldiers in to get him. They dragged him outside onto the grass, but the barn was blazing by that point, and we all had to move away or get roasted. They carried Booth over to the front porch of the Garrett house. At first I thought he was dead, but someone threw some water in his face, and I saw that he was trying to say something."

C.V. took another swallow of his whiskey, and Grady knew that he was having a very difficult time, that he was now reliving a part of his life which had been so terrible that not until this moment had he ever spoken of it.

"Here was a man, a fellow human being, in the last moments of his life on earth, trying, pitifully, to speak. I should have had some compassion for his suffering. Instead, I hated the son of a bitch."

"What did he say?" Wyatt asked. "Could you understand him?"

"Yeah," C.V. said. "He said, 'Tell my mother I died for my country, and,' he had to stop and draw another breath then, a rasping, torturous breath before he finished in a whisper, 'I did what I thought was best.' Can you imagine that? He was dying, but he was totally unrepentant. He actually wanted the message taken to his mother that he had done what he thought was best. I wanted to kill him. Then he asked someone to lift up his arms so he could see his hands. His last two words were, 'Useless. Useless.' I've never been able to figure out what he meant by that. I don't know if he meant that his hands were useless, or that his act had been useless. At any rate, he lingered on for another couple of hours. He didn't say anything else, he just labored to breathe. Then, at about sunrise, he breathed his last."

C.V. closed his eyes for a moment and leaned his head back. Grady thought he was through with his story, but he went on.

"Lieutenant Doherty reprimanded Boston for shooting Booth. It was my intention to tell the lieutenant that I ordered him to shoot, but the sergeant insisted I keep my peace."

"I was going to shoot the bastard anyway." Corbett interjected. "Besides, you were an officer and a lawyer. I figured you had a lot more to lose than I did."

"I thank you. my friend, for what you tried to do for me," C.V. said. "But the truth is. it didn't work. You see, we lost sight of one important thing: I was my own judge and jury. Here I was, a man dedicated to justice and the Law. But at a critical moment I abandoned my principles. I totally disregarded that which was the guiding tenet of my life. I wanted the taste of blood. Boston Corbett may have held the gun, but I pulled the trigger, not only with my order, but with my heart. Afterwards, I couldn't face being a lawyer again. I drifted around for several years, worked as a gambler on a riverboat, did some prospecting, did some scouting. It wasn't until I found a twelve- year-old kid out on the plains that I started to put my life back together."

"And I had to come along and remind you of all that," Boston said. "I'm sorry. Major. I really am."

C.V. smiled at Boston. "Don't worry, it's all behind me now. I saw a part of me that I didn't know existed, and I never want to see again. But in the long run, I think it has helped me to a better understanding of others. I tell myself that, anyway. I have to believe that there is some purpose to my life."

Grady laughed. "Well, listen C.V., you won't get any argument from me," he said. "After all, I wouldn't even be here if it weren't for you."

"And I wouldn't be here if it weren't for you." Boston put in. "So you see. it has all come full circle. Welcome to Tombstone, fellas. Out here, a man needs to know who he can count on, and I for one am glad to know I've got a few good men in my camp."

Chapter Seven

GRADY BUMPED INTO her as she was coming out of the Pioneer Boot and Shoe store. She was carrying three parcels stacked one on top of the other, so she didn't see him. He didn't knock her down, but he did send her parcels scattering in every direction.

"Oh! Why don't you watch where you're going, you clumsy oaf!" she shouted in frustration.

"I'm sorry, Miss," Grady apologized quickly. Embarrassed, he picked up the packages for her, then looked at her as she was brushing off her dress. The girl appeared to be no more than twenty years old. She was exceptionally pretty, slender and of medium height, with hair the color of spun gold. Her eyes were blue-green, like Arizona turquoise, and flecked with silver. Except for a pretty dusting of freckles across her nose, she was fair of complexion. He started to hand the packages back to her, then thought better of it.

"Please," he said. "Let me carry these for you."

"I can carry them my . . . " the girl started, then she stopped and gave a small laugh. "I'm sorry," she said. "I was raised with two older brothers, and I guess I'm more used to fighting with men than to being nice. It wasn't really your fault. I had the packages so piled up that I couldn't see where I was going. I have a buckboard over at the O.K. Corral. You can carry them for me if you want."

"I'd be happy to," Grady said. "I'm Grady Ford."

"I'm Sally Clanton."

"Clanton?"

"You've heard of me?"

"I've heard of N.H. Clanton."

"N.H. Clanton is my father," Sally said.

"I see."

Grady had never met N.H. Clanton, but he knew that Clanton was the person against whom he and C.V. were bringing suit on behalf of Bianca.

"You say that as if you don't approve of my father," Sally said defensively.

"I've never met the gentleman," Grady said.

"You haven't? Where have you been? I thought my father knew everyone between here and Tucson."

"That may be, but my partner and I are from Kansas. We've only recently arrived in Tombstone," Grady said.

"Your partner? Are you prospecting for silver or gold?"

"No," Grady said, laughing. "I mean my law partner," Grady said. "I'm an attorney."

"That's good," Sally said. "If there's anything Tombstone doesn't need, it's another prospector or miner. And it would be nice to have some real law for a change. The way it is now, the Earp brothers run the whole town just to suit themselves. Why, if it weren't for Sheriff Behan, the honest ranchers who live outside of the town wouldn't have a chance."

"I gather that you don't think Wyatt and Virgil and Morgan Earp are good lawmen?"

"You should ask my brother Ike," Sally said. "He's had a few run-ins with the Earps already. Billy has gotten along with them all right, but Billy gets along with just about everyone. Oh, that's my buckboard over there."

Grady put the packages in the buckboard for Sally, then

helped her climb into the seat. She reached for the reins, then looked down at him.

"Mr. Ford, the Cattlemen's Association is having a barn dance tonight," she said. "Will you be coming?"

Grady hadn't heard anything about a Cattlemen's Association dance, but if this girl would be there then the idea of going was greatly appealing.

"Yes," he said. "I plan on it. I wouldn't miss it for the world."

Sally smiled at him.

"Perhaps I'll see you there."

"Only if you promise to save a few dances for me," Grady said.

"We'll see," Sally replied, smiling at him coquettishly. She snapped the reins and the team pulled the buckboard ahead. She looked back over her shoulder and smiled at him one more time as she drove away. Grady waved at her as the buckboard turned onto Third Street.

After the buckboard was out of sight, Grady continued on his errand. He walked on down to the depot to wait for the morning train. Two days ago he had telegraphed the Territorial Capitol in Phoenix and asked that they send him, by Rail Express, copies of all the documents they had pertaining to the land that was in dispute between Bianca and N.H. Clanton.

Grady, C.V. and Bianca had been in Tombstone for nearly a month now, and in that time they had learned that everyone was divided into two camps. One camp was composed of the miners and merchants of the city. They were supporters of the Earp brothers. The other camp was composed of the cowboys and ranchers, who were supportive of Sheriff Behan.

Most of the cattlemen had been in this area since long before the birth of the town of Tombstone, and they considered the city and all its inhabitants to be nothing more than interlopers who were trespassing upon their range.

The townpeople, on the other hand, considered the cattlemen and the cowboys who worked for them a bunch of ruffians—hell-raisers who had grown wild on the range and were only too anxious to let out steam when they came to town. Often, letting off steam meant shooting their guns, if not at each other in some spontaneous duel, then at any target which caught their fancy.

The Earps had quickly aligned themselves with the townspeople. This wasn't unusual, since they had been introduced to the trouble cowboys could cause while they were peace officers in Dodge City, Kansas.

The leading troublemakers of all included Ike Clanton, one of the sons of N.H. Clanton, and his friends Frank and Tom McLaury. The Clantons and the McLaurys had been friends long before the town of Tombstone came to be. Their ranches lay along the San Pedro River, west of town.

Of the two Clanton boys, Ike was the older, and Billy the younger. Ike was a bully, a crude ruffian who was unwelcome in most of the saloons, restaurants and pleasure houses of the town. Billy, on the other hand, was a well-behaved young man who was welcome just about anywhere. Most of the townspeople felt sorry that Billy was burdened with such a no-count brother as Ike, His popularity was such that no one allowed Ike's indiscretions to color their perception of Billy. He was, after all, not responsible for the sins of his brother.

Billy was extremely aware of Ike's shortcomings, and he was always trying to do what he could to keep his brother out of trouble, or extricating him from trouble when he was unable to keep him out of it.

Grady stepped up onto the station platform. He smiled as he saw the black skillet sitting on the stump. The three men who had caught him with their trick some time back were sitting in the shade, drinking beer, waiting for the morning train and their next victim.

"Well, here's a fella who don't take long to examine a skillet," one of the men chuckled.

"How are you doing?" Grady asked good- naturedly.

"We didn't get anyone yesterday," one of the men said.

"We hope to do better today."

"I see you've got your bait set."

"Yep. You wanna check it out again?"

"No thanks," Grady said, laughing and raising his hands. "I've seen it."

Grady walked into the station to talk to the Express dispatcher. "Would you check the express packages right away please? I'm expecting something from Phoenix."

"Sure thing, Mr. Ford," the dispatcher said. Grady walked over to sit on one of the wooden benches and wait from the arrival of the train. He saw a woman and a little girl waiting and when the little girl caught his eye she smiled at him.

"We're goin' to see gramma," she said. "You know where she lives? She lives in St. Louis."

"My," Grady said. "That's a long way for a little girl to travel."

"It's all right," the little girl said. "Mama's goin' with me."

"Nonnie," her mother scolded, "don't bother the man."

The train was right outside the station now, and the heavy engine made the windows shake. The little girl squealed with delight and put her hands over her ears as the train drew alongside the platform. It stopped with a hiss of steam and a squeal of brakes, then the baggage car door opened and the express sack, a canvas bag, was dropped out. Grady leaned against the wall of the depot under the shade and awaited for the dispatcher to go through the bag.

"You sons-of-bitches!" an angry voice suddenly shouted. "I'm gonna gut-shoot ever'one of you," The voice came from someone who had just picked up the hot skillet. Grady looked over and saw that it was a young man, about his own age, wearing a pistol strapped low and tied down on his right side.

"Hold on here, mister, we was just funnin' with you," one of the men said, holding out his hand in fear. "I ain't packin' a gun. We ain't none of us packin'a gun."

The young man reached around behind him, under his jacket, and came up with a pistol. He slid it across the baggage

Warriors of the Code

cart.

"Use it," he said menacingly.

"Wait a minute, friend," Grady put in quickly. He smiled at the would-be gunman. "I got roped in on this little trick myself a month back. It doesn't mean anything."

"You sidin' with them?"

"Yes," Grady said. "To the extent that they shouldn't be forced into a gunfight over a harmless little joke."

"Dutch Brown don't like bein' made a fool of," the young gunman said.

"Who is Dutch Brown?"

"I'm Dutch Brown, mister. Who are you?"

"I'm Grady Ford. I'm a lawyer, representing these men." Grady stuck his hand out but Brown backed away.

"You ain't packin' a gun either? What is it with this town? Has ever'one got a yellow streak down their back, or what?"

"We have a law," Grady said. "A very sensible law, which says no one shall be armed except law enforcement officials."

"Yeah? Well, I ain't no lawman, 'n I don't intend to give up my gun. Now, since you've throw'd your lot in with this bunch, whyn't you make the first move for the gun?"

"What? What are you talking about? You can't be serious!" Grady said. He had come down here, innocently, merely to check on an express delivery. Now he was on the verge of a gunfight! And it wouldn't be a fair gunfight either, for it would be much more difficult to pick the gun up off the baggage cart than it would be if it were in a holster by his side. This young ruffian had stacked the odds neatly in his own favor.

"I'm not going to pick up that gun," Grady said.

Brown pulled his gun and shot it at Grady's feet. The bullet hit the platform between his feet, then ricocheted out behind him. He felt the spray from the bricks pepper his legs.

"Pick it up, mister, or I'll shoot you anyway."

"Put the gun away, mister, or die with it in your hand," a calm, clear voice said.

Grady looked with relief toward the speaker, but saw that it wasn't any of the Earps. This man was almost emaciatedly thin, dressed in somber black, and with a drooping black moustache. His face was pallid, almost yellow in color. But it was his eyes which startled Grady the most. They were so dark a brown that the pupil was almost indistinguishable. Surprisingly, he had no weapon in his hand, though he was wearing a pistol.

Brown turned toward the sound of the voice as soon as Grady did, and he, too, saw that the man was unarmed.

"What did you say to me, mister?" Brown said.

"I said drop your gun, or die with it in your hand," the emaciated stranger said.

Grady had never seen the man before, but he suddenly realized who it must be. He had heard Wyatt Earp speak of a friend of his, a dentist named 'Doc' Holliday who suffered from tuberculosis and often spent time in a sanitarium. From Wyatt's description, this had to be Doc Holliday. He had just gotten off the train, perhaps returning from the sanitarium.

Brown laughed, and waved his pistol around.

"Mister, you must be some kind of a fool," he said. "I'm standin' here holdin' a gun in my hand and you're tellin' me to drop it?" He pointed his pistol at the older man. "Now, I'm sayin'—"

The man never finished his statement. As quick as the blink of an eye Doc Holliday had pulled his pistol, cocked it as he was raising it into position, then fired as the gun came level. The ball crashed into Brown's chest, and his gun clattered to the brick platform.

"How did you do that?" Brown gasped as the front of his shirt reddened with gushing blood. He clutched his chest, then pitched forward onto the platform. Grady hurried over to him and reached down to feel for a pulse, but there was none. By this time, Wyatt Earp had arrived, drawn to the station by the first shot Brown had fired. Wyatt saw the gunman lying face down on the platform, and he saw Doc standing there with his

Warriors of the Code

pistol still drawn.

"Well, Doc," Wyatt said easily. "I see you're back."

"Marshal, if there was ever a fella needed killin'," one of the three jokesters said, "it was this one. He come off the train try in' to goad ever'one into a fight. He even tried to take on Lawyer Ford."

"That right, Grady?" Wyatt asked.

Grady nodded.

Wyatt looked toward the train and saw that there were faces in every window. The vestibules were full and a few who had been in the process of boarding were still standing on the platform, looking back toward the scene of violence just passed.

"All right, folks, it's all over now," Wyatt said to them. "If you're boarding the train, get it done. Conductor?"

"Yes, sir?"

"Signal the engineer. Get the train on out of here."

"Yes, sir," the conductor said. He looked around the platform. "Board!" he called. He waved at the engineer who gave a couple of short blasts on his whistle. The people on the platform and the people in the vestibules moved quickly on into the train. Seconds later the train began moving, starting its run to Lordsburg.

"You know this fella. Doc?" Wyatt asked.

"The one I killed or the one I saved?" Doc asked.

"Both."

"I take it the one I saved is one of those two lawyer fellas you wrote me about."

"Grady Ford," Grady said, reaching his hand out to take Doc's. "You couldn't have picked a better time to make an appearance."

"Don't be misled, Doc," Wyatt said. "I've seen Grady here in action. He's pretty good at taking care of himself."

"Maybe, but you keep all the men naked in this town," Doc said. "No matter how good he is; a man can't defend himself if he isn't armed."

"I know, I know," Wyatt said, chuckling. "Doc is, officially, one of my deputies," he explained to Grady. "That way he gets to keep his gun. It saves a lot of arguments."

"No argument," Doc said easily. "The only way anyone is ever gonna get my gun is off my dead body. That fella is Dutch Brown. Ever heard of him?"

"Dutch Brown? No, I can't say as I have," Wyatt said.

"Too bad. He's heard of you. He came here to kill you."

"Oh? How do you know?"

"I was drinkin' in a bar in Tucson last night," Doc said. "This fella was in conversation with another fella at a nearby table. I heard him tell how Ike Clanton had sent him a letter, offerin' to pay him two hundred and fifty dollars a head for any of the Earps. I been keepin' an eye on him ever since then. When he braced these folks, I figured I'd step in and take a hand,"

Wyatt squatted down beside the body and searched through all his pockets. He pulled out a billfold, opened it and looked through it, finding forty-seven dollars and the stub of a Tuscon-to- Tombstone train ticket. There was also a receipt from a gunstore in Tucson showing that Brown had bought two boxes of .44 caliber shells. Unfortunately, there wasn't a letter from Clanton, or anything else that might incriminate him.

"Damn!" Wyatt said. "What did he do with the letter?"

"I don't know," Doc said. "I never saw it. I just heard him talking about it."

Wyatt looked at Grady. "What about it, Grady?" he asked. "Can I arrest Ike Clanton?"

"On what charge?" Grady asked.

"On the charge of attempted murder," Wyatt said. "He paid this fella to come over here and kill us Earps."

"We don't know that he did," Grady said.

"Sure we know that he did," Wyatt insisted. "Doc overheard them."

"That's just it," Grady said. "You believe Doc and I believe Doc. But that isn't evidence. If we went to court with that, it would be thrown out as hearsay evidence. Clanton would get off scott-free and the situation would be even worse because he would get the feeling that he is above the law."

"Damn!" Wyatt said. He looked down at the still figure of Dutch Brown.' "Too bad you had to kill the son-of-a-bitch. We might've gotten something out of him."

"Mr. Ford? I believe you were looking for this?" the dispatcher said then, bringing a large brown envelope over to Grady.

"Yes, thank you," Grady said. He hefted the envelope. "It feels full. Maybe it's all we'll need to make our case."

"That the case where you're tryin' to get Bianca's land back from old man Clanton?" Wyatt asked.

"Yes. So whatever plan you have in store for N.H. Clanton; don't do anything until after this' claim is settled."

"N.H. Clanton is slowing down some in his older years," Wyatt said. "He mostly just stays out on the ranch without worryin' that much about what's goin' on in town. I reckon any dealin's I'm gonna have will continue to be with Ike. And sometimes Billy."

"I've heard Billy is not like the rest of them," Grady said.

The undertaker arrived then, and he directed the three jokesters to put the body on the back of his wagon. Wyatt watched them, stroking his chin thoughtfully.

"As a matter of fact, he isn't like the others," Wyatt finally said. "I believe Billy could be a pretty good kid if he didn't have to deal with his brother and the McClaury's. But the fact is he does have to deal with them. And they're leading him straight down the path to hell in a handbasket." Wyatt sighed. "When the trouble comes, Billy will be right in the middle."

"You're convinced that there will be trouble?"

"You've been here a month, Grady," Wyatt said. "Do you think there's any chance that there won't be trouble?"

"No," Grady said. "I wish I could say otherwise, but I can't. What about the Clanton girl?"

Wyatt smiled. "You mean Sally?"

"Yes," Grady said, thinking about the pretty young woman he had spoken to earlier. "I believe that's her name." He knew full-well it was her name, but he was trying to hide the interest he had in her.

By now the undertaker had stretched a tarpaulin over Dutch Brown's body, and he started taking him back to the hardware store where he also ran a mortuary. Wyatt watched the wagon pull away, then he started back toward town.

"Come on Grady, I'll walk you back to your office," he said. When they'd walked for awhile in silence, Wyatt suddenly said, "Listen, you don't want to get mixed up with Sally Clanton."

"Who said anything about my getting mixed up with her?"

Wyatt chuckled. "Nobody had to say anything. I saw you carry her packages for her. I know you aren't blind. You can see what a beautiful girl she is. Have you ever seen a coral snake?"

"Of course I have."

"Probably one of the most beautiful snakes there is," Wyatt said. "And easily the most deadly. There's some folks like that, and I reckon Sally is one of them."

"Are you saying that just because she's a Clanton?"

"That would be reason enough," Wyatt said. "But that's not the only reason. Reckon you never heard about the little incident at Bitter Wells last year." '

"No, I haven't."

"No reason you should have," Wyatt said. "You've not been here long enough to catch up on all the gossip. Anyway, it seems that Sally Clanton, that pretty young girl you were carrying the packages for, was taking a stage to Contention last year. The stage was jumped at Bitter Wells by some Commancheros."

"Commancheros? You mean white men and Indians

riding together?" Grady asked. He remembered his parents' murder, many years ago. They had been killed by a band of Indians and white men who rode together. At the time, he didn't know what such gangs were called. Now he knew they were referred to as Commancheros.

"Yeah," Wyatt said. "Anyway, they held up the stage and they kidnapped Sally Clanton. I guess they figured they could hold her for ransom. Old man Clanton certainly is rich enough to pay for his daughter's release."

"How much did he have to pay?" Grady asked. They were nearly back to the law office by now, and they stopped in the middle of the street while Wyatt finished his story.

"He didn't pay anything," Wyatt said. He chuckled. "That's the story. It seems that the white man left to take the ransom message to the old man, leaving two Indians behind to watch over her. The Indians got to drinking whiskey and Sally managed to work her ropes loose. Then she grabbed a pistol and started blazing away. She killed both the Indians, took one of their horses, and beat the white man back to her father's ranch. When Clanton found out that a Commanchero was coming to demand ransom money from him, he and Ike and the two McClaury's waited for him. They shot him to pieces."

"Seems to me like Sally was justified in doing what she did to the two Indians," Grady said.

"Didn't say she wasn't right," Wyatt said. "I just said she was dangerous, that's all. And of course, her being a Clanton and you being one of the lawyers suing her father isn't going to help the situation any. Just be careful, Grady, that's all I'm saying."

"Thanks for the warning, Wyatt. I'll keep it in mind," Grady said.

They'd reached Grady's office at this point, and the two parted. Wyatt crossed the street and climbed up on the board sidewalk to continue his patrol of the town, while Grady climbed the stairs to the offices of Battenburg and Ford.

Bianca was sitting at a desk working on something, and

C.V. was leaning over her. Grady saw his hand move quickly as he stepped through the door.

"My," Grady teased. "Don't tell me I almost caught you with your hand in the cookie jar."

"Grady!" Bianca gasped, and her cheeks flamed in embarrassment.

"I'm sorry," Grady said gently, surprised at Bianca's reaction to his joking remark. "I mean nothing by it."

"What have you there?" C.V. asked, pointing to the brown envelope as he deftly changed the subject.

"Oh, this came by express," Grady said, dropping the envelope on Bianca's desk. "It's all the information recorded relating to Bianca's land. I haven't had a chance to open it yet."

"Well, let's not waste any time," C.V. said, eagerly tearing open the packet.

"Do you think it will do us any good, C.V.?" Bianca asked.

"Well, if it has the tax history, and if we can prove that your husband had paid the taxes for the years in question, then all we have to do is petition the court to return the land to you." C.V. took out the papers and began looking through them. After a moment, he let out a frustrated sigh and dropped the papers on the desk. "I might have suspected it," he said.

"What?" Grady asked. "What is it?"

C.V. pointed to the papers. "Every piece of information ever recorded about that land is there, from the original Spanish land grant, which was nearly two hundred years ago, all the way down to Santa Anna. There's also information about the land since N.H. Clanton took over. But there's not one word in there to suggest that Bianca's husband ever even owned the land, much less paid taxes on it."

"What? But that's not possible, is it?" Bianca asked, picking up the papers and looking through them anxiously.

"See for yourself," C.V. said glumly. "The records for thirty years are missing."

"Well, doesn't that suggest something to you?" Grady said.

"Of course it does. It suggests that Clanton paid someone in the Territorial Capital to pull any papers which might dispute his claim," C.V. said.

"So?" Grady said.

"So nothing," C.V. said. "We could ask the court to consider that the pages were purposely pulled, but without any other supportive evidence, it would be very risky."

"What do we do now?" Bianca asked.

"I don't know," C.V. said. He saw the long look on Bianca's face. "But not to worry, my pretty one. Battenburg and Ford have just begun to fight. Right, my lad?"

"Right," Grady said. "For Bianca we will fight to the bitter end. Look at her beautiful green dress, C.V. Doesn't that remind you of the song, *Greensleeves?*" Grady began singing: "I have been ready at your hand; To grant whatever you would crave."

C.V. picked it up from there: "I have both waged life and land; Your love and goodwill for to have."

Both sung the chorus: "Greensleeves was all my joy, Greensleeves was my delight; Greensleeves was my heart of gold, And who but Lady Greensleeves?"

On the last line Grady took one of Bianca's hands and C.V. took the other, and both raised her hands to their lips for a kiss. Bianca laughed and blushed again, but it was a happy blush. Even though the chances of her recovering her land looked bleak, she felt an almost giddy happiness around these two men.

Chapter Eight

FROM LATE AFTERNOON on, ranchers and their wives, cowboys and their girls, began arriving in town for the Cattlemen's Association Ball. Many came into town in wagons and buckboards carrying their entire families.

For the most part, this was the rancher at his best. With their wives and children along, none of the ranchers were anxious for any trouble, and the cowboys, aware that their jobs might depend upon their good behavior, also managed to put their best foot forward. The townspeople managed to put their hostility toward the ranchers aside for the duration of the Ball, and some of them even managed to smile and wave at the wagons and buckboards as they arrived.

By dusk, the excitement which had been steadily growing down around the ballroom of the Homestead Hotel was full blown. The musicians could be heard practicing, and children had gathered around the glowing windows to peek inside. The ballroom floor had been cleared of tables and chairs and the band was installed on the platform at the front of the room.

Even though everyone wasn't yet there, the band reached such a point of fine tuning that they were no longer able to hold back. They plunged into their first song, 'Buffalo Gals.' After that came 'Little Joe the Wrangler,' and then 'The

Gandy Dancers Ball.'

By now, horses and buggies were beginning to pile up on the street in front of the hotel. Every hitching post was full and the large lot at the livery was crammed with buckboards and wagons. Men and women were streaming along the board sidewalks headed for the hotel, the women in colorful ginghams, the men in clean blue denims. Many of them were sporting brightly decorated vests as well.

Grady wore a tan suit with highly polished boots, and a dark silk vest covering a white frilled shirt for the dance.

C.V. whistled when Grady came down into the dining room of the hotel, where he and Bianca were having dinner together. "Well, you certainly are dressed to the nines," he said with a grin.

"Grady, what a handsome young devil you are!" Bianca said, smiling up at him.

"Thank you," Grady said. "I hope a certain female party shares your feeling."

"If she doesn't she's blind," Bianca said.

"Are you going to tell us who this mysterious girl is?" C.V. asked.

"I ... I don't know," Grady said. "I'm not sure how the two of you would take it."

"Take it? How are we supposed to take it?" C.V. asked. "What gives us the right to approve or disapprove of anyone you might want to see?"

"I'm glad you feel that way," Grady said. He looked at Bianca. "Bianca, it's Sally Clanton." Bianca's eyes flashed momentarily, but she brought them under control almost immediately.

"Sally Clanton is a lovely girl," she said. "I can see why you are taken with her."

"I'm not taken with her, exactly," Grady said. "I never even knew she existed until this morning. I bumped into her, literally. I knocked some packages out of her arms, then, by way of apology, carried them to her buckboard for her. She mentioned this dance and I said I thought I'd come."

"Sounds innocent enough," C.V. said. "Is she pretty?"

Grady's face lit up with a smile. "C.V., I've seen two women who could have been the inspiration for Lord Byron's poetry . . . Bianca is one and Sally is the other."

"She walks in beauty, like the night; Of cloudless climes and starry skies," C.V. started.

"And all that's best of dark and bright; Meet in her aspect and her eyes," Grady went on.

"Thus mellow'd to that tender light; Which heaven to gaudy day denies," Bianca concluded, laughing. "You two aren't the only ones who know poetry," she said. "Even I can finish that verse."

"Bianca, I hope you don't feel I am betraying you in any way," Grady said.

Bianca smiled. "No, of course I don't," she said. She kissed Grady on the cheek. "Go on, Grady. Have a fine time."

"Thank you," Grady said, smiling at her.

"We aren't the ones you have to worry about anyway," C.V. said.

"What do you mean?"

"If your girl is anything like the other Clantons, she'll need some placating once she learns who you really are. Or does she already know?"

"She knows that I'm a lawyer," Grady said.

"Does she know you are suing her father?"

"I don't know. I didn't tell her."

"What happens when she finds out?"

"I guess I'll just cross that bridge when I come to it," Grady said. He reached down and took C.V.'s pickle. It was something he had done since he was twelve years old, and discovered that C.V. didn't like pickles. Though they weren't actually father and son, nor even older and younger brother, this unconscious action showed the closeness of the relationship that had developed between them. He smiled and waved at them as he left their table. "Be seeing you," he called over his shoulder.

"It's a shame," C.V. said quietly to Bianca as Grady left the dining room.

"What's a shame?"

"That his folks didn't live to know what a fine young man he has become."

Tenderly, Bianca reached across the table and took C.V.'s hand in his. "Who's to say that they don't know?" she asked softly. "And they also know who is responsible for it. You have done a fine job with him, C.V."

Grady could hear the music of the band from halfway down Fremont Street. He hummed along with the music as his boots trod loudly on the board walks. He tipped his hat to the wife of one of the cattlemen as they were approaching the front of the hotel, then, gallantly, held the door open for them.

Inside, the lights glowed, the music played, and men and women laughed and whirled about on the dance floor. Grady stood just inside the door for a moment, looking out over the sea of girls in butterfly-bright dresses and men in denim and leather. Finally, he saw Sally. She was standing on the other side of the room surrounded by half a dozen young men. She was wearing a light blue dress, embroidered with beads of many colors. The dress was cut daringly low in front, showing off her figure to perfection. For some inexplicable reason, Grady had ambivalent feelings about the lowcut neckline. On the one hand, it certainly displayed her beauty to appreciative eyes, and Grady was one who took advantage of it. On the other hand, he realized he wasn't the only one appreciating the scenery, and he felt an unexpected twinge of jealousy toward the men who had gathered around her like bees around a flower.

The music stopped and one of the musicians lifted a megaphone.

"Ladies and gents! Choose up your squares!" he called.

The cowboys started toward the young women, who, giggling and turning their faces away shyly, accepted their invitations. Grady noticed that Sally seemed to be turning down all the invitations which were offered her, and he hesitated about going over to her, for fear she would turn his down as well. Then he caught her eye and she smiled, and crossed the room to him.

"Aren't you going to choose me for the square dance?" she asked.

"I saw you turning everyone down," Grady said. "I thought you weren't going to dance."

"I had to turn them down," Sally said with a low, throaty laugh. "If I had accepted one of their invitations, I wouldn't be free to accept yours. That is, if you intend to issue one."

"Oh, yes," Grady sputtered. "Of course." Sally put her arm through his.

"We'd better hurry," she said. "Otherwise the squares will all be full and we'll be left out."

By now there were three squares formed, or forming, and Grady and Sally moved into one of them to wait for the music to begin.

The music began, with the fiddles loud and clear, the guitars carrying the rhythm, the accordion providing the counterpoint, and the dobro ringing out over everything. The caller began to shout. He laughed and clapped his hands and stomped his feet and danced around on the platform in compliance with his own calls, bowing and whirling as if he had a girl and was in one of the squares himself. The dancers moved and swirled to the caller's commands.

Around the dance floor sat those who were without partners, looking on wistfully; those who were too old, holding back those who were too young.

At the punchbowl table, cowboys added so much of their own alcoholic ingredients to the punch that though many drank from the bowl, the contents never seemed to diminish.

That dance finished and Sally fanned herself and smiled at Grady. Her face was covered by a sheen of perspiration and a curl of blonde hair stuck to her forehead. She blew a stream of air across her face and the lock of hair was dislodged.

"Would you like to go outside and get a breath of fresh air?" Grady invited.

"Sure," Sally answered. "Why not?"

Two of the cowboys had gotten into an argument over the attentions of one of the girls and they were glaring and growling at each other, though cooler heads seemed to be prevailing, and the argument was settled by the time Grady and Sally stepped outside.

It was cooler outside, and half a dozen other couples were also taking advantage of the fresh air.

"Let's walk," Sally suggested.

"All right."

Arm in arm they walked the entire length of the board sidewalk until they reached the edge of town. They continued on for another hundred yards or so until the sound and the lights of the town were behind them. Now the loud cranking of the pianos from the dozen or so saloons was barely audible. They heard a woman's scream, not of fear, obviously, because it was followed by her laugh which carried clearly above everything else.

Ahead of them lay the Dragoon Mountains, great slabs of black and silver in the soft wash of moonlight.

"The moon makes the mountains look silver," Grady commented.

"They are silver," Sally answered. "At least, they are loaded with silver. We'd all be a lot better off if they weren't."

"Do you dislike the town that much?" Grady asked.

Sally ran her hand through her hair. As she raised her arm, the action brought one of her breasts into prominence, the more visible because of the lowcut dress she was wearing. Grady's eyes were drawn to the subtle light and shadows thus presented.

"I guess not, really," she said, answering his question. "Before Tombstone I never got to go into town unless we went all the way to Tucson. And with no other towns out this way there was no railroad, and there were no stagelines. We had to go by wagon, and we only went about once or twice a year. This way, at least, I have a chance to get into town whenever I want."

"Well, then, you see? The townspeople and the ranchers should get along well," Grady said. "The merchants in town need the ranchers as customers, the ranchers need the merchants for their goods and supplies."

Sally chuckled. "You sound like a lawyer," she said.

A sudden blaze of gold zipped across the sky, and Sally squealed with delight.

"Oh, look!" she said. "A falling star!" She shivered. "Oh."

"What is it?"

"Someone just died."

"What?" Grady asked, chuckling. "Why do you say that?"

"That's what a falling star means. There's a star in heaven for everyone on earth, and when someone dies, his star falls."

Grady shook his head. "You're serious, aren't you?"

"That's what I've always heard," Sally said.

"That's just a myth," Grady said. "Anyway, stars don't fall."

"What? Of course they do. We just saw one."

"What you just saw was a meteor," Grady said. "They are actually small chunks of rock which are traveling through space. Occasionally one of them falls to earth."

"Really? Have you ever seen one?"

"Yes, as matter of fact, I have."

"Oh, I bet they are beautiful," Sally said. "They must look like a large diamond, they glow so when you see them at night."

"They glow only because they are heated up as they are falling. Actually, they just look like any other rock. There isn't anything spectacular about them."

"That's a shame," Sally said. "I rather like thinking of them as beautiful things."

"Well, they are beautiful when you see them the way most

people see them," Grady said.

"You're a strange one, Grady Ford."

"Why do you say that?"

"You aren't like any of the other men I know. You're different."

"I've had the advantage of a good education," Grady said.

"Did you go back east to go to school?"

"No. My education came from a remarkable man named C.V. Battenburg."

"That's the man who's your partner, isn't it?"

"Yes, but he's much more than that. He raised me from the time I was twelve years old. My parents were killed by Commancheros, and he . . ." Grady saw Sally flinch, then he felt her stiffen. "What is it?" Grady asked. "What's wrong?"

"Nothing," Sally said. She sighed. "I ... I once had a run-in with some Commancheros." Grady remembered the story Wyatt had told him about Sally. As he looked at her now, so soft and beautiful in the moonlight, so feminine in her ball dress, it seemed impossible that this could be the same woman Wyatt had been talking about.

"Oh? What happened?"

"I don't want to talk about it," Sally said.

"All right, we won't talk about it." Grady put his hands on Sally's shoulders and turned her so that he was looking into her face. "I don't understand what has gotten into me anyway."

"What do you mean?"

"Here I am out under a beautiful, starry sky, with an even more beautiful woman, and I'm spending all my time talking about nonsensical things. I should be telling you how pretty you are . . . how the moon does something to your hair so that it glows like a welcome lantern on a dark night. I should be telling you how much I've been thinking about you all day, ever since I met you this morning."

Sally smiled. "Have you really been thinking about me?"

"Every moment of the day," Grady admitted.

"I've been thinking about you, too."

"What have you been thinking?"

"I've been wondering what it would be like to have you kiss me," Sally said.

Grady pulled her to him, and felt her lips on his. They were as sweet as nectar, and he felt them open to his kiss, inviting him to probe more deeply. She leaned into him and he could feel the heat of her breasts, the eager press of her pelvis against the awakening thrust of his manhood. Grady's mind was whirling; he had thought to keep himself aloof from any involvement with this girl, but it was too late for that now. She had drawn him into her perfumed lair and there was no way out.

Suddenly, Sally broke off the kiss and looked up at Grady with an expression of total wonder on her face.

"We can't . . . " she started, then pulled away from him and ran her hand through her hair. The expression of surprise on her face hadn't changed. "We'd better get back now," she said.

"Must we?"

"Yes," Sally said. "We have to."

"All right." Grady reached for her hand but she pulled it away. "Sally," he said, "is something wrong?"

"I ... I don't know what kind of woman you think I am."

"I think you're a wonderful woman," he said.

"But you're thinking that a good girl wouldn't do what I just did."

"You mean let me kiss you?"

"I didn't let you kiss me, Grady Ford, and you know it. I kissed you."

"There's no shame in that, Sally."

"The shame wasn't in the kissing," Sally said. "The shame was in the feelings the kiss caused."

"What feelings?"

"I can't explain it. I got all hot and cold and shaky at the same time," she said. "I ... I wanted . . . more. Only I know it isn't right to want more. Especially if you're just trifling."

"Sally, I wasn't trifling with you," Grady said.

"I know that. But I was trifling with you. That is, I thought I was. Only when you kissed me the trifling stopped, and I . . . well, I just think it would be best if we went back to the dance."

"All right."

They walked in silence for a moment and as they approached the town again the cacophony of noises from the busy nightlife of the little town once more reached their ears. A piano rendition of 'Buffalo Gals' held sway for a moment, then that was replaced by another piano playing 'Camptown Races.'

"Sally, I'd like to see you again," Grady said. "I expect I'll be in town now and then," she answered.

"No, I don't mean that. I mean I would like to come calling on you. I would like to pay you court."

"You . . . you don't think I'm too fast?"

"Not at all," Grady said. "I think you're a very special girl."

Sally looked up into his eyes for a moment before answering. "All right, you can—"

"So, there you are!" a loud, unpleasant voice called. "I was wonderin' where you got off to. You promised the next dance to me, 'n the next thing I know'd you was out galavantin' with this townie."

A cowboy stood in front of them, having just emerged from the dance. Grady didn't know who he was, but he had seen him around Sally earlier in the evening, and he had seen him at the punchbowl—where he had evidently spent quite a bit **of** time.

"Jason, you just go back on inside now," Sally said.

"Sure, I'll go back inside, 'soon as you're ready to go with me. You owe me a dance, Sally Clanton, 'n I aim to collect."

"You're drunk, Jason. I told all you boys before the night began that I wouldn't dance with anyone who got drunk."

"Maybe I would'na got drunk iffen you had'n run off with that feller. Now, come on in and dance with me." Jason lurched toward Sally and reached for her. Sally let out a little squeal, and Grady stepped forward, pushing Jason back.

"She said she doesn't want to dance," Grady said.

Suddenly the expression in the cowboy's face grew cold and he glared at Grady.

"You shouldn't ought to've done that," he said coldly. "You shouldn't 've put your hands on me like that."

"I just didn't want to see you hurt Miss Clanton," Grady said. "I could've hit you. Now just go on away and leave us alone."

After a long hard look at Grady, the cowboy turned and stalked off into the night. Grady watched him for a moment, then turned to Sally.

"Is he a friend of yours?"

"He's a friend of my brothers'," Sally said. "Actually, he's Ike's friend—I don't think he and Billy get along too well."

"I think the more of Billy because of it," Grady said. "Well, come on, let's get back inside."

"I'll have to dance with someone else now," Sally said, almost in way of apology.

"I know."

"You won't be upset?"

"Devastated," Grady said, smiling at her. "But I'll manage to hold it in."

They re-entered the ballroom, and someone was asking Sally to dance almost immediately.

Grady smiled at her, then walked around to the table. There were at least a dozen men leaning up against the wall behind the punch table, all of whom were holding a glass of the drink.

Grady poured himself a glass of punch, the first one of the night, then made a face as he drank it. It was not only too strong from the cowboy's spiking, but it had been spiked with perhaps half a dozen different whiskeys and blends.

"After the dance winds down, what say we go down to the Oriental?" One of the men against the wall was saying. He was tall and rangy, with stringy blond hair.

"Ike, if you go to the Oriental you're just asking for trouble," another said. He was also blond, though not quite as tall as the first man. His features, though similar, seemed more pleasantly arranged.

"Listen to my little brother, will you?" Ike said. "Sometimes he's just like a mother hen, protectin' his little chicks. Cluck, cluck, cluck," he said, and the other men laughed.

Grady knew Ike and Billy Clanton. No one could live in Tombstone and not know them. They were frequent visitors to the town, they were prominent ranchers, and Ike was universally known as a hell-raiser.

Billy's cheeks reddened a bit. "Do what you want to," he said, gruffly. "I'm not goin' to get you out of any more trouble."

"Nobody asked you to get me out of trouble, little brother," Ike said. "I'm capable of takin' care of myself."

"WHERE IS THAT EGG-SUCKIN' SCUM?" a loud voice suddenly shouted. A couple of women screamed, the music tattered to a ragged stop, and everyone moved quickly to get out of the way. Several chairs were knocked over.

Grady looked toward the door and saw the same cowboy there who had accosted Sally outside a few minutes earlier. At the same time he saw the cowboy, the cowboy saw him.

"Fill your hand you son-of-a-bitch!" the cowboy shouted. "I'm gonna shoot you to hell!" Grady felt himself breaking out into the cold sweat of fear. He had seen men die in this town for the slightest affront, and he knew this drunken fool was about to kill him. For the second time in one day he was being braced, and for the second time he was without a gun.

"Jason!" Billy shouted. "Jason, he isn't armed."

"Don't tell me that," the cowboy slurred. "All the townie bastards carry sleeve guns or somethin'. I know he's armed."

"You're prob'ly right," Ike chuckled. "Why don't you shoot 'im?"

"Ike! Shut up!" Billy said. "He's just drunk enough to think you're serious."

Ike took a swallow of his drink and studied Grady over the edge of his glass.

"How do you know I'm not serious, little brother? This is the fella who took our little sister for a walk in the moonlight awhile ago."

"Seems to me like it's Sally's business who she walks with," Billy said.

"Maybe. Only this here is the same fella who's tryin' to sue us, to take away our ranch."

Billy looked at Grady, and for a moment, Grady saw an expression of contempt in Billy's face as well. Then the expression softened.

"That don't matter none. The point is he's not armed. If Jason shoots him down, Jason's gonna hang. This is Earp's territory, you know that."

"That's Jason's problem, not mine," Ike said easily.

Jason raised his pistol and pointed it at Grady. He cocked it, and Grady heard the dreaded sound of clicking steel as the cylinder rotated. As if mesmerized, Grady stared down the large hole at the end of the gun barrel.

Suddenly Billy stepped between Jason and Grady.

"Jason, you're gonna have to kill me first," he said.

Jason wavered for a moment. "Get outta the way, Billy. I got nothin' ag'in you."

"You're gonna have to kill me before you can kill this fella," Billy said. "Then you'll hang for sure."

Subconsciously, Jason put his finger to his collar and pulled it away from his neck.

"He shoved me, Billy," Jason said. "He hadn't ought to've shoved me like he done."

"He shoved you because you were grabbing me," Sally said.

"Well I wouldn't 've grabbed you iffen you had danced with me like you said you would. Instead you danced with him and you went walkin' with him."

"Who I dance with and who I walk with is my own business," Sally said. "Now why don't you just put your gun away?"

At that precise moment Wyatt Earp stepped in through the door of the ballroom, right behind Jason. Wyatt had his pistol drawn.

"Jason?" Wyatt said.

Jason turned around toward Wyatt, and when he did, Wyatt brought his gun down on Jason's head, clubbing him sharply. Jason went down, then out like a light.

"A couple of you men get him out of here," Wyatt said.

"You get 'im out of here, Marshal," Ike said. "You're the one hit him."

"All right, I'll get him out of here," Wyatt said. "But if I take him he's gonna wind up in jail." Wyatt bent over to pick Jason up, but a couple of cowboys came out of the crowd.

"We'll take 'im back to the ranch, Marshal," one of them said.

Wyatt smiled. "I think that's a good idea." Wyatt touched the brim of his hat. "You folks have a real good time now, you hear?"

Wyatt left with the two cowboys right behind him, following with Jason's prostrate form. A moment after they left, the band started up again, and a few more people got out on the floor to dance. Grady walked over to talk to Billy.

"I want to thank you for what you did, Billy," he said.

"Yeah, well, I was probably doin' it more for Jason than for you," Billy said. "I didn't want to see him hang."

"Good point," Grady said. "Nevertheless, I'm thankful."

"I know how thankful you are," Billy said. "You're so thankful you're tryin' to steal our land."

Billy turned and walked away, leaving Sally there with Grady.

"What did Billy and Ike mean about your tryin' to steal our land?" Sally asked. "You aren't, are you?"

"My partner and I are representing someone who has brought suit against your father," Grady said.

"Who?"

"Senora Esteban de Santa Anna," Grady said. "Though she prefers to be called Bianca."

"Bianca? The Mexican woman?"

"Yes."

"I know about her," Sally said, her eyes flashing angrily. "My father loaned her husband money to pay his taxes. Then, when Sheriff Behan went out to collect, Santa Anna tried to gun him down. Sheriff Behan had to shoot him in self-defense."

"I've heard another version."

"I suppose you would have," Sally said. "Especially if you are representing that . . . that woman."

"I think she has a legitimate claim."

"Well I don't think so," Sally said, her eyes flashing in anger. She turned and started to walk away, then stopped and looked back toward Grady. "Oh, and incidentally, you can forget about calling on me. I've no intention of keeping company with anyone who would try and use the courts to steal another person's land."

Grady watched Sally melt back into the crowd and he felt a sinking sensation in his stomach. He had only known her one day, but already he felt that having her walk out of his life like this was a very great loss.

Chapter Nine

BIANCA LAY WITH her head on C.V.'s shoulder, listening to his soft, even breathing. They had made love during the night just passed, and she was still heavy with him. She could feel his naked skin against hers and she felt a small chill of excitement pass through her.

Bianca was hopelessly in love with C.V., so much so that it frightened her. In every relationship in her past, no matter what the relationship was, she had been in control. Her husband had been twenty-five years older than she, and the marriage had been arranged by her family, but despite all that, she had been in control of the situation. Her older husband was so in love with her that he would do her bidding, no matter what that might be. Now she suddenly found the shoe on the other foot. Her entire life was wrapped up in C.V. Battenburg, so much so that if he suggested she give up the quest to regain her lands, she would do it, He hadn't suggested such a thing though, and in fact was pursuing the lawsuit with great enthusiasm, calling it his 'Crusade for the Holy Grail.' Someone else might believe that C.V. was motivated in his quest by the monetary reward that would be his when the case was successfully concluded. Bianca knew better. She knew that C.V. was primarily interested in seeing the law work out here in this last frontier. If, in the middle of wild cowboys, rough miners, indiscriminate peace officers and reckless gamblers, the court could be used for the peaceful settlement of a question which meant thousands of dollars for the litigants, then it would be a triumph for law. That, Bianca knew, was what motivated C.V. Battenburg.

Bianca eased out of the bed and walked over to the window to look out on the street. It was soft and quiet under the early morning light. She saw two heavily loaded freight wagons with their drivers sitting on the seats holding the reins, already looking tired from the long day's haul they had in front of them.

Bianca had learned that there were actually two Tombstones ... the Tombstone at night and the Tombstone at day. The night-time Tombstone began at about six in the evening and generally ended by six in the morning when all the revelers were drunk and just getting in bed. The daytime Tombstone was no different from any other town. It consisted of the men and women who worked to make a living and a home for their families. The freight drivers were two such men.

By now the wagons were even with the hotel where the Cattlemen's Association had held their dance last night. The drivers of the wagons were probably unaware that there even was a dance the night before, because both of them were probably asleep, preparing for their day's work today.

Grady hadn't said much about the dance when he came back to the hotel. Bianca and C.V. had been in the bar downstairs having a quiet drink when he came in. He sat with them for a moment or two, but it seemed obvious that he wasn't in the mood to answer any questions about his evening.

Bianca liked Grady. She had a difficult time in the beginning, because she had the distinct feeling that Grady had fallen in love with her. Grady never mentioned it, never even suggested it, but Bianca didn't need it put in words. She had the type of fiery beauty which had aroused passion in men from the time she first blossomed into young womanhood. She knew, without having to be told, exactly what a man was thinking when he was around her.

Bianca had to be very careful around Grady; she cared for him a great deal and she had no wish to hurt him by spurning his attentions, even though he never said anything about it. On the one hand she considered herself too old for him, and on the other, She knew from the very beginning that she was going to fall in love with C.V. The relationship between C.V. and Grady was too important to be endangered by any type of jealousy over a woman.

Grady had evidently come to the same conclusion independently, for now the situation between them was quite comfortable. She could almost look upon Grady in somewhat the same way as C.V. saw him, if not as a son, then certainly as a younger brother.

"Hey," C.V. said softly from the bed behind her.

Bianca turned toward him. His arms were folded with his hands locked behind his head. He was smiling at her.

"Hi," she said.

"What are you doing out of bed so early?"

"I just wanted to look out at the town," she said.

"See anything?"

"No. Just a couple of wagons."

C.V. patted the bed beside him. "Well," he said. "You could stand there and watch those wagons if you want to. Or . . . " he let the word hang.

Bianca smiled at him. "Or what?"

"You could get back into bed."

Bianca, who was totally uninhibited by her nudity, walked across the room to join C.V. on the bed. She met his mouth with her own, and as they kissed C.V.'s hand went to her breast, then burned a searing path down her body and across her stomach, finally coming to rest at the junction of her thighs. His fingers dipped into the center of all her turbulent feelings.

As she had when they made love last night, Bianca floated in the stupor of languorous sexual arousal. Her blood was hot and there was a sweet hunger in her loins. Beneath C.V.'s skilled and loving fingers, her body trembled with fire and need.

They had made love many times by now, and that had created in each of them an awareness of the other's pleasures and wants. Bianca knew how long C.V. could ride the building wave of desire before he reached the crest, and he knew exactly when she was ready for him. He moved over her, then into her and Bianca experienced the sweet, exquisite pleasures she had come to expect from their lovemaking.

Bianca was not a passive lover. She gave as well as took, at times becoming as much the aggressor as he. Then, as they loved, she felt the building up of pleasure inside her, a tensing of energy which gathered, then released at that supreme moment of rapture when she abandoned all thought save her desperate quest for culmination.

The pleasure burst over her in waves, sweeping her from pinnacle to pinnacle where she hung precariously balanced for a time which was far too short and yet encompassed an eternity.

Finally, C.V.'s own shuddering moan told her that he, too, had experienced the exquisite moment of pleasure. She locked her arms and legs around his naked back, holding him to her, keeping him inside her, as they shared one final moment of ecstasy.

Grady was in the hotel dining room eating his breakfast. A shadow fell across his table and he looked up to see a tall, bearded man wearing a badge. He smiled as he recognized Boston Corbett and he invited Corbett to join him.

"What brings you here to Tombstone?" Grady asked.

"The Army asked me to check around for some mules," Boston said. He chuckled and reached for one of Grady's biscuits. "Do you mind?"

"Help yourself," Grady said, and he held up his hand to get the attention of the waiter, then pointed to the plate of biscuits indicating that he wanted some more.

Boston spread butter and jam on his biscuit. "Seems to me like a United States Marshal could come up with a better way to spend his time than looking around for mules," he said.

"Do you have any idea where they may be?" Grady asked.

Boston sighed. "Yeah," he said. "I know exactly where they are."

"Well, then there's no problem."

"They're on the Clanton spread," Boston said. He finished the biscuit just as the waiter came, then he started preparing another one.

"The Clantons stole some mules from the Army?"

"No, they didn't steal 'em," Boston said. "Fact is, they bought 'em, all fair and proper. But the fella they bought 'em from stole 'em. That means they're still U.S. Army property. I got to go get 'em back. I don't think the Clantons are going to like that much."

"They don't have any choice," Grady said.

"Yeah, well, try tellin' ol' man Clanton that. Or that crazy son of his, Ike." Boston demolished another biscuit. "If Billy's there, it should go all right. He's got more sense than the rest of 'em put together."

"I have to agree," Grady said. Quickly, he related the story to Boston of what had happened last night, and how Billy had prevented the cowboy from shooting him.

"You're one lucky fella," Boston said. "These fool cowboys have been known to shoot a man just for snorin'. Uh, listen, Grady, I'm not just passin' time with you. I came to ask you to go with me."

"You want me to go with you? Why?"

"I thought maybe you bein' a lawyer, you could explain things to 'em better'n me. You know when a fella pays good money for some stock he has ever' reason to believe it is his.

And if that person is N.H. Clanton, he's gonna be willin' to back up that belief with guns, no matter who comes for the animals."

"What you're saying is, if I can't explain it to their satisfaction, then you may want my gun. Is that it?"

"I've seen you use that thing, remember? You're pretty handy with it."

"Why don't you get one of the Earps?"

"In the first place, they would have no jurisdiction out there unless I deputized them first. And in the second place, taking one of the Earps out there to do something like this would be like waving a red flag in the face of a bull."

"I'm afraid you're right there," Grady agreed. "And Sheriff Behan is worthless when it comes to dealing with the Clantons. They have him in their hip pocket."

Grady rubbed his beard and looked across the table at Boston.

"I'll tell you what," he said. "I'll go with you. But I don't intend to take a gun with me."

"That might prove to be pretty risky," Boston said.

"That's the only way I'll go, take it or leave it."

C.V. and Bianca came into the dining room then, and C.V. smiled when he saw Boston. Boston stood and they shook hands, then C.V. and Bianca sat when a waiter came over to take their order. After breakfast was ordered, Grady told C.V. what Boston had asked. "Do you think it could jeopardize our case?"

"I don't see how it could," C.V. said. "After all, you're only going to explain the law to them. You might even be helping matters if you can keep them out of trouble."

"Grady, be careful," Bianca said.

"Like I was walking on eggs," Grady replied.

It was a good half hour ride to the Clanton Ranch. Grady had been out this way before, having once climbed an overlook with C.V. and Bianca to look at the land which had been her family's, and at the ranch which the Clantons worked. From the overlook it was easy to see why the Santa Anna land had been so important to N.H. Clanton. Most of Clanton's land was watered by undependable creeks and streams, whereas the Santa Anna property had the San Pedro River. It wasn't a large river, but it had water most of the year and that made it a very valuable river.

On those earlier trips out here Grady had seen the main house and bunk houses, barns, stables and graineries which made up the Clanton Ranch, but he had never visited before. This would be his first time. He told himself that he was doing it for Boston, and for the case he was trying, to make certain that nothing went wrong with Boston's attempt to recover the Army mules. In truth, he was doing it because he wanted to see Sally again.

And yet, even as he admitted that to himself during the ride out he knew that he was engaged in risky business. If Sally was already against him for his participation in the lawsuit, how much more would she be against him when he showed up with Marshal Corbett to serve notice that they must give up some stock, and not stock which they came by dishonestly, but stock for which they paid good money.

They passed under a gate which featured a set of polished longhorn steer horns, then rode up to the front of the house, By the time they reached the front of the house, old man Clanton was standing on the front porch, cradling a shotgun.

"Mr. Clanton?" Boston said, touching the brim of his hat. He pointed to the shotgun in Clanton's arm. "That doesn't seem very neighborly."

"You're a U.S. Marshal, ain't ya?" Clanton asked.

"Yes, sir, I am."

"I don't reckon any U.S. Marshal's gonna be payin' me a neighborly visit. What do you want?"

"Could I get down and talk for a while?"

"I can hear you real good just where you are," the old man said. He looked at Grady. "This here your deputy?"

"No, Mr. Clanton. I'm Grady Ford. I'm a lawyer."

"A lawyer? Ha! A lawyer?"

"Yes, sir."

"They ain't no need for lawyers in the Arizona territory," Clanton said.

"I don't agree with you, sir."

"I don't reckon you would. You one of the fella's tryin' to take the old Santa Anna property away from me?"

"Yes, sir."

"Is that what this is about?" The shotgun had been broken open at the breach, but now Clanton snapped it shut with an ominous click. He didn't raise the barrel, but the threat had been implied, nevertheless. "'Cause if you're here about that property, I ain't a'talkin'."

"No, sir, it doesn't have anything to do with the property, sir," Boston said.

"It don't?"

"No, sir."

"What does it have to do with?"

Grady saw a movement of the curtain in the window, and, without being too obvious, he glanced in that direction. He saw Sally's face disappear just as he looked toward her.

"Mr. Clanton, did you come into a team of mules recently?"

"A team of mules? Yeah, I reckon I did. They belong to Ike. I think he had some fool notion of prospectin' or somethin,' I don't know. What about 'em?"

"They belong to the U.S. Army, Mr. Clanton. I'm here to take 'em back."

"What? Look here, are you tellin' me my boy stole them mules?" Clanton asked.

"No, sir, not at all," Boston said. "Ike bought the mules from a man named Coleman Peterson."

"Well, I don't understand. If you're sayin' Ike didn't steal 'em, then how can they still belong to the Army?"

"Because the mules weren't Peterson's to sell," Boston

said.

Clanton squinted his eyes and looked at Boston. "Seems to me, then, like that's a matter between the Army and Peterson. Don't see as to how it effects Ike."

"It effects Ike because he has the mules and they still belong to the Army," Boston said.

"I don't understand quite what you're sayin'," Clanton said. "But if Ike paid for the mules, fair and proper, then you ain't gettin' 'em."

"Mr. Clanton, under the law, Ike is technically guilty of larceny, just as if he had stolen the mules himself," Grady explained. "You see, he is guilty of receiving stolen goods. Now my understanding is that the government is willing to accept the plea that Ike didn't realize they were stolen, is that right, Boston?"

"Yes," Boston said, shaking his head in the affirmative.

"Therefore, no charges will be filed," Grady went on. "But since the mules never belonged to Coleman Peterson in the first place, they weren't his to sell. That would be like me selling some of your cattle. If I went to Tucson and sold a hundred head of your cattle and a cattle buyer came out here with a receipt, you wouldn't give him the cattle would you?"

Clanton scratched the stubble of a two day growth of beard.

"No," he said. "No, I reckon I wouldn't."

"Well, Ike's receipt is no good either. The mules still belong to the Army."

Clanton broke open the shotgun and pulled out the two shells. He leaned the gun against the front of the house.

"All right, mister, I reckon you made your point," he said. "Never wanted the worthless critters in the first place, and can't figure out why Ike thought he did. They ain't done nothin' from the day he brought 'em in but eat. I'll go out to the barn 'n get 'em 'n bring 'em to you, 'n good riddance."

"Thank you, sir," Boston said.

"Mr. Clanton?" Grady called as Clanton started toward the

barn. Clanton stopped and looked back toward him.

"Yeah?"

"If you like, I will see to it that a claim, on your behalf, is filed against Coleman Peterson."

"What good will that do?"

"Maybe none," Grady said. "On the other hand, he may have some unencumbered property, in which case a judgment would be made in your favor. You might get your money back."

"You'd do that for me?"

"Yes, sir, I would."

"Why? I thought you were tryin' to take my land away from me."

"I'm a lawyer, Mr. Clanton. I would like to see more disputes settled by Mr. Blackstone's Lawbooks, and fewer by Mr. Colt's pistols."

Clanton chuckled. "Don't reckon any of us are likely to live to see that day come," he said.

"It will come," Grady said. "The court is already the arbitrator of disputes in the East."

"This ain't the East," Clanton said. He turned to go. "I'll get them mules."

"Grady," Boston said quietly, after Clanton left.

"Yes?"

"There's someone in the house behind the curtains, and someone around the corner of the house. Be ready if I have to pull my gun."

"No!" Grady said. "The person in the house is Sally. She's not doing anything."

"Maybe not, but I don't aim to be cut down by whoever's behind the corner there."

Boston got off his horse and began adjusting the bridal. Then, moving so quickly that Grady was scarcely able to follow him, he pulled his gun, dropped, and rolled toward the corner. He was lying in the prone position with his gun out and pointed toward the person behind the corner of the house before anyone knew he was about to make his move.

"Come on out from behind there," Boston said. Grady looked toward the comer and saw Billy Clanton stepping out from behind the building with his hands up, hesitantly. He was wearing a gun.

"What were you doin' back there, Mister?" Boston asked. "Plannin' on shootin' us in the back once we got the mules?"

"No," Billy said. "I was just listening to what was going on, that's all."

"Why didn't you come 'round front?"

"I didn't want to interfere."

"Shuck outta that gun."

"Marshal," Billy said, his face growing red in anger. "Don't make me do that. This is my ranch, these are my men. If you make me drop my gun it'll make me look bad in front of 'em."

"I can't worry about that none. Shuck outta that gun."

"Boston," Grady said. "Let him keep his gun. I don't think he meant us any harm."

"Yeah? How do you know?"

"If he had wanted me harmed, he could've let it happen last night."

"Yeah, well I wasn't with you last night, and you weren't tryin' to take anything of his. I think it's better to be safe than sorry."

"Don't do this," Grady said.

Boston looked at Billy for a moment longer, then he sighed and put his gun away.

"All right," he said. "You can keep your gun. But I'm gonna keep an eye on you."

"Mr. Ford?" Billy said.

"Yes?"

"This squares us, Mr. Ford. Don't be doin' me no more favors' 'n don't look for any from me."

"All right," Grady said. "If you want it that way."

"I do," Billy said.

Old man Clanton returned then, leading two mules. He handed the ropes to Boston.

"The halters 'n rope belong to me. I'd be obliged to have 'em back when you're done with 'em," he said.

"I'll get new halters and ropes in town," Boston said.

"I'll keep up with your stuff," Grady offered.

"Mr. Clanton, I appreciate your cooperation, sir," Boston said. He clicked at his horse and he and Grady started back down the road.

They were near the overlook when Grady saw her. She was riding fast, across the open pasture. It was really quite a pretty sight to behold as the horse raised a high rooster tail of dust behind him and the girl, an accomplished rider, was bent low over the animal's head.

"Who's this cornin' up on us?" Boston asked.

"It's Sally."

"Sally?"

"The girl behind the curtain, remember?"

"Oh, yes," Boston said. He scratched his beard. "I wonder what she wants?"

"I hope she wants to talk to me."

"To you? What for?"

"I, uh . . . " Grady started, then stumbled. Suddenly Boston realized what Grady was trying to say and he smiled broadly.

"Well, damn, boy, why didn't you say somethin' earlier?" he asked. "Listen, why don't I just take these mules on back and leave you here to talk to her?"

"Yeah, thanks," Grady said.

Boston clucked at his horse again, then started on toward town while Grady turned back to meet Sally.

Sally reined up when they drew even.

"Anything wrong?" Grady asked.

"Let me get down and give the horse a blow," she said. "I ran him pretty hard to catch up with you. I didn't want Pa or Billy to see us together."

Grady looked around. "You want to go over there in those rocks?"

"No," she said. "This'll be all right. We can see anyone if they're comin' up on us."

Now Grady and Sally were both off their horses, and Sally was patting her horse gently, on the neck.

"Thank you for takin' up for Billy back there," she said.

"Seemed only fair," he said. "Billy certainly took up for me last night, and in a big way. I guess that man would've shot me."

"No he wouldn't have," Sally said easily.

"He wouldn't? You couldn't prove that by me. He looked ready to pull the trigger."

"So was I," Sally said.

"So were you? What do you mean?"

"Ike had his guns hanging up in the cloak room," she said. "I was standing just inside the cloakroom aiming at him. I would have shot him before I would have let him shoot you."

Grady chuckled. "Sally Clanton, you're a surprising woman," he said. "Like this. This is a surprise, your coming to see me like this. I thought you didn't want to see me anymore."

"Well," Sally said, smiling at him, "I sort of surprised myself on this."

"Really?"

"Yes, I . . . thought about you last night," she said. "The fact is, I thought about you a lot."

"And what did you think?"

"I thought I'd like to see you some more," she said.

"Sally, do you mean it?" Grady asked happily.

"Sure, I mean it."

"Yaahoo!" Grady said, and he grabbed Sally and pulled her to him, kissing her, and squeezing her so hard that she could barely breathe.

"Grady Ford, let me go, I can't breathe," she said, squealing and laughing at him.

"Oh, I'm sorry," he said, letting her go quickly. He

brushed her off. "Are you all right? Did I hurt you?"

Sally laughed, and brushed her hair back from her forehead.

"You're crazy, Grady Ford, did you know that?"

"I've been called worse," Grady said. "When can I see you? Can I come out this afternoon? Tomorrow? Maybe I can see you tomorrow."

"Wait a minute, wait a minute," Sally said. "Not so fast. Lands, a body would think you'd never called on a girl before."

"I haven't," Grady admitted.

"What?"

"I mean, well, not a proper girl," Grady said. "Not what you would call courting."

Sally laughed again. "You mean with all your education there might be a few things you can learn from me?"

"I'm sure there are many things," Grady said. He smiled broadly. "But I'm a fast learner, you'll see."

"All right," she said. "The first thing you have to learn is not to come out to the ranch again."

"What? But I thought you said you would see me again."

"I will," Sally said. "But I don't think Pa would approve of me seein' you, since you're the one that's tryin' to take his land away from him."

"I'm just representing—"

"You're just the lawyer, I know," Sally said. "I reckon I can see that. I don't quite understand it, but I can see it. But Pa won't understand it, and Ike sure won't. Pa wouldn't do no more than get real mad. There's no tellin' what Ike might do if he got wind we were courtin'. So, I don't want any of them to know about it. Is that all right?"

"If you say so. But how are we going to see each other without anyone knowing about it?"

"I've got that all figured out," Sally said. "You're goin' to start callin' on Miss Sylvia Collins. Everyone will think you are courtin' her. But I'll be there too, and it'll be me you're courtin' all along, only nobody will know it but Sylvia."

"Who is this Sylvia Collins?"

"She's a friend of mine. Probably my very best friend, and she's in love with my brother Billy."

"Oh no," Grady said, holding his hands out. "Wait a minute, Sally, do you know what you're saying? You want everyone to think I'm courting Sylvia Collins, which means Billy will think that too, right?"

"Billy, most of all."

"I don't think that's all that good of an idea, do you? I mean, if your brother is the jealous type."

"Oh, I hope he is," Sally said.

"What do you mean, you hope he is? You want him to come after me?"

"No, I want him to go after Sylvia."

"Sally, you're going to have to explain this to me. I don't know what you're talking about.

"Don't you see? It's absolutely perfect, and it'll solve two problems: for one, it'll let us see each other with nobody getting the wiser. Secondly, it'll make Billy notice Sylvia, and maybe even get jealous of her. You see, Sylvia is crazy in love with Billy, but so far Billy just acts like he doesn't even know she exists. Maybe if he thinks someone else is courting her, he'll get interested."

"Yeah, well, maybe," Grady said. "I just hope he doesn't get too interested too quickly. I don't want him coming after me."

"Don't worry about that," Sally said. "So what do you say? Are you willing to see me under those conditions?"

Grady smiled broadly. "I'll see you under any conditions you name."

"Then call on Sylvia tomorrow. And bring an appetite. We're going on a picnic."

"I'll be there," Grady said.

Sally started to climb on her horse, then she stopped and smiled at Grady. She walked over to him and kissed him on the mouth.

"I'll see you tomorrow," she said.

Grady watched Sally as she rode away, back across the open pasture to her house. He rubbed the back of his fingers against his mouth, where he could still feel the heat of her kiss on his lips.

Chapter Ten

BECAUSE GRADY WANTED to take the next day off for his picnic with Sally, he agreed to relieve C.V. and Bianca for the rest of the afternoon. He spent all day in the office, meticulously going over every detail of the information which had been sent from the territorial capitol. He examined every land transaction, every tax payment, every item which pertained to the Santa Anna land, trying to find something they could use.

At about eight o'clock that evening, he heard C.V.'s voice and Bianca's laugh as the pair trooped up the stairs, returning from their rounds. They had rented a buggy and rode to as many ranches and farms as they could reach in one day, collecting affidavits from cooperative witnesses. It had been a much more pleasant assignment than going over the files.

The door opened and C.V. and Bianca came into the room.

"Well, my friend, are you still toiling over those extracts?"

Grady lay the pencil down and pinched the bridge of his nose.

"Yeah," he said. He stretched, then pointed to a page he had filled with his own writing. "I'm not sure how much good this'll do," he said. "But I've got a complete history of all the taxes paid on that place, even when they were being paid to the

Spanish King."

"If nothing else, we can establish a long family history of responsible stewardship for the land," C.V. said. "We have a few affidavits which support our case," C.V. went on. "As well as a commitment to testify from one man who went to Phoenix with Esteban to make the tax payment. All in all, I would say it was a very successful day."

"Good," Grady said.

"You look tired," Bianca said.

"I am," Grady replied. "It's funny how something like this can tire you faster than physical labor."

"Why don't you knock off?" C.V. suggested. "Go have a few drinks, enjoy the night life of this bustling community."

"A cool beer would be nice," Grady said. He stood and slid his chair back under the table where he had been working. "Uh, C.V., you're sure now there won't be any problem with my taking off tomorrow?"

"No problem," C.V. said easily. He looked at the pages Grady had filled. "In fact, it looks to me like you did two days work today anyway. You deserve a day off. Go, lad, and rejoice in your freedom." C.V. put his arm easily, comfortably, around Bianca's shoulder and pulled her to him. Though he had never said so, by that very gesture he told Grady that he was appreciating the time he was having alone with Bianca. Grady smiled in the sudden realization that C.V. was as anxious to get rid of him as he was to go.

"All right. I'll see you later," Grady said. He left the couple to themselves and hurried to the saloon, already able to taste the big, cool mug of beer he would soon be drinking.

The piano was playing merrily but the noise in the saloon was such that no one could hear it from more than ten feet away. In one comer, a group of raucous cowboys had started their own singing in competition with the piano. One of those cowboys, Grady noticed, was Ike Clanton. Ike didn't seem to notice him, and Grady was glad of it. He didn't know how Ike would take the loss of his mules this morning, and the last thing he wanted was a confrontation.

"Hello, Grady. Beer?" the bartender asked as Grady stepped up to the bar.

"Yeah, George, make it a tall and cool," Grady said.

The bartender drew the beer, leaving a small head on it, and handed the mug to Grady. Grady blew off the suds, then took his first drink, while George went back to rubbing his rag on the bar. If you had asked him, he would have told you he was cleaning the bar. In reality he was just spreading the spilt liquor around, which did nothing toward improving the bar surface.

There was a commotion on the floor, then a loud burst of laughter, and Grady turned around and leaned back against the bar to watch. One of the cowboys had shoved several tables aside, and was doing his interpretation of the Mexican Hat Dance.

"Hey, Tom," Ike called. "What are you tryin' to do? Learn to dance the Fandango?"

The dancing cowboy, Grady knew, was Tom McClaury. His brother Frank was standing beside Ike Clanton.

"He'll never make it," Frank laughed. "He can't dance any better'n he can punch cows."

"Oh yeah?" Tom answered. "Well just watch this step."

Tom jumped up and attempted to kick his heels together, but his spurs got entangled and he fell to the floor in a heap. His fall was greeted with loud laughter and Ike tossed him a bottle. Tom turned the bottle up and took several deep swallows while still seated on the floor.

Grady laughed with the others.

"Hey, are you gonna just sit there on the floor, suckin' on that bottle like a baby on a tit, or are we goin' over to Belle's Whorehouse?" Ike called.

"Ike, you know we ain't welcome at Belle's," Frank said, shaking his finger back and forth. "McClaury's and Clantons just ain't welcome there."

"That's not true," Tom said. "Us McClaurys ain't

welcome, 'n of Ike there ain't welcome, but little Billy Boy, why, he's welcome as rain. Why is that, Ike? Why is Billy welcome where you ain't?"

"'Cause Billy's got good manners," Ike said. "He's my little brother 'n I raised him up proper." Tom and Frank laughed at Ike's comment.

"Too bad you didn't learn some of them manners yourself. If you had some of 'em, maybe we wouldn't get turned away ever' time we tried to get into a whorehouse."

"We'll get in there tonight," Ike said.

"Yeah? What makes you think so?"

"'Cause I don't intend to be turned away tonight," Ike said. "And if you're men, you'll go with me."

"Sure, why not?" Tom said. "Hell, I'll go with you." He stood up, drained the last of the bottle and tossed it over his head casually. It hit the corner of the bar and smashed into little pieces, but the three men didn't even look around at it as they stepped outside.

"They's gonna be a shootin' sure," someone said. "I seen the Earps down there a while ago."

"Come on, let's go watch!" another said, and a moment later there was a mad rush for the doors.

Grady was swept along by the crowd, and soon he, and nearly everyone else who had been in the saloon at the time, were arrayed in a half circle in front of Belle's. Grady saw the Earps standing on the front porch of the building. They just stood there, like magnificent statues, looking down at Ike Clanton, Tom and Frank McClaury. Clanton and the McClaurys were standing in the dirt of the street, looking up. The only light came from a gas street lamp which hissed on the wall right behind the Earps. It cast a golden bubble of light which splashed out onto the street, making deep shadows on the faces of everyone present.

"I believe you gentlemen have come to a place where you aren't wanted," Wyatt said. He spoke in a low, quiet voice, all the more menacing because of its apparent lack of emotion.

"Get out of the way, Earp," Ike called. "Me 'n my friends is comin' in." In contrast, Ike's voice was loud and threatening. And, Grady thought, frightened.

At this point of the showdown, the advantage definitely lay with the Earps. They were deathly calm, without a twitching muscle among them. Ike Clanton and the two McClaury brothers were all three displaying nervous tics. "You got that, Wyatt Earp? We're comin' in."

"No, I don't think so, Clanton," Wyatt answered, as calmly as before.

"What makes you think we ain't?"

"Because I aim to stop you," Wyatt said.

"The only way you gonna stop us is to shoot us," Ike said.

"I'm prepared to settle this issue once and for all in just that way," Earp said. Now he dropped his arm loosely by his side.

All conversation halted then, and there was a collective holding of the breath as the crowd waited for the play to unfold.

Grady realized that what had started out as fun and laughter in the saloon a few moments earlier was about to end in a shootout. If so, it would be disastrous for Ike and his friends. Even under normal conditions, Grady believed the Earps would be more than a match for Ike Clanton and the McClaurys. But these weren't ordinary conditions. Ike Clanton and his two friends were drunk. Tom McClaury was so drunk, in fact, that it was all he could do to stand on his own two feet. If a shootout did develop now, it would be little more than murder.

Suddenly Grady thought of Sally Clanton. He was going to see her tomorrow. How could he call on her in innocence tomorrow, if he stood by and watched her brother shot down tonight?

Slowly, Grady moved through the crowd until he was standing right behind Ike Clanton. Then, so quickly that few in the crowd saw what he was doing, he pulled Ike's pistol from his holster and brought it crashing down on Ike's head. Ike dropped like a sack of potatoes.

When Tom and Frank McClaury saw that Ike was down, they suddenly lost their taste for fight, and they threw up their hands.

"We ain't gonna draw, Earp!" Frank said quickly. "See, our hands is up. We ain't gonna draw!"

Earp stood there with his temple throbbing in anger, looking down at the prostrate form of the man who had been his adversary. For one, brief moment, Grady had the fear that Wyatt was going to draw anyway. Then he saw the muscles in Earp's neck and shoulders relax.

"What the hell did you do that for?" he asked, indicating the unconscious body of Ike Clanton.

"Looked to me like there was about to be a fight," Grady said easily. "I thought it was my civic duty to stop it if I could."

"You didn't stop it," Wyatt said easily. "You just delayed it."

"Wyatt, you don't mean you're going to wait until he regains consciousness?"

"No, I don't mean that," Wyatt said. "But there'll be another time he'll come at me, and at that time the party will commence. Seems to me like it would have saved a lot of worry and time if I had just gone ahead and killed him here 'n now."

"You two men," Grady said. "Take Ike and get on out of here."

"Take 'im down to the jail," Wyatt said.

"On what charge?" Grady asked.

"What?" Wyatt looked at Grady with a surprised expression on his face. "Grady, what are you talkin' about, what charge? Disturbin' the peace."

"Wyatt, you can't make that charge stick," Grady said. "All he did was come down here and try to enter a business establishment."

Wyatt took a step toward the edge of the porch, then

hooked his fingers in his belt. He bent over slightly at the waist and looked down at Grady.

"In case you haven't noticed, this here business establishment is a whorehouse," Wyatt said. "I'll arrest him for tryin' to enter a place of prostitution."

"In most of the states that would be illegal, I agree. But there is no Federal or territorial law against prostitution, nor is it prohibited by city statutes. Therefore, this is a legal place of business, and whether Belle wants him in or not, he has every right to try and enter."

"He doesn't have a right to shoot his way in," Wyatt said in exasperation.

"He didn't do that."

"He was about to."

"We don't know that," Grady said. "I knocked him out before it got that far. If you must arrest someone, arrest me for assault."

Wyatt shook his head and clucked his tongue in frustration.

"I can't figure you, Grady Ford. For the life of me, I can't figure you." He sighed in disgust, then made a jerking motion with his thumb. "All right, you two McClaury boys, get him out of here." With the possibility of a gunfight effectively defused, the crowd which had gathered for the excitement now began to disperse.

"Virgil, you go on home to the wife," Wyatt said. "Morgan and I'll take the rounds."

"Okay, Wyatt, thanks," Virgil said. "I know she's had to wait supper tonight." He nodded to Grady, then started down the street toward his house and the late supper his wife had waiting for him. In that respect he was no different from any other working man whose business kept him long hours. The only difference was his job could have quite easily erupted in a blaze of gunfire.

"Morgan, you go that way, I'll go this way."

"All right, Wyatt," the youngest of the Earp brothers said.

"Well, Grady, that just leaves you and me," Wyatt said. "You want to walk with me for a bit?"

"Sure," Grady said. "Why not?"

Grady walked along the line of closed business establishments with Wyatt, as Wyatt tested the doors on all of them. Their boots clumped loudly on the wooden planks of the sidewalk.

"Grady," Wyatt said after they had walked a few buildings. "That was a damn fool thing for you to do back there."

"I admit I'd be hard pressed to make a case for intelligence over the move," Grady said.

Wyatt checked another door.

"Why did you do it?"

"I told you, to stop the fight."

"I know that," Wyatt said. "The question is, why did you want to stop it?"

"Are you serious?"

They passed a place where there was a space between two of the buildings, and a little fence bridged that space. There was a gate on the fence, and Wyatt opened the gate and looked inside, to make certain no one was up to no good between the two buildings, out of sight.

"Yes, I'm serious," Wyatt went on. "Seems to me it would have been better to go ahead and get this thing over with now. The way it is, Clanton or one of his friends might just waylay me from an alley some night. You see what I'm doing here, don't you? How I'm walkin' along dark rows of buildings, checkin' on things?"

"Yes."

"Grady, ever'body knows I do this. If Ike Clanton wanted to do me in, this would be a perfect time for him to do it, don't you think?"

"I suppose so."

"I'm a law abidin' man, Grady. I can't ambush Clanton, even though I know he probably has some such trick planned for me. I can't even push him into a fight without just cause. I can't believe that when the opportunity came up for me to take care of it, once and for all, you came along and stopped it. Do you see now why I'm mad?"

"You forget, Wyatt. Even if you had killed Ike and the McClaurys tonight, it would have left Billy, and Jim Spence, and half a dozen others who are in the Clanton camp. So where does it all stop? Are you going to have to kill all of them?"

"It may come down to that," Wyatt said. "I don't really believe they are going to leave me any choice."

"Maybe not, but I can't see any reason to rush into it, either."

"You sure it isn't just the girl?"

Grady stopped and looked at Wyatt. "What girl?" he asked.

"Boston stopped by today to tell me about how you and he recovered the mules. He also told me that as you were leavin', Sally Clanton came ridin' out on a horse to talk to you."

"What if she did?"

"Nothing, nothing," Wyatt said. "She's a beautiful girl, 'n there's no law against you seein' her, even if she is a Clanton. It's just that I would hate to see your head so turned and your eyes so blinded by a pretty girl that you forget who your friends are."

"Wyatt, if you really are my friend, you won't push this issue," Grady said.

"Well, I reckon I am your friend," Wyatt said. "So I reckon I won't push. But I will give you one little word of caution. The time's comin', Grady, when there's gonna be a showdown between Ike and Billy Clanton and those damn McClaurys, and my brothers and me. I expect when that time does come there are gonna be a couple of Clantons left dyin' in the dirt. Sally won't be able to understand the whys and wherefores of all that, and you won't be able to explain it no matter how hard you try. She's gonna wind up powerful hurt, 'n she's gonna take some of it out on you. There's no gettin' around that. I just thought I'd let you know."

"Thanks," Grady said. "I'll keep that in mind." Wyatt smiled broadly. "Well, now that we got all that behind us, what say we go down to The Grotto and have a bite to eat? My treat."

"I sure can't afford to pass up an opportunity like that," Grady said, returning Wyatt's smile. "You're on."

Grady slept late the next morning, then, around ten, rented a buggy from the O.K. Corral. It was an easy drive out to the Collins Ranch, where Sylvia lived with her mother. Her father had died two years earlier and now Sylvia and her mother lived on the money they made by renting out their pastureland to other ranchers.

Sylvia was a very pretty girl, somewhat shorter than Sally, and with hair which was more red than blonde. Grady was a little nervous when he arrived, because he didn't know if Sally had let Sylvia in on their arrangement. To his relief, Sylvia set him at ease right away, coming out on the front porch to greet him.

"Mr. Ford," she said. "Sally will be along shortly. I've made some lemonade—would you like to sit-in the front porch swing and have some?"

"I can think of nothing more pleasant," Grady said.

Sylvia laughed. "Heavens, don't let Sally hear that," she said. "I don't think she would appreciate that at all."

"Oh, I didn't mean that," Grady said. "I'd much rather be with Sally . . ." suddenly he realized what he was saying and he stopped and apologized again. "I'm sorry, I didn't mean that either, it's just . . . "

"Pay no mind to Sylvia, Mr. Ford," Sylvia's mother said, coming to the porch and brushing her hands against her apron. There was about her the smell of flour and cinnamon, as she had been baking in the kitchen.

For a sudden, brief moment, Grady recalled his own mother. How well he remembered that smell. He looked at Mrs. Collins with an intensity which surprised her.

"Heavens, I must be a mess," she said, laughing nervously. "I didn't even think how I must look." She turned to go back into the house.

"No!" Grady said. "Please don't go." Mrs. Collins stopped. "My mother used to bake a lot," Grady went on, explaining his reaction. "I like the look of flour and the smells of baking. It reminds me of her."

"Where is your mother now?" Mrs. Collins asked.

"She's dead," Grady said. "She and my father were killed by Commancheros when I was twelve."

"Oh," Mrs. Collins said, and the look in her face and in her eyes told Grady that her compassion for him was genuine. "How terrible that must have been for a twelve-year-old child."

They heard the hoofbeats of an approaching horse then, and Sylvia smiled.

"Here comes Sally now," she said. "I guess that means you're saved from a fate worse than death."

"I'd better get back inside," Mrs. Collins said. "I've packed a nice picnic lunch for you and Sally. I hope you enjoy it."

"Oh, I'm sure we will," Grady said. He stepped down from the porch and walked out front to meet Sally.

"Good morning," Sally said brightly, swinging down from her horse.

"Good morning," Grady and Sylvia replied. "Oh, Sylvia, what a pretty dress," Sally said, her eyes flashing with humor. "I hope you haven't been trying to make time with my beau."

"I've been trying," Sylvia said. "But so far, without much success,"

Sally laughed, they turned to look at Grady. "I heard what you did for Ike last night," she said. "I want to thank you for that."

"What did he do?" Sylvia asked.

"He knocked him on the head with a gun," Sally said.

"I thought you said he did something *for* Ike— not *to*

him."

"That *was* for him," Sally said. "Ike was drunk and about ready to go up against Wyatt Earp and his brothers. If he'd done that he would've been killed."

With the picnic lunch loaded in the buggy, Grady drove while Sally gave directions. She led him onto a trail which worked its way back into the Dragoon Mountains to a spot she called her 'secret' place.

"I've come here often," she said. "I don't think anyone else has ever discovered it, for in all the years I've been coming I've never seen another."

"I hope your brothers don't know about it," Grady said.

"Don't worry about them."

The trail climbed up a large rock outcropping, past the silent vigil of towering saguaro cacti, across a level bench of sand peppered with fluttering yellow, red and blue cactus flowers, to a prominent overhang. When they reached the overhang Sally told him to stop, then she got out and walked out to the ledge.

Grady knew they had climbed quite a distance during the drive out, but he had no idea of high they had actually come until he walked over to stand beside Sally. Then he saw that they were actually several hundred feet above the desert floor, and, from here, could see for miles in every direction, including the town of Tombstone, far in the distance.

"You are the only person I've ever shared this with," Sally said.

"I'm flattered that you would bring me here," Grady said sincerely.

"Do you think I'm crazy for thinking the desert is beautiful?" Sally asked.

"Not at all," Grady answered. "Why should I think such a thing?"

"I've been in Tucson or Phoenix and heard the folks from back east talk about the desert as a great wasteland. I know they would laugh at the thought of someone finding it beautiful."

"Perhaps they would," Grady agreed. "But only because they have never seen it as you and I have. They don't know what it's like at twilight when the clouds are lit from below by the setting sun so that they glow pink and gold against the purple sky. And I don't think they have ever looked at it like this, with the cactus flowers carpeting the desert floor with every color of the rainbow. And I'd be willing to bet that they've never slept out here at night and watched the stars sparkle like diamonds on velvet, nor have they listened to the owls talk quietly among themselves. If someone has never done all those things, then they have no right commenting about it."

Sally took Grady's arm and held it, while she looked up into his face. Her eyes were shining with a sheen of tears.

"Oh, how I wish I could put it in words like that," she said. "You've said exactly what I feel." The little lock of hair which was always falling out of place fell against Sally's forehead then. Grady brushed it away for her.

"Sally, when you feel something as intensely as you feel for your desert country, you don't need to put it in words. People who are with you will know, believe me."

Sally's eyes penetrated to Grady's soul and he knew then that she wanted to be kissed. He moved his lips to hers and her mouth opened on his and her arms went around him. He felt a quivering in his stomach and a sudden giddiness. He wanted to make love to Sally. He wanted her more than he had ever wanted any woman. But he didn't want her just for the moment, he wanted her forever. He broke off the kiss, because he was afraid that if he let it go any further he would lose control.

"Oh," Sally said, leaning against him. "That took my breath away. Grady, do you ... do you feel the same way I do when we kiss?"

Grady laughed.

"What is it?"

"Don't you know you are supposed to fake a nonchalance about such things?"

"Fake a what?"

"You are supposed to pretend that you don't feel anything when you kiss."

"Why?"

Grady laughed again. "Come to think of it, I don't know why."

"Let's kiss again," Sally said spontaneously, arid she put her arms around his neck and pulled his lips down to hers.

This kiss started where the other one left off, and Grady felt a dizzying heat overwhelming him. If he didn't regain control of himself soon, he was going to ruin everything. This time, though, it was Sally who stopped.

"Oh," she said. "I ... I think we'd better not do that again for a while."

"All right, what do you say we eat? Is Mrs. Collins a good cook?"

"Oh, yes," Sally said. "She's really a great cook. Whatever she fixed us will be wonderful, you can bet on it."

"What have we here?" Grady said as he and Sally looked eagerly through the straw basket.

"Sliced ham and freshly baked bread," Sally said. "And potato salad, and some canned peaches. And, of course, a bottle of wine."

"Sounds good," Grady said, reaching for the loaf of bread.

"Just be patient, I'll set it out for you," Sally said. She spread a blanket, then put out the food. Grady made himself a big sandwich and took a healthy bite.

"Fantastic," he said, smacking his lips in appreciation. "Absolutely fantastic."

"Wine?" Sally asked, pouring some into a glass. After they'd both eaten, and they sat enjoying the wine, they talked for a long while. Up until this point their attraction for each other had been mutual and physical. The intensity of their attraction had overshadowed everything else, so that only now were they beginning to learn about each other. And so it was that, for the first time, Grady heard from Sally the story of her kidnapping.

"After I was taken off the stage, they took me to a line-shack," Sally said, running her finger nervously around the rim of her glass. "There were three of them, two Indians and a white man."

"Sally, I know this is uncomfortable for you," Grady said. "You don't have to tell me this if you don't want to."

"I want to tell you," Sally said. "I've never wanted to tell anyone else, but I want to tell you."

Grady put his arms around her and held her while she told him, word by painful word, what had happened to her.

"The white man had his way with me first," she said. "Then the Indians. There was no difference between them, they were all filthy, disgusting beasts. Then, when the Indians were finished, they tied me up. The white man asked for directions to my house, so he could get the ransom money. I was confused, I gave him the wrong directions though I didn't intend to. Then, after he left, the Indians started drinking some whiskey which had been on the stage. They started getting drunker and drunker, and paying less attention to me. There was a nail sticking out of the wall where I was, and I managed to use that nail to work the ropes loose. When I finally got my hands free, I untied my feet and legs, then tried to sneak out. I thought they were asleep, or passed out drunk. But, somehow, they heard me, and they came after me. I tried to run but my legs were numb and I fell down. One of them laughed, and he fell down on top of me and started undoing his clothes. I knew he was going to rape me again and I. . . I couldn't stand the thought. "

Sally paused for a long moment while Grady just held her quietly.

"I was trying to fight him off," she said after awhile, "when I felt his gun. It had been jammed down in his belt, and when he loosened his belt it fell. I pointed the gun at him and yelled at him to get away. I didn't really intend to shoot, in fact I don't even remember doing it. Suddenly I heard the gun go off, then I heard someone screaming. I was the one screaming and I was the one shooting, but it was like I was watching someone else. When it was all over, both of the Indians were dead and I was standing there holding an empty pistol, still pulling the trigger, even though there were no bullets left. After that, I was terrified that the white man was going to come back for me, so I grabbed one of the Indian ponies and rode home as fast as I could. When Pa and Ike found out what had happened, they went into a rage. They were going to go look for the third man when, all of a sudden, he rode up into the front yard. That was when I remembered I had given him the wrong directions. I…I started screaming and shouting that he was the one. When he saw me he was so shocked that he couldn't speak. Pa and Ike began shooting then and I think both of them emptied their guns in him. He was dead before he ever hit the ground."

When Sally finished her story Grady held her tightly for a long, long time while she cried, relieved at last to be able to share all the horror with someone else, to be rid of it once and for all. Finally, the tears stopped, and, tenderly, Grady tipped her head back and kissed each tear track, and then her lips.

Gently, but with the supreme confidence now that he wouldn't be resisted, Grady began to loosen the buttons of Sally's dress. As the buttons were opened and her breasts were exposed, the nipples hardened, sensitized by the gentle breeze. Sally twisted and turned to allow him to completely undress her, so that within a few moments she was totally naked.

Grady began removing his own clothes then, while Sally lay back and watched from the blanket which had served them for their picnic.

When Grady was as naked as she, he lay down beside her, but he didn't touch her yet. He thought of the terrible ordeal she had been through, and he knew that she might be easily frightened. If, in her fear, she turned against him, he would never forgive himself.

"Sally, I want you to be sure," he said. "I want you to be perfectly sure."

"I'm sure, Grady," Sally said. "I'm very sure. Can't you tell? Don't you know that I need this to ... to blot out forever what happened to me before?"

'"Sally took his hands and moved them over her own body, along the smooth curve of her hips, and then up across her breasts. She rubbed the palm of his hand across her nipples, then moved his hand down again, across her belly, hips and thighs. As his fingers explored her secret place, gently stroking, she leaned back and sighed.

As Grady smelled the perfume from the flowers of the desert, and Sally's own delicate scent, every ounce of his being was caught up in the sensations of the moment. Still, he moved gently, cautiously, lest he frighten her.

Sally cried out with desire then, and grew impatient because Grady was proceeding so slowly. She pulled him down over her and guided him into her. Grady looked across their bodies, to where he and Sally had joined to become one. He began to make love to her then, and the golden haze of sensual delight which lay over them began to undulate through both of them in wave after wave of pleasure.

Sally let herself go, to explore the outer limits of sensation. She was using Grady as a cleansing device to put away forever the terrible scars of that afternoon of horror. She gave herself to him, not only physically, but emotionally as well. There was no pain, there was no fear. There was just pleasure, pure and simple, with no sense of guilt or feeling of shame.

With Grady and with Sally, there was a conjoining of the spirit, a commingling of desire which drove them toward a mutual goal.

She thrust against him and he pushed against her as pleasure continued to sweep over them in wave after delightful wave. Her entire body seemed ready to dissolve under the white hot flames which licked at her.

Then it happened. Sally was first. It hit her body with such intensity that it was not possible to separate the individual ripples of pleasure. It felt like one sustained period of rapture which burst over her, sending tinglings throughout every part of her body.

Then Sally became aware of Grady's own release, and she shared the pleasure he felt with him, joining him at the supreme moment.

"I love you."

They laughed, for both had spoken the words at the same time.

And both knew that no truer words had ever been spoken.

Chapter Eleven

FOR THE NEXT MONTH and a half Grady and Sally continued to meet, secretly, at Sylvia's ranch.

The wisdom of their decision to keep their relationship secret was clearly bourne out by developments in the lawsuit which Bianca, through Battenburg and Ford, was pursuing. The animosity which naturally existed between the townspeople and the ranchers was exacerbated by the situation because the ranchers, to a man—including those who had never been particularly friendly with the Clantons— believed that some 'slick city lawyers' were going to use 'slick city tricks' to rob N.H. Clanton of his land and water.

On those occasions when Sally would come into town, she would carefully avoid all contact with Grady, even looking away from him if they happened to pass on the street.

Most of the time Sally was accompanied by one of her brothers, or her father, or a few of the ranchers. At other times, she was accompanied by Sylvia Collins. Sylvia would always smile graciously and nod at Grady, though they were never actually seen together on the streets, despite the fact that everyone knew, or thought they knew, that Sylvia and Grady were 'keeping company.'

"I'm tellin' you, he rides out there three or four times a

week," someone said. "I've seen 'im myself."

"Yeah, and the stage driver to Contention said he's seen Grady out to Sylvia's several times. You mark my words, there's gonna be a weddin' in this town soon."

So ran the gossip of the townspeople. The comments of the ranchers and cowboys were less kind, and poor Sylvia was the one who was suffering the brunt of it. The ranchers and cowboys thought Sylvia should 'stay with her own kind,' and they were openly jealous of her seeing so much of the lawyer who was trying to 'steal' the Clanton land. They were all the more critical of her because she was supposed to be a friend of Sally Clanton's, and they often wondered aloud how she could keep company with a man who was out to ruin her best friend's family.

One who was particularly upset with Sylvia was Billy. He commented on it one day as he and Sally were returning from town with a wagonload of supplies.

"What do you mean you don't like the way Sylvia is acting?" Sally asked, responding to Billy's comment.

"Well, it's obvious, isn't it? I mean, there's all that talk about him going out to her ranch so often. And the way they carry on in town."

"Billy Clanton, the only thing Sylvia has ever done in town is give the man a smile."

"Yeah, well I don't like her doin' even that," Billy said. "She should have more pride than to throw herself at him like that."

"Have you ever considered the fact that it might just be the other way around?" Sally asked. "Don't you think that Grady Ford may be throwing himself at Sylvia?"

"Well if he is; she's letting him do it."

"What's wrong with that?" Sally asked. "She's a pretty, marriageable young woman and he is a handsome, marriageable young man."

Billy looked at his sister. "Sally, you don't think . . . look here, are they about to get married?"

"I don't know," Sally said. She smiled and felt a secret thrill inside. Was her brother jealous? Was the plan she and Sylvia had worked out finally bearing some fruit? "Would it make any difference to you?"

"Yes," Billy said. "I always thought that I—uh, that is, I would hope that Sylvia would do better than pick out someone like Grady Ford to marry."

"Billy, are you interested in Sylvia?"

"Well, we do live on neighboring ranches, and we more or less grew up together, as you know. I've known her since she was a little girl, that's all. I just wouldn't want to see her make a mistake."

"Why don't you tell her?"

"What?" Billy asked.

"Why don't you ride over to see her and tell her that you don't want her to see Grady Ford anymore?"

"That wouldn't stop her."

"It might," Sally said. She was playing with a double-edged sword here, she knew. If her brother did ask Sylvia to stop seeing Grady, and if something happened between her brother and Sylvia, it would make it all the more difficult for her to see Grady. And yet, she would be thrilled if her brother and her best friend were to fall in love. She and Grady would find some other way to meet if need be. She smiled.

"What are you smiling about?" Billy asked.

"Nothing in particular," Sally said.

As Billy and Sally were driving back to their ranch, Grady was back in Tombstone, having lunch with C.V. and Bianca. They were at The Grotto, as usual, and they were at the table which was permanently reserved just for them.

C.V. was entertaining them with one of his endless supply of stories . . . this one about a balloon ascension he once made with Professor Lowe. He had them convulsing with laughter when a shadow suddenly fell across their table. They looked up to see Boston Corbett.

"Boston, my old friend," C.V. said. He pointed to the

empty chair at the table. "Have a seat, join us for lunch."

"Oh, I've already eaten," Boston said as he sat. "But I will join you."

"The chef made a special coconut cream pie," C.V. said.

Boston smiled broadly. "Well, maybe I will join you for dessert," he said.

"What brings you to Tombstone?"

"I brought some new wanted circulars to the marshal's office," Boston said. By now a piece of pie had been placed in front of him, and he took a big bite, beaming in pleasure.

"I told you it was good," C.V. said.

"Have you heard from the judge?" Grady asked.

"Oh! Yes! That's why I came over here to see you," Boston said, embarrassed that his love affair with the pie had made him temporarily forget his mission. He reached into his inside coat pocket and pulled out a paper and handed it to C.V.

"What does it say?" Bianca asked.

C.V. smiled broadly.

"My friends, the day of reckoning is nearly here," he said. "Listen to this." He cleared his throat, then read a few mumbling words until he got to the important part. ". . . therefore, be it known that on Thursday, the 27th of October, 1881, all interested parties will assemble in court in Tombstone, Arizona Territory, to litigate the matter pertaining to rightful possession of the land known, as the Santa Anna land, the boundaries of such land already being mutually agreed upon by both parties. Federal Judge William J. Donlevy, presiding."

"C.V., that's great!" Grady said.

Bianca had her own way of showing enthusiasm, and she embraced C.V. happily.

"Boston, don't you see what this means?" C.V. asked.

"It means Bianca is going to have a chance to get her land back," Boston said.

"Yes, that of course, but much more," C.V. said. "It means

that for the first time in the Southwest, a dispute of this magnitude is going to be settled by legal means. The Lincoln County Wars in New Mexico and the Pleasant Valley War here in Arizona have been fought over land disputes, but ours will be decided in court."

"Maybe," Boston said.

"What do you mean, 'maybe'?" Grady asked. Boston finished his pie, then when he saw that Bianca hadn't eaten all of hers he looked at it longingly. She smiled and shoved it over to him.

"What if the decision goes against you?" Boston said. "What if Judge Donlevy rules in favor of the Clantons?"

"I will accept the decision," Bianca said.

"Even though you feel in your heart that you are right?" Boston asked.

"Yes," Bianca said.

"We've discussed this, Boston," C.V. said. "Bianca agrees with me. The important thing here is not what decision Judge Donlevy renders. The important thing here is that the Judge be given the opportunity to render his decision. It is the triumph of law we celebrate, and not the outcome."

"Yeah, well, I'm glad you feel that way," Boston said. "But the problem isn't what will happen if the decision goes against you, but if it is in your favor."

"What do you mean?" Bianca asked.

C.V. took Bianca's hand in his and patted it gently.

"I think he means, my love, that if the decision goes against the Clantons, they may not accept it as graciously as we."

"There's no may not to it, C.V.," Boston said. "They won't." He drained the last of his cup of coffee, then wiped the back of his hand across his mouth. "And if they don't that's where I come in. Since Judge Donlevy is a Federal Judge, and I'm a U.S. Marshal, it's gonna be up to me to back up his ruling."

"Will the Judge give you help if you need it?" C.V. asked.

"He'll empower me to deputize as many men as I need," he said. He sighed. "I might have to ask the Earps for help. That's a little like setting a fox to watch over the chicken coop, but I probably won't have any choice."

"Maybe we're anticipating more problems than there will actually be," C.V. suggested. "Anyway, it's two week's away. There's no telling what might happen between now and October 26th."

With the news of the setting of the court date, Grady and C.V. worked hard to get their case in order. Grady felt an ethical responsibility to the Clantons, as well as a personal responsibility to Sally, to inform them of the setting of the date, and to recommend that they hire a lawyer. Sally insisted that she was trying to talk her father and brothers into hiring a lawyer, but they either didn't think it was necessary, or else they had so little regard for the proceedings of the court that they refused to do so. If.it had been up to Billy, Sally might have been able to talk him into it. But Billy's father, and his brother Ike, were against it, and Billy didn't want a lawyer badly enough to go against them in a family argument. So Billy continued to work hard around the ranch, brooding about the relationship between Grady and Sylvia.

Ike, on the other hand, and his constant companions the McClaurys, continued to be the scourge of Tombstone's nightlife, and a constant irritation to the Earps. There were several occasions when one or the other of the three troublemakers would push Wyatt or one of his brothers to the edge of gunplay. That nothing had happened as yet seemed only a pregnant pause. The tension between the Earps and the Clantons and McClaurys was increasing like a spring being tightly wound. Everyone agreed that soon the spring would snap.

There were two innocent Clantons who suffered from Ike's almost psychotic behavior. One of them was Sally, of course, who had to carry on her love affair in total secrecy lest she be discovered; the other was Billy, who was torn between his desire to live a normal life and his loyalty to his brother. On the one hand. Billy tried to appease the other ranchers and the townspeople for the trouble his brother caused. On the other hand, he tried hard to maintain some contact with his brother, for they were, after all, blood relations, and. despite everything, Billy knew he could never completely turn his back on Ike.

Despite Billy's pleas to Ike to settle down, Ike continued to be a hellraiser. One night Ike and Tom and Frank McClaury, as well as several cowhands from the McClaury and Clanton spreads made a shambles out of the Alhambra Saloon. The Alhambra was virtually the only place left in town where no drink limitations had been put on Ike and his friends, and for their generosity the owners had paid a price. Their tables and chairs were smashed, their windows were broken, and a sizeable amount of their liquor stock was destroyed in an impromptu 'target practice.' As a result, the Earps were brought in, and all the hellraisers, including Ike, spent the night in jail. Because Ike, Tom and Frank were property owners, Judge Spicer released them on their own recognizance, subject to a heavy fine and costs. The cowboys would have to serve fourteen days.

The wagon had already seen quite a few years of duty and over that time the sun had bleached the wooden body of the wagon white. When it got hot, as it was now, it also gave off pungent smell. The wagon was loaded with fence posts, tools and barbed wire. With so many of their cowboys in jail, there was a great deal of extra work to be done around the ranch, and when there was extra work to be done, it was like Billy to take this, the least desirable of all jobs.

Billy cut the strand of wire from the spool, then strung it up between the two poles. He nailed the wire in place and was admiring his job when a lone horseman approached.

Billy pulled out a handkerchief and wiped the sweat off his face as he watched the rider approach. He saw then that it was Grady Ford.

"Hello, Billy," Grady said, swinging down from his horse.

"Ford, I don't find you particularly welcome out here," Billy said.

"I guess I can see that," Grady replied.

"So why are you here?"

"I thought I'd ride out and tell you that I petitioned Judge Spicer to release your men early. You'll have your crew back soon."

"Thanks," Billy said. He started rolling up the wire to take it back to the wagon. When he had it rolled up, he picked it up and set it in the back of the wagon. The wagon dipped with its weight.

"The question is, why did you do it?" Billy asked.

"My reason wasn't entirely unselfish," Grady said. "I wouldn't want you and your father and your brother to claim that, with all your hands in jail, you couldn't make the court appearance this week."

"What court appearance?"

Grady sighed. "Billy, you know what court appearance. You've been served with a summons to appear in court this Thursday at ten o'clock."

"Oh, yeah, that court appearance," Billy said. "I hadn't given it much thought."

"Billy, you've got to think about it," Grady said. "If none of you show up the judge will rule for the plaintiff by default."

"What does that mean?"

"It means the judge will rule that the land belongs to Bianca."

"He's gonna rule that anyway, ain't he?"

"Not necessarily." Grady said. "I think we have a strong case. I think we have an excellent chance of convincing the judge to rule for us, but it certainly isn't guaranteed. If you had hired a lawyer when you were offered the opportunity . . . " Grady let the sentence drop.

"I don't get it, Ford," Billy said. "Whose side are you on, anyway?"

"I'm on the side of justice," Grady said.

"There's only one justice out here," Billy said. "And it's not the kind you get in a courtroom."

"Now you sound like your brother," Grady said. "You're not like your brother, Billy. You and Sally, you're different. You're . . ."

"What do you know about Sally?"

"I've visited with her."

"Oh? Where?"

"At Sylvia Collins' place."

"I don't want you seeing Sylvia anymore."

"Why not?"

"I just don't," Billy said. "She's my girl."

"Oh? Does she know that?"

"Yeah, she knows it."

"Have you told her?"

"I don't have to tell her. She knows it," Billy insisted.

"She's never told me"

"Yeah, well, just stay away from her," Billy said.

"Billy, Sylvia doesn't mean anything to me," Grady said. "She's just—"

"That's enough!" Billy shouted, and before Grady could finish his sentence, Billy hit him in the mouth. The punch was so sudden and unexpected that it caught Grady totally off-guard, and it dropped him to his knees.

Grady tried to stand up, but before he could, Billy hit him again, this time with a powerful blow to the jaw, knocking him down again.

Grady landed flat on his back with his arms and legs spread out. Billy bent over and put his left hand on him halfway up, then drew his right fist back ready to hit him again, but Grady twisted out from under him and hopped back up to his feet. Billy lunged for him and missed, and Grady took advantage of his off-balance position to send a whistling right hand crashing against the side of his head knocking him down. Billy raised up on his elbows, then put his hand on his chin as if testing it. Grady was ready to hit him again if need be, but Billy made no further effort to continue the fight.

"I guess you do care for her," Grady said.

"Suppose I do," Billy growled.

"Then dammit, man, tell her. She's one of the finest young women I've ever known and she loves you."

"What?" Billy asked. "How do you know?"

"Because she told me she did," Grady said. Billy got up and brushed off the seat of his pants.

"I don't get it," he said. "Why are you telling me this?"

"If you had let me finish my sentence a moment ago, you would know," Grady said. "I was going to say that Sylvia doesn't mean anything to me except as a friend."

"Yeah? Well you sure go to her place a lot for her to be no more than a friend."

"I only go there,.Billy, so I can meet Sally." Billy looked at Grady with a look of shock on his face.

"Sally?" he said quietly. "My sister?"

"I love your sister, Billy, and she loves me," Grady said. "And we want to get married if this crazy bickering ever settles down."

"Does anybody else know this?" Billy asked.

"Only Sylvia and her mother," Grady said. "And now you. We've kept it a secret because we were afraid of how certain people would react if they knew."

"By certain people, you mean us, right? Ike and Pa and me?"

"Mostly Ike and your father," Grady said. "Sally has always believed she could trust you. I only hope she is right."

"Jesus!" Billy said. "I can't believe it! Here you are, tryin' to steal half of what's ours, 'n you got the nerve to tell me you're in love with my sister. What the hell are you tellin' me for?"

"I need an ally, Billy," Grady said. "I need a friend in the family."

"No," Billy said resolutely. "No, you ain't got that. I

can't be your friend, Ford. You got no right to ask me that."

Grady sighed. "All right, I'll accept that," he said. "But, Billy, if you won't be our friend, will you at least keep our secret? For your sister's sake?"

Billy walked over to the wagon and slapped the side of it with his hand, then he turned and pointed at Grady. "If you hurt her, Ford, in any way, you've got me to deal with. You hear that?"

"Will you keep our secret, Billy?"

"Yes, dammit, I'll keep your damn secret. You just remember what I said about not hurtin' her, that's all."

The next morning, Sally got up with the sun and walked through the quiet house to stand on the front porch. The sun was a glowing, orange ball just poised over the rim of the distant cliffs. In this early morning light the world looked as if it were painted in hues of red, orange and burnt ochre, except for patches of deep purple where the blue veil of night still clung in the notches and draws of the hills.

Behind her, inside the house, her family was sleeping soundly and contentedly. Last night, Billy told her that he knew about her and Grady. At first she was frightened, but he assured her he wouldn't tell anyone else, then she gave a squeal of delight and hugged him affectionately. After that she was even emboldened to ask him if he would go over to Sylvia's house with her the next time she went for a visit.

"When are you going again?" Billy asked.

"Wednesday afternoon," Sally said.

"Yeah," Billy said. "I guess I'll go."

Now Sally was beside herself with happiness. Everything was working out just as she had hoped. Maybe all of her family didn't know about her relationship with Grady Ford, but Billy knew, and as far as she was concerned, his acceptance was the most important.

The door opened and Sally looked around to see her brother Ike coming outside. He was carrying a towel and a sliver of lye soap. He walked over to the pump and started pumping water into a washbasin.

"What are you doin' out here so early in the mornin'?" he asked Sally.

"I might ask you the same thing," Sally said. "This is about the time you've been going to bed lately, isn't it?"

"The work gets done," Ike said.

"That's only because Billy does his share and yours too."

Ike soaped up his face, then splashed water on it before he answered.

"You two is just alike, you know that? If I hadn't watched the both of you bein' borned, I'd wonder if you two was really from this family."

"You're the oldest, Ike," Sally teased. "Have you ever considered the possibility that maybe *you* aren't from this family?"

"What's that supposed to mean?"

"Nothing. I was just wondering, that's all."

Ike finished washing, then he put on a clean blue cotton shirt.

"You aren't going to string fence in that, are you?" Sally asked.

"What makes you think I'm gonna string any fence?"

"I heard Pa talking last night. He said there was a lot more fence to be strung."

"The hands come back from jail yesterday. They can string it."

"Pa said it was gonna take everyone. Ma and I are cooking up a big dinner for them."

"Yeah, well, there's gonna be enough people around here without me. That's why I got up early. I'm plannin' on sneakin' outta here before Pa gets up. I'm goin' into town 'n I'm gonna have me a little fun."

"You remember what happened the last time you went into town, don't you?" Sally said. "You wound up in jail."

"Don't worry about it," Ike said easily. "There ain't no

way I'm gonna wind up in jail this time." As Ike spoke the words, he loosened his gun in his holster.

"What do you mean by that?" Sally asked.

"What do I mean by what?"

"You touched your gun when you said that."

"Oh, that's just a nervous habit," Ike said. "It don't mean anythin'." Ike started out to the barn to saddle his horse.

Suddenly, and inexplicably, Sally felt a chill. "Ike?" she called.

Ike put his finger to his lips to quiet her, and he took several steps back toward the porch.

"Shhh! I told you I was tryin' to sneak outta here before Pa come awake," he said. "You ain't helpin' any."

"I'm sorry," Sally said, more quietly.

"Well, what is it? What do you want?"

"Don't go into town, Ike," she finally said. "I've got a bad feeling about it."

Ike chuckled. "Oh, I can see that," he said. "When a few of the fellas ask me why I missed the card game, I could say that my little sister got a bad feelin' about the place and she asked me not to go."

"I'm serious, Ike," Sally said. "I don't want you to go."

"I'm goin'," Ike said.

"I suppose there's nothing I can say or do that will stop you," Sally said. "But I do want you to remember the court hearing day after tomorrow. Dad will be counting on you and Billy to be there."

"Me 'n Billy will be there, don't worry about it," Ike said. He smiled broadly. "We'll be all dressed up in our funeral suits, lookin' so proper that you'll never know it's us."

The house sat on the edge of town. It needed a coat of paint, but the roof was sound and all the windows had glass. There were even the remnants of a rose garden alongside, and though the roses were gone now, with a little effort they could be brought back. The house had a living room, dining room, parlor, kitchen, and two bedrooms. It had been built by the owner of the Silver King Mine, but after a year; he sold his interest in the mine and went back east. The house had been standing empty for almost a year now.

"Well?" Bianca asked, smiling brightly. "What do you think?"

"What do I think?" C.V. asked, looking around. "The question is, what do you think?"

"I think it's beautiful," Bianca said.

There was an old piece of carpet rolled up in the comer, and C.V. unrolled it to look at it. A cloud of dirt and dust rose into the air from his efforts.

"Of course," Bianca admitted, coughing and fanning herself, "it will require a little cleaning up. But you'll see. It'll be lovely."

"Is this really what you want?" C.V. asked. He seemed somewhat less than enthusiastic at the prospect.

"Sure," Bianca said. "C.V., you are going to make an honest woman out of me—aren't you? You haven't just been leading me on, I hope?" She touched a long, cool finger to his temple as she spoke. She was teasing him, but there was a tiny, submerged element of concern to her tease.

C.V. put his arms around her and pulled her to him. He kissed her just on her hairline.

"You and I have a date with the preacher next month," he said. "Don't you dare try to wiggle out of it."

"Well, if we are going to get married, having a house is all a part of it," Bianca said.

"I can barely remember the last time I lived in a house," C.V. said. "I've always been camping out, or living in a hotel, one or the other."

"Then it's about time you settled down."

"What about Grady? How will he feel about you and me moving out of the hotel?"

Bianca chuckled. "What about him? C.V., even if he was your own son, he'd be on his own now. Besides, he's so crazy in love that he probably won't even notice we're gone."

"In love? Grady's in love?"

"Of course he is," Bianca said. "C.V., don't tell me you're so blind that you.can't see that."

"You mean he's in love with that Collins girl?"

"I guess so," Bianca said, putting her finger on her cheek and depressing her dimple. "I'm really not sure. He does act like he's in love, but he never mentions the girl's name. I find that most unusual."

C.V. laughed. "That's my partner, all right," he said. "He always has marched to a different drummer."

Chapter Twelve

IKE CLANTON TOOK a room at the Cosmopolitan Hotel when he reached Tombstone, but he needn't have bothered. The only bed he saw that night was a bed at Big Nose Kate's, and that bed wasn't for sleeping.

After Ike left Big Nose Kate's place, he decided to make a long, sodden night of it, and he hit one saloon after another, downing shot after shot of whiskey until well past midnight.

At around one o'clock in the morning he decided to get something to eat. The lunchroom he chose happened to be occupied by Wyatt and Morgan Earp, but they didn't seem to notice him. He chose a table in the back and ordered a fried ham sandwich.

About halfway through his sandwich, Doc Holliday came in. Doc saw Ike, and he went over to his table.

"You son-of-a-bitch of cowboy, pull your gun!" Doc said angrily.

"I don't have a gun."

"The hell you don't, you back-shootin' son-of- a-bitch" Doc said.

Wyatt heard the commotion, and he looked over toward them.

"Doc," he called easily. "Let 'im be."

"I'll let 'im be," Doc said. "When he's six feet under, I'll let 'im be."

"I said let 'im be," Wyatt said, and Doc, still muttering, left the cafe.

"Ike, why don't you finish your sandwich, then go on to bed before there's trouble?" Wyatt suggested.

"I'll go where I damn well please," Ike replied. After the meal Ike left the cafe, not to go to bed, but to continue his rounds of the saloons. He drank right through until sunrise the next day.

The next morning, Wednesday, Sally got up before dawn to make breakfast. The coffee she had started earlier was done now, and its rich aroma filled the kitchen. Billy wandered into the kitchen and poured himself a cup. He leaned against the sideboard drinking the coffee, watching his sister preparing breakfast.

"Have you seen Ike this morning?" Billy asked.

"No," Sally said. She opened the oven and removed a pan of golden brown biscuits, then set them on the table.

"Maybe I ought to go into town and get him," Billy suggested. "If we're going to make an appearance in court tomorrow, we ought to at least talk over a few things."

"Then you are going to court?"

"Yes," Billy said. "I certainly don't intend to just set back and let them take the land away without putting up some kind of a fight for it."

"Billy, what if we lose the land?"

"What makes you think we will lose it?"

"Grady says they can prove that Senor Santa Anna paid his taxes, and that Pa and Sheriff Behan cheated him out of his land."

Billy finished his cup, then walked over and poured himself a second cup.

"Is that true?" Sally asked.

"Maybe," Billy said.

"Billy, you mean all this time I've been defending Pa, and

he was wrong? He did cheat Senor Santa Anna out of his land?"

"It wouldn't be the first time an honest rancher threw a long rope down here," Billy said.

"Do you condone what Pa did?"

"Sally, you've got to understand. If Pa hadn't gotten title to that land, we would've been locked away from the water."

"What if the court rules against us? Will Pa accept it?"

"Not without a fight."

"You mean a real fight? A range war?"

"Sally, you know how important water is to a cattle ranch. Without it, we won't survive. We may as well set up ranchin' out in the middle of the desert somewhere."

Sally put fried eggs and bacon onto a plate and put it on the table for Billy.

"Billy, what if Bianca guaranteed our access to water?"

"She wouldn't do that," Billy said.

"Yes she would. Grady told me she would." Billy chewed thoughtfully for a moment.

"If they guaranteed us access to water, I think we would deal with them," he said.

"Billy, do you think Pa would?"

"Yeah, I think he might."

"Then that just leaves Ike," Sally said. "Oh, Billy, if Ike would go along with it, we could settle this thing once and for all."

"You'd like that, wouldn't you? Then you could marry your lawyer boyfriend."

"Yes." Sally said.

Billy rubbed his hand through his hair. "You're sure he's the man you want? Not Tom or Frank McClaury?"

"Uggh," Sally said. "Billy, you know what I think about both the McClaurys."

Billy laughed. "Yeah, I know. I was only foolin'. All right, don't you worry about Ike," he said. "I'll go into town and get him this morning, and I'll talk him into going along with a guarantee."

"I'm going with you," Sally said.

"You don't have to do that."

"I know I don't have to," Sally said. "But I want to. Afterwards, you and I can go see Sylvia."

"What for?"

"Billy, you promised, remember? You're going to see her this afternoon."

"Oh, yeah," Billy said, smiling at his sister. "I guess I did say that, didn't I? All right. I'll hitch up a team to the buckboard and we can ride in together. But get ready in a hurry, will you, Sis? Ike's been in town long enough as it is. If we don't collect him pretty soon, there's no telling what kind of trouble he'll get into."

A little over an hour later, Billy and Sally arrived in Tombstone. It had been a very pleasant drive in, and Sally couldn't remember when she had enjoyed being with her brother more. She had even extracted a confession from him that he was looking forward to the visit with Sylvia this afternoon. And he promised to be on his best behavior with Grady Ford.

"After all," Billy said. "If he's goin' to be my brother-in-law, I better learn to get along with him, I guess."

They stopped the buckboard in front of the General Store. Carl Moore, the proprietor of the store, was sweeping off the store's front porch.

"Have you seen my brother Ike, Mr. Moore?" Sally asked.

"Not since yesterday, Miss Clanton," Moore answered. "I'm sorry."

"Don't worry, I'll find him," Billy said. As he got out of the buckboard, Sally saw that he was still wearing his pistol.

"Oh, Billy, you don't need that," Sally said, pointing to the gun.

"I feel better with it," Billy said. "Don't worry, it'll be okay." He started down the walk toward the Cosmopolitan Hotel.

"Mornin', Billy," someone said, as he passed Billy on the board sidewalk.

"Good mornin' to you," Billy said.

"You should have seen your brother this mornin'," the passerby said, laughing. "He come out of Big Nose Kate's place with three women hangin' on to him. Three, mind you. I don't know what he's got, but if you could put it in a bottle you could make a fortune sellin' it."

"Do you know where he is now?" Billy asked. "Sure, he's havin' his breakfast over at the Alhambra."

Billy left the sidewalk and crossed the dirt street, picking his way gingerly through the horse droppings. He pushed the door open at the Alhambra Cafe, and saw Ike sitting at a table in the back. It was all Ike could do to hold his head up.

Billy walked back to the table and sat down. "Billy," Ike said, grinning broadly. "I knew you'd come. I knew you wouldn't let your brother down."

"Look at you," Billy said. "Did you even go to bed last night?"

"Last night?" Ike said. He hiccupped, then smiled. "Last night ain't over yet," he said. He pointed toward the front window. "Oh, it might be light out, but the night ain't over till it's over, if you know what I mean."

"You're so damn drunk, I don't think you even know what you mean," Billy said.

The waitress brought a plate of eggs, potatoes and fried ham to set before Ike. Ike looked at it stupidly for a moment, as if having difficulty making his eyes focus. Then he smiled.

"Oh, yeah," he said, grinning. "I was sittin' here waitin' on another drink, but I must've ordered breakfast." He looked up at Billy. "Want some?"

"I ate at home."

"Oh, yeah, I forgot," Ike said. "You're the good boy of the family." Ike put a forkful of eggs into his mouth, and the yellow dribbled down his chin and dripped on his shirt. His shirt was already stained with whiskey, perfume, powder and rouge from his night of carousing. "Sally and Pa both think I should be more like you," Ike said. "Tell me, Billy, do you think I should be more like you?"

"Would it do any good if I said I thought you should?"

"It might," Ike said. 'Course, first, I got me this little score to settle with the Earps. But you know that, 'cause you come to town to help me out."

"Ike, come on," Billy said. "Let's go back home. We've got to be in court tomorrow, and there are a few things we need to talk about before we go."

"I'll go back after I've settled accounts with the Earps."

"Let it be, Ike. We've got more important things to worry about than the Earps."

"There ain't nothin' more important than standin' up like a man," Ike said. "Now what's it gonna be, Billy? Are you gonna stand up like a man? Or are you gonna turn coward and run?"

"Ike, I don't have a quarrel with the Earps."

"Well I do." Ike said. "And if you're really my brother, my fight is your fight."

"Let it go, Ike."

"No!" Ike shouted, slamming his fist on the table with such force that his knife and fork clattered to the table. A few of the others who were eating their breakfast looked around nervously.

"You're making a scene, Ike," Billy cautioned.

"I don't care. This here thing with the Earps has gone far enough. We're gonna settle it today, once and for all."

"You aren't in any condition to settle anything," Billy said. "Look at you. Hell, you can't even stand up."

"If I say I'm gonna stand up to the Earps today, are you gonna back me up? Or are you gonna turn tail 'n run?"

"I've got my gun on, don't I?" Billy said.

"If it actually come to gunplay, Billy, would you back me up?" Ike asked again.

Billy sighed. "Yes," he said. "You're my brother. If it

comes to gunplay, I'll back you."

Ike grinned broadly. "I was hopin' you would say that," he said. "Just knowin' I can count on you makes me happy. Come on."

"Where are we going?"

"We're goin' home," Ike said. He laughed. "Didn't you say we have things to talk about? If the Earps wanna have a shootout, why, they can just have it amongst themselves."

Billy laughed happily. "Now you're making sense," he said. "Come on, Sally's outside waitin' for us."

"Sally came with you, huh?"

"Yes. She was worried about you."

Ike laughed, drunkenly. "I got me a good sister, I got me a good brother. Tell me, Billy, how did I come to be the black sheep of the family?"

Ike left some money on the table for his uneaten breakfast, and he and Billy started out the front door.

Sally had moved the buckboard up the street, across from the Alhambra, waiting for Billy to bring Ike out. She breathed a sigh of relief when they stepped outside and Billy waved and nodded at her. It was his signal that he had talked Ike into coming home peacefully.

Sally watched them as they turned to head for the corral and Ike's horse.

Suddenly Sally saw a quick movement in the alley. She saw two men step up behind Billy and Ike, then she saw them bring their guns crashing down on the heads of her brothers. Both of her brothers went down.

Sally let out a little scream and jumped out of the buckboard. She started across the street to her brothers, but at that moment a wagon loaded with ore came clattering down the road.

"Look out Miss!" the driver shouted in angry alarm, and Sally jumped back out of the way just in time. She was pelted with dirt thrown up from the street by the whirling wheels of the wagon.

By the time the wagon had passed, she saw Billy and Ike both trying to stand up. Ike got to his hands and knees, then one of the two men who had been waiting in the alley kicked him in the ribs. Sally saw the glint of a star on the jacket of the man who was doing the kicking, and she realized it was Wyatt Earp. The one with him was his brother, Virgil.

Billy looked up and saw Sally trying to cross the street.

"No!" he shouted. "Sally, stay there!"

Sally stopped then, but she was close enough to hear what was being said.

"You two boys huntin' for us?" Wyatt asked. "If I'd seen you a second sooner I'd of killed you," Ike said, rubbing the top of his head.

"Oh you would, would you? How about it, Billy? Are you in this with your brother?"

"Am I in what?" Billy asked, gingerly rubbing the back of his own head.

"Are you as anxious as Ike to have it out with us?"

"I was taking him home," Billy said.

"That ain't the way the McClaurys are tellin' it all over town," Wyatt said. "They're makin' the claim that you four boys are goin' to face us down today."

"The McClaurys don't talk for us," Billy said. "We're goin' home."

"I'll be damned if I'm goin' home," Ike said then, seething with anger. "I'm gonna finish this." Oh, Ike, Sally thought. Why can't you just keep your mouth shut so Billy can get you out of this mess?

"Yeah, well, let's see what Judge Wallace has to say about that," Virgil suggested. "Get up, boys, we're goin' to court."

"You can't take them to court like that," Sally said angrily. She came over and helped both her brothers to their feet. "They need to see a doctor. They could be badly hurt."

"Sally, get on out of here," Billy said. "This is no place for you."

Sally touched the bleeding knot on Billy's head and he

winced.

"You could have killed them," Sally said.

"It's probably goin' to come to that, ma'am," Wyatt said laconically.

"I'm taking them to the doctor," Sally said.

"No, ma'am," Wyatt said. "I'm takin' them to court, 'n if you don't stay out of the way, I'll be takin' you down there too, for obstructin' justice."

"I'm going to go see Grady about this," Sally told Billy. "He's a lawyer, he'll know what to do."

Ike, who had been tending to his wound, looked at his sister with a surprised expression on his face. "You're gonna see who?"

"You aren't going to see anyone," Billy said.

"Grady? Grady Ford? Why would you go see him?" Ike asked.

"She's not going to see him," Billy said with an angry look at Sally. She realized that Billy was warning her with his glance that now was not the time to introduce a new irritating factor, and if Ike knew the true nature of the relationship between Sally and Grady it might push him over the edge.

"Come along," Wyatt said. "Ma'am, you want to step back out of the way?"

Sally stepped back off the sidewalk as Wyatt ordered, then watched as her brothers started down to the courtroom with Virgil and Wyatt walking along behind them, keeping them covered with drawn pistols. Sally walked along with them, though she stayed in the street, out of the way. They passed a horse trough.,

"If you boys wanna dunk your handkerchiefs in the water there, go ahead," Wyatt invited generously.

"Thanks," Billy muttered. He and Ike wet their handkerchiefs, then dabbed at their bloody heads.

"This is your day, Earps," Ike muttered. "You're gonna die today."

"Ike, you've threatened my life enough times," Wyatt

said. "I want this thing stopped, now."

"It'll stop when you're dead," Ike replied. "You damn, dirty cow thief," Wyatt said. "If you're anxious to fight, I'll meet you."

"I'll see you after I get through with the judge." Ike answered. "All I want is four feet of ground." After the men had dabbed at their heads a bit more, Wyatt waved the barrel of his pistol, indicating they should go on. Judge Peach Wallace's court was just three more doors down from the water trough. Sally followed them to the court. Ironically, the door was held open for her by Morgan Earp, the youngest of the Earp brothers. He smiled at Sally, and gave her a courtly bow. Sally looked away in a show of her disdain for all of them. She wished Grady was here. She wished Billy would let her go get him.

"We're gonna have our showdown, Earp," Ike muttered again, just as they entered the courtroom.

Morgan, who walked in just behind Sally, heard Ike's final taunt, and he couldn't let it pass without comment.

"I can see to it that you are accommodated, Ike," Morgan said. "For example, if you don't have the money to pay your fine, I'll pay it for you."

"I'll pay my own fine," Ike said. "It'll be worth it to get at you. I'll fight you anywhere or any way," Ike said.

Sally heard a commotion at the front door and she looked around to see Tom McClaury.

Great, she thought bitterly. This is just what we need, another hothead.

"What's goin' on?" McClaury asked Wyatt. "I hear you've arrested Ike and Billy."

"That's right," Wyatt said.

"What were they doin'?"

"Disturbing the peace," Wyatt replied.

Billy had been very quiet up to now. He took the handkerchief away from the back of his head and looked at it. It was completely bloodsoaked.

"We weren't disturbing the peace, Marshal," Billy said quietly. "In fact, I had talked Ike into going back home with me."

"From where I saw it, you were disturbing the peace," Wyatt said. "Ain't that about the way you saw it, Virg?"

"Yeah," Virgil said. "That's pretty much the way I saw it." They were disturbing the peace."

"They were not!" Sally put in angrily, unable to keep quiet any longer. "They had just left the restaurant and were walking along when you two stepped out of the alley and hit them over the head."

"Miss Clanton, if you don't be quiet now. I'm gonna have to arrest you for disturbin' the peace as well," Wyatt said.

"And that'd be a shame." Morgan said, his eyes flashing in bright humor. "You're much too pretty a thing to be put in jail."

"Look," Billy said, angry now. "I told you, I had my brother talked into going home with my sister and me. Now why don't you just let us out of here and we'll go."

"I'm afraid it's not gonna be that easy, Billy," Morgan said.

"What do you mean?" Billy asked.

"This thing has come to a head. It's best we go on and get it settled, here and now."

Morgan's words weren't angry, they were cold and deliberate, and Sally felt a chill run down her spine. Until this very moment she had hoped matters could be settled before the situation got out of hand. Now she was afraid it had already gotten out of hand.

"Morgan?" Billy asked, and his voice was quiet and heavy. "Morgan, are you telling me that we're going to come down to it now?"

"I'm afraid so," Morgan said.

"No!" Sally screamed, raising her hand to her mouth. "No, Billy, no! Don't listen to him! Pay your fine and let's go home. We'll take Ike with us if he'll go, but if he won't, we'll leave him here. Please, Billy!"

"Billy may turn yellow, but if you fellas are wantin' to make a fight. I'll make a fight with you anywhere," Tom McClaury put in angrily.

"All right," Wyatt answered. He slapped Tom in the face with his left hand, and clubbed him in the head with the revolver he was holding in his right hand. Tom fell to his knees. "Make a fight right here." Tom McClaury was so dazed that for a long moment he couldn't get up off his knees.

"You are awfully quick to hit people with your pistol," Sally said. "Are you going to hit me next?"

"I may," Wyatt retorted.

"Sally, for God's sake stay out of this," Billy hissed.

There was a moment of silence, then the Justice of the Peacecame in, and Wyatt and Virgil holstered their guns.

"All right," the judge said. "What's going on?"

"Disturbing the peace, Your Honor," Virgil said.

"How do you plead?"

"We ain't—" Ike started, but Billy interrupted him.

"Your Honor, we'll plead guilty," Billy said. "If you'll let us pay our fines and go on home."

"No, you yellow livered coward!" Ike shouted at him.

"I'll take my brother home," Billy said again.

"All right," Judge Wallace said. "Ten dollars," he announced with the rap of his gavel.

"Marshal?" Billy said, looking at Wyatt. "Are you going to let us go in peace?"

"Please, Marshal Earp," Sally pleaded through her tears.

Wyatt sighed. "All right, Billy, you take 'im on home now."

"Come on," Billy said to Ike as he pushed him out onto the board walk. "We're goin' home."

"Wait just a—," Ike started.

"Ike, please!" Sally begged.

"All right, I'll go home," Ike said. "But first, let's go down to Bauer's Meat Market and collect the money they owe us."

"Then you'll go?"

"Yeah," Ike promised. "Then I'll go."

"Where is your horse?" Sally asked.

"It's at the O.K. Corral."

"I'll go down and have the liveryman saddle it," Sally said.

"All right," Ike said. "You do that. Come on, Billy, let's go get our money from ol' man Bauer." Billy, Ike, and Tom McClaury started for the meat market, and they were joined by Frank McClaury, and Billy Claibourne, a rider for the McClaurys. Sally started back for her buckboard. "Where you fellas goin'?" Frank asked.

"Home," Billy said. "We got a court date tomorrow, we have to get ready for it."

"You can't go home," Frank said. "You can't go home now. We got to have this thing out now. If we don't have this thing out now, we ain't ever gonna have any peace around here."

"Yeah, well if we go up against the Earps, the only peace some of us are going to have is eternal peace," Billy said. "Now Ike and I are going to collect our money from Mr. Bauer, then we're goin' on home. I'd advise you all to do the same."

"You think the Earps are just gonna let you go?" Frank asked. "You think they're just gonna stand back and let you go home as if nothin' happened?"

"They said they would. I see no reason why they wouldn't."

"You don't, huh? Well take a look back there," Tom McClaury said. "The Earps are followin' us.

They're just waitin' for their chance. I tell you, if we don't stop and make a fight of it, they're gonna just shoot us down."

"They won't shoot us down," Billy said. "Just keep walking."

Sally was in her buckboard now, and she was riding

alongside them. She had the feeling, perhaps irrationally, that if she shepherded them all the way to the livery nothing would happen to them. She watched as the five men, including Billy Claibourne, crossed Third street. Bauer's market was just beyond Fly's Photograph Gallery, and the O.K. Corral was just beyond that. Sally was beginning to feel a little better now. The corral was in sight. All they had to do now was get their money from Bauer then get their horses, and they could leave town before the situation got any worse. Sally let out a long sigh of relief. It seemed as if she had been holding her breath in fear for hours. Everything was going to be all right now.

Then, suddenly, her worst fear was realized. Ike let out a curse and jumped off the walk into the open lot between the corner house and Fly's Photograph Gallery.

"Ike, what is it?" Billy asked. "What are you doin'?"

"I ain't goin',"," Ike said angrily. "I ain't showin' yellow to the Earps. I ain't takin' another step."

"Ike, it isn't showing yellow, it's just good sense," Billy insisted.

"Ike, please!" Sally called from the buckboard.

"No," Ike said. He pointed his finger at Billy. "You've made a coward outta Billy, but you ain't makin' one outta me. I aim to finish this here 'n now."

The two McClaurys and Billy Claibourne stepped off the walk and into the alley with Ike, leaving Billy alone on the sidewalk.

"Wait!" Billy said. "Wait, you don't know what you're doing. Ike, let's go home. I didn't come in town to fight anybody. I don't want to fight anybody and no one wants to fight me."

"Well, then you and your sister go ahead and skedaddle," Frank said to Billy. "You can leave the fightin' to the men."

"Yeah," Ike said. "You should'a told me if I couldn't count on you."

"Ike, you're talking about killing," Billy said. "And if it's the Earps we're going against, it's going to be some of us that wind up dead."

"I never took you for no coward, Billy," Ike said.

"Billy!" Sally pleaded. "Billy, please, come on! Leave him! If he's crazy enough to get himself killed, just leave him!"

Sally looked at Billy and the others, then she looked toward the three Earp brothers. All three of the Earps were dressed in black suits, white shirts, and ties. They were as dapper looking as if they were going to a party. Sally couldn't see one ounce of emotion in the faces of any of the three. She looked at her brothers. Billy's face showed resignation, while Ike's and the McClaurys' reflected fear and excitement. The foolish bravado of Ike and the McClaurys would be no match for the cool professionalism of the Earps, Sally thought.

And to make matters worse, she saw Doc Holliday hurrying up the street to join the Earps.

"Wyatt, wait for me," Doc called.

Wyatt looked back over his shoulder at the emaciated little man with the dark, brooding eyes. "Doc, this is our fight," he said. "There's no call for you to mix in."

Doc looked hurt, as if the Earps were all going to dinner and he hadn't been invited.

"That's a hell of a thing for you to say to me."

Wyatt wiped his chin, then nodded at Virgil.

"Deputize him, Virg."

Virgil deputized Doc, then took away the cane Doc was carrying and handed him a shotgun.

Sally looked back toward her brothers, then felt a sudden ray of hope. Sheriff Behan had stepped out of Camillus Fly's photo gallery.

"Oh, Sheriff, thank God!" Sally said. "Please, talk some sense into them."

"I'll do what I can," Sheriff Behan said. He pointed to

Sally. "You stay right there in your buckboard and don't get in the way."

Sally sat perfectly still as she was told. She watched Sheriff Behan approach Billy and the others, then she turned and looked down toward the three Earps and Doc Holliday. The Earps had gone to Bauer's Meat Market, and they were standing there under the awning. For the moment, they seemed content to stand there and watch.

"Okay, boys, let me have your guns," Sheriff Behan said.

"No," Ike said. "I'm not givin' up my gun to you, or to nobody."

"There's going to be some killin' otherwise," Sheriff Behan said.

"Sheriff, see if the Earps will give up their weapons," Billy suggested.

"You know they won't, Billy. They are the law in this town."

"You're the law in the county. Doesn't that mean anything?" Sally called from her position in the buckboard.

"Give me your guns, boys," Behan said again. "I'll give 'em back to you when you're out of town. They won't do anything if you aren't armed."

"Get their guns, and we'll give you ours," Frank McClaury said.

"Frank, I know you," Behan said. "You're a pretty good shot, better than any of these other boys, maybe even better than me. But you are no match for any one of those four men down there. And the rest of you won't have a chance at all."

"Are you with us, or ag'in us?" Ike asked.

Behan sighed. "Stay here," he said. "I'll go see them."

Sally watched Sheriff Behan as he walked down to the market. A few people had come onto the front porch of the Papago Cash Store, and they stood there watching the unfolding drama.

"No call for you to be hangin' 'round here, Sheriff." Virgil Earp said as Behan approached them.

"I'm tryin' to prevent trouble." Behan answered.

"There's no way to prevent it now, it's gone too far," Doc said.

"I saw you talkin' to 'em," Wyatt said. "Did you get their guns?"

"They won't give 'em up unless you agree to give yours up too."

Virgil looked at Sheriff Behan with an expression of surprise on his face.

"Are you kiddin' me, Sheriff? We're city marshals, duly constituted to carry firearms."

"It might help," Behan said.

"I'm goin' to talk to them," Virgil said.

"Earp, for God's sake, don't go down there!" Behan called to Virgil.

"I'm going to disarm them," Virgil snapped back over his shoulder.

Wyatt, Morgan and Doc brushed by Behan, following after Virgil.

"Stop!" Behan called to them. "I'm sheriff of this county, and I'm ordering you to stop!"

Sally felt her heart go to her throat. She raised her hand to her mouth and watched, numbed with fear.

As the three Earps and Doc Holliday drew even with Sally, who was parked in the street in front of Fly's Gallery; Billy, Ike and the two McClaurys backed into the vacant lot which was between Fly's and a small house which Sally knew belonged to William Harwood. Mrs. Harwood had once sold baked cookies with Sally during a Fourth of July Celebration.

The two parties of men faced each other, standing no more than six feet apart. The Clantons and the McLaurys were now boxed in. The Earps and Doc Holiday were standing in the open place toward the street. The house and Fly's Gallery blocked the sides, and only the rear, which led to the open lot of the O.K. Corral, offered any means of escape. Billy Claibourne, the cowboy who had joined so brazenly with them before, now slipped out that way, and he and Sheriff Behan stood behind the corner of the photo gallery to watch. There was a moment of silence as the men confronted each other, then Virgil called out to them: "You men are under arrest. Throw up your hands."

Billy and Frank McLaury cocked their holstered pistols. The click of the hammer coming back was audible, even from Sally's position across the street.

"Hold!" Virgil called. "I don't mean that! I've come to disarm you!"

Tom McLaury made the first move. "You son- of-a-bitch!" he shouted as he reached for his .45.

"No," Ike suddenly shouted, throwing his gun down. He took a couple of hesitant steps backwards. "No. wait, we'll be killed!" Ike ran toward Wyatt. "No. don't shoot us. don't shoot us!" he begged.

"Ike!" Billy shouted.

"It's too late," Wyatt said, pushing Ike away from him. "The fight's started. "Get to shootin' or get to runnin'!" By now the Earps had their own guns out and the first shots were already fired.

Sally saw Billy aim at Wyatt, holding his gun at arm's length. There was something unreal about it, as if she were watching a drama on stage. But Wyatt, who was the most skilled of all of them, had his gun out as quickly as any of them, and the first shot came from Wyatt's gun.

Despite the fact that Billy was aiming at Wyatt, Wyatt concentrated his aim on Frank, known to be the best shot of the four. Sally saw the recoil kick Wyatt's hand up, and she saw the great puff of smoke from the discharge. She heard Frank call out in pain, then she saw him grab his stomach as blood spilled between his fingers. Frank went down. As Ike fled from the scene of battle, he ran between Billy and Wyatt, preventing Billy from getting off a clean shot. Billy fired at Wyatt, but missed.

After that guns began to roar in rapid succession. The

next person to be hit was Billy. A bullet from Morgan's pistol tore through Billy's right wrist. Another hit him in the chest.

"Billy!" Sally screamed.

Billy staggered back against a window of the Harwood House. It was the same window Mrs. Harwood used to cool her baking cookies. Billy slid slowly to the ground, then switched his pistol to his left hand. He sat there on the ground with his legs crossed, resting his pistol on his shattered arm, shooting with his left hand. He hit Virgil in the leg, but Wyatt hit Billy again, this time in the lower ribs.

"Billy, oh my God!" Sally said. Out of the corner of her eye she saw Ike running across the open lot of the O.K. Corral.

Doc saw Ike also, and he fired a shotgun blast toward him, but by now Ike was out of shotgun range.

Tom McClaury, who had been the first to draw a gun, drew blood from Morgan, hitting him in the left shoulder.

Doc turned the other barrel of his shotgun toward Tom then and pulled the trigger. The buckshot tore through the cowboy's vest and opened up his right side. He stumbled out into the street, right by Sally's buckboard. He grabbed the wheel of the buckboard and looked into Sally's face, then, inexplicably, smiled, before he pitched face down into the dirt.

Frank, who had been the first hit, was still on his feet, and he Fired a shot at Doc Holliday. The bullet hit Doc in the hip. Morgan, Wyatt, and Virgil all fired at Frank at the same time. Frank was hit once in the head and twice in the heart.

Now there was only Billy. He had been knocked flat on his back by Wyatt's last shot, but he managed to work himself upright again. He aimed his pistol at Wyatt and pulled the trigger. The hammer fell on an empty cylinder.

Billy kept pulling the trigger over and over again, but by now the last shot of the fight had been fired, and there remained only the echoes from the distant, hills, and the click,

Warriors of the Code

click, click, of metal on metal as the hammer of Billy's gun kept falling on empty chambers.

Wyatt stood there watching Billy as he worked the gun. Of those who had started the fight, only Wyatt was still standing unscathed. Virgil, Morgan and Doc were wounded. Tom and Frank McClaury were both dead, and Billy was dying.

Billy Claibourne, as well as Ike, had run.

"Give it up, Billy," Wyatt said quietly.

Now that the gunfire had died, Sally jumped out of her buckboard and ran across the street to Billy. She got down on her knees beside him, and took his gun from him.

"One more shot, God," Billy said. "Please, one more shot."

"Billy!" Sally called. "Oh, Billy, why? Why did you do it?"

Billy leaned back against the wall of the house and looked at his sister. Sally watched in horror as the light began to fade in his eyes. It was as if she were watching him die in stages.

"No!" she called. "No, Billy, no!"

Sally cradled Billy's head in her lap and looked up as the townspeople approached. The fight had been witnessed by dozens of people; and now Sally could see them looking down at the bodies of the slain, and at the wounded, and even at her. None of the townspeople said anything. Their looks weren't of pity, or compassion, or even hate. Most were of morbid curiosity as if they were experiencing a sensual pleasure from being so close to death, while themselves avoiding it.

"Did you ever see anythin' like this?" someone asked.

"Never," another answered. "Did you see ol' Ike skedaddle? I never seen such a coward."

"It was over in a hurry, wasn't it?" someone asked.

"Thirty-seven seconds," another said, holding a watch in his hand. "I timed it."

By now, Wyatt had helped Virgil and Doc back to their feet, and Sheriff Behan came out from behind the gallery.

"You men are all under arrest!" Behan called.

Wyatt looked at him.

"For what?"

"For murder!" Behan said. "I'm taking you all to jail! Let me have your guns!"

"Not today, Behan," Wyatt said. "Not tomorrow. Not ever."

"I'll see you in court, Wyatt Earp!" Sally called from her position at her slain brother's side. Tears were streaming down her face but she didn't care. "I'll see you in court if I have to go to President of the United States!"

Chapter Thirteen

GRADY, WHO WAS supposed to see Sally at Sylvia's place that afternoon, knew nothing of the gunfight. He had gone to Contention on an errand. He timed his return so as to arrive at Sylvia's in time to keep his date with Sally.

To Grady's surprise, there was no one home at Sylvia's place, neither Sylvia, or her mother. And since it wasn't a working ranch, there weren't even any hands to ask where everybody was.

Grady waited around until almost an hour beyond the time he was supposed to meet Sally, then he decided to ride over to the Clanton ranch to see if Sally was there.

About a mile from Sally's house, two riders suddenly appeared. They were both carrying guns, and they ordered Grady to stop.

"I'm coming to call on Miss Clanton," Grady said.

"Mister, you must be crazy if you think you can come callin' on a day like today," one of the cowboys said.

"What do you mean?" Grady asked. "What's different about today?"

"Where you been? China?" the other one asked derisively. "You had to be, not to have heard."

"Heard what?" Grady asked, not only curious, but a little

worried by the strange words. "I've been in Contention all day. Has something happened to Miss Clanton?"

"Naw, nothin's happened to Miss Clanton," one of the riders said. "It was her brother, The Earps kilt 'im this mornin'."

"Ike?" Grady said. He shook his head. "It's been coming, everyone could see it."

"Naw, it wam't Ike," the cowboy said. "It was Billy."

"Billy?" Grady gasped. "Are you sure?"

"I reckon I know the boys as well as anyone in this world, mister. You sayin' I don't know the difference between Billy 'n Ike Clanton?"

"But why Billy? Ike has been the one who . . ." Grady stopped. "Poor Sally, how she must be taking this. Where is she? I must see her." One of the two riders cocked his gun and when he did, the other cocked his as well.

"Mister, Ike 'n the ol' man told us not to let anyone come down this here road, 'n I reckon that means you. Now, iffen you're hell-bent on tryin', well you just go right ahead, but I'm tellin' you I'm gonna shoot you if you try."

"And I'll be shootin' right alongside 'im," the other rider added, ominously.

Grady sighed. "All right," he said. "But will one of you at least tell Miss Clanton that I came here to call on her?"

"We'll tell ol' man Clanton," one of the riders said. "If he wants to pass that on, well I reckon it's up to him. After all, she's his daughter." Grady knew that the old man didn't even know he had been seeing Sally, and certainly wouldn't have approved had he known.

"Never mind," he said with a frustrated sigh. He turned and started riding back to town. Why did it have to be Billy who was killed? Though Grady was sure that Sally had a sisterly love for Ike, he also knew that she was particularly close to Billy. She would be taking his death very hard and there was nothing he could do to comfort her. Ironically, the fact that it was Billy instead of Ike who was killed also left him without any other contact within the Clanton family. Slowly, and sadly, Grady rode on into Tombstone.

By the time Grady reached Tombstone, it resembled an armed camp. The mines had all blown their emergency whistles, not to signal a mine cave-in, but to summon their employees to a large joint meeting. At the meeting, the miners had been told that there was a possibility the cowboys would gather in strength and attack the town. The miners then collected weapons and posted themselves at strategic points around the town, behind barricades and on rooftops, ready to repel any attack which might be launched toward them.

The only two cowboys to come to town that first afternoon were Ike Clanton and Jim Spence, a cousin of the McClaurys'. They went to Ritter and Ream, the undertakers, to make arrangements for the bodies.

Grady heard that Ike was in town, so he hurried over to the undertakers to talk to him.

There were several people gathered around outside the undertakers' parlor, which was located in the rear of a hardware store, and they were all peering in through the front window. Grady had to pick his way through the crowd to get inside.

"Are you goin' inside, Mr. Ford?" someone asked.

"Yes, I am."

"Ask 'em how much longer it'll be."

"How much longer what will be?" Grady asked. "Till they put the bodies on display. I hear tell Ike is gonna have 'em laid out in the hardware store window."

"I hardly think so," Grady said in barely concealed disgust.

"Sure is," another said. "I seen Ritter layin' out the green felt awhile ago. He's got the curtains shut now, though."

Grady shook his head, then went on in to the undertakers' parlor. He saw Ike and Spence talking with Mr. Ritter. Ritter was dressed all in black, as was his custom, and he was wearing a stovepipe hat. Behind them, Grady could see the bodies of the three young men. The corpses were all naked and Grady could see the neat black-holes in Billy's and Frank's bodies. Tom's body was not so neat. Doc's shotgun blast had opened him up and Grady could see his rib cage. On another table lay the clothes the men would wear: dark suits, stiff, white shirt fronts, silk bowties.

"You know the coffins we want?" Ike was saying to Ritter. "We want them shiny black ones with the silver trim."

"Yes, sir," Ritter was saying, taking notes on the instructions. "Those are our most elegant caskets. They have a viewing window, of course, and they are lined with white satin. They are really quite comfortable."

"Haw!" Spence laughed aloud. "I don't reckon ol' Frank and Tom are givin' two hoots right now 'bout bein' comfortable."

"I ... I suppose not," Ritter apologized. During the exchange between Spence and Ritter, Ike looked around and saw Grady.

"What the hell are you doin' in here?" Ike asked.

"I came to extend my condolences," Grady said.

"Yeah, I'm sure you're real sorry," Ike said.

"I am."

Ike looked at him for a moment, then chuckled. "Yeah, you prob'ly are at that. You're sorry it's Billy, 'stead of me lyin' there."

"I'm sorry anyone has to be lying there," Grady said. "I wish there would have been a way to avoid it."

"There wam't no way. The Earps was determined to spill blood. I was just lucky I wasn't killed along with my brother."

By now Grady had already heard the story of how Ike had provoked the fight, then ran when it started, leaving his brother to hold the bag.

A couple of funeral home employees began dressing the corpses then, and, morbidly, Grady watched for a few moments.

"Is that all?" Ike asked.

"Not quite." Grady said. "Ike, I tried to call on your sister today but I was turned away by two of your riders."

"I told 'em not to let anyone by," Ike said.

"I would very much like to see Sally."

"What for?"

"To ... to express my sorrow over this," Grady said.

"I'll tell her you mentioned it."

"I'd like to tell her myself."

"No," Ike said. "I told you. I ain't lettin' no one from town come out to the house. Them that tries is likely to wind up right here, alongside Billy and the McClaurys."

Grady saw that it was useless to continue the discussion so he started to leave.

"I've got the window cleaned out, Mr. Clanton," Ritter said. "We'll have the bodies on display in about half an hour."

"Good," Ike said.

"Ike!" Grady said. "You can't be serious? You don't intend to put your brother on display for all of Tombstone?"

"Yeah, I do intend to do that," Ike said. "The Earps murdered my brother 'n I want the whole town to see it."

"Think of your sister and your mother." Grady said. "How do you think they would feel knowing Billy's body was being displayed like some . . . some freak in a circus show?"

"Seems to me, mister, like you got an awful lot of interest in my sister," Ike said.

"I just don't want to see her hurt any more than she has already been."

"You just leave that to me. Us Clantons take care of our own." Ike turned to Ritter. "Get 'em out there as fast as you can," he said.

Grady left the parlor in disgust. By the time he got back out front, well over a hundred people were gathered by the window, staring at the drawn curtains as if waiting for the opening of a play over at the Trivoli.

Grady walked back down the street toward his office. Half a dozen kids were playing in the front yard of a house.

"Bang, bang!" one of 'em called. "You're dead!"

"Charlie, you be Ike Clanton, and when we start shootin', you skedaddle."

"Not me! I ain't gonna be no coward!" Charlie answered.

Grady continued on down the street, then climbed the stairs to his office. C.V. and Bianca were waiting in his office for him.

"What's the mood of the town?" C.V. asked.

"Strange," Grady answered. "They're all waiting in front of the hardware store to view the bodies."

"View the bodies?"

"That's right," Grady said. "Ike has made an arrangement with Ritter and Ream to display Billy and the McClaurys in the window of the hardware store."

"Ike should have been in show business," C.V. suggested.

"He's just going to get the whole town worked up," Grady said.

"That's precisely what he intends to do," C.V. said. "I just spoke with Wyatt a short while ago. He and Doc are in jail."

"In jail? What for? From everything I've heard it's an open and shut case of self defense."

"Sheriff Behan and Ike Clanton are two witnesses who didn't see it that way," C.V. said. "Behan has arrested Wyatt and Doc for murder. I told Wyatt we'd defend him. You don't have any qualms about that, do you?"

"No, of course not," Grady said. "Why should **I ?**"

"Behan and Ike Clanton aren't the only prosecution witnesses. There's another witness whose testimony promises to be the most damning of all."

"Who?"

"Sally Clanton," C.V. said easily.

"Sally?" Grady said, with a quick intake of breath.

"I'm afraid so," C.V. said. "And she's going to be a devastating witness because she had a box seat to the whole affair."

"You mean . . . you mean Sally actually saw it happen? She saw her brother killed?"

"She saw everything," C.V. said.

Grady shook his head. "My God, what an ordeal that must have been for her," he said quietly.

"She's the one, isn't she?" Bianca asked. "Sally Clanton is the one you're in love with."

Grady didn't answer, he just nodded his head in the affirmative.

C.V. reached over and put his hand on Grady's shoulder.

"If you want to, Grady, you can withdraw yourself from this case," he offered.

"No," Grady said. "Why would I want to do that?"

"Because if she is the principle witness for the prosecution, then we're going to have to break her."

"I thought all we had to do was see that justice is served," Grady said.

"Yes."

"Then it doesn't hold that we will, necessarily, have to break her. All we have to do is get the truth."

"Yes," C.V. said. "Well, in the meantime. I've petitioned Judge Donlevy to grant a thirty day extension on the land claim. With Billy dead and the old man, Ike, and Sally in mourning, I think it would be inappropriate to pursue the land case at this time, don't you?"

"It's Bianca's case," Grady said. "How do you feel about it?" he asked Bianca.

"I think C.V. is right. I don't think this is the time for it."

"All right," Grady said. "Uh, what about Virgil and Morgan? Were they arrested as well?"

"They are recovering from their wounds," C.V. said. "They aren't under arrest now. I imagine their fate depends upon what happens to Wyatt and Doc."

"Well, if they are defendants in the case, then they will at least be friendly witnesses," Grady said. "Perhaps I'd better go interview them."

Grady picked up a tablet and a pencil and started for the door.

"Grady?" C.V. called quietly.

Grady turned and looked back toward his friend.

"Yes?"

"I'm sorry about the way things are turning out. I mean, first you were representing the plaintiff in a lawsuit against Sally's family, and now you are representing the man she feels murdered her brother."

"Yeah," Grady said. "Well, whatever happens, happens, I suppose."

"Listen, why don't you research the case? I'll argue it."

"All right," Grady agreed.

Grady knocked on the front door of Virgil's house and Virgil's wife, Allie, answered.

"Grady," she said. "How nice of you to call. Come on in, Virgil's in the bedroom with his leg propped up. He'll be so glad to see you."

"How's he doing?" Grady asked.

"It's been troublin' him some, but I think he's goin' to be all right. Can I get you some coffee?"

"Yes, thank you," Grady said.

Grady walked through the little house to the room in back. James, the oldest of the Earp brothers, who was himself wounded in the Civil War and therefore no longer a battler like his brothers, was in the bedroom with Virgil.

"Grady, hello," Virgil said. He stuck out his hand and Grady shook it.

"How are you doing?"

"When you consider the alternative, I can't complain," Virgil said. "Billy got me in the leg. If he'd shot just a little higher, I might be dead now. Have you seen Morgan or Wyatt?"

"No," Grady said.

"Morgan was hit in the shoulder. I guess he's hurtin' 'bout

as much as I am. Wyatt, the lucky dog, didn't get a scratch."

"Yes," Grady said. "I hope we can keep him that way."

"What do you mean?" Virgil asked.

"Virgil, Behan has arrested Wyatt and Doc for murder."

"What? What the hell is he thinkin' about? Those men pulled on us first."

"He's telling a different story," Grady said. "And he has Ike and Sally Clanton to back him up."

"Sally can talk," Virgil said. "She sat right there in the buckboard the whole time. I remember thinkin' when I was goin' down toward Billy and the others what a cool customer she was. She's got a lot of grit, that girl. I hate it that she's gonna be goin' ag'in us, but you could hardly think she'd do otherwise. But Ike? What the hell can he tell about it? Unless he has eyes in the back of his head, he didn't see anything. He was runnin' to save his own hide the whole time."

"Did he start running before or after the shooting started?" Grady asked.

"At about the same time, as I recall. He threw his gun down and ran toward Wyatt."

Grady had been taking notes, and on that he looked up in surprise.

"Wait a minute. Did you say he ran toward Wyatt?"

"Yes. He ran toward Wyatt and tried to push Wyatt's gunhand up."

"What did Wyatt do?"

"He just pushed him away and told him it was too late to stop now. I think he told him to get to shootin' or get to runnin', one or the other."

"That's interesting," Grady said.

"What's so interesting about it?" James asked. "What difference does it make which direction he ran? The point is, he ran."

"It's interesting that he ran toward Wyatt," Grady said. "Because if Wyatt had intended to murder, he could have shot Ike then. That information could be used to convince the judge and jury that Wyatt was only shooting in self defense."

"What about Morgan and me?" Virgil asked. "Are we under arrest too?"

"No," Grady said. "And that's good, because we can use you as witnesses for the defense. Now, as clearly as you can remember, tell me everything that happened leading up to, and including, the fight."

Grady finished with Virgil, then started over to the Cosmopolitan Hotel where Morgan was recuperating from his wound. Grady had to walk by Ritter and Ream's Hardware store, and he looked in at the three bodies which were on display under a large sign which read:

MURDERED IN THE STREETS OF TOMBSTONE

The three coffins were side by side. They were, as Ike had ordered, shiny black with ornate silver trim. The hinges were of silver, and at the foot and bottom lid of each coffin was a spray of silver oak leaves. Just under the viewing glass was a large, spreadwinged, silver eagle, and right above the eagle, a silver plate with the name of the deceased inscribed.

The head and shoulders of each of the men were visible through the viewing glass. Frank looked as peaceful as if he were asleep. Tom also looked as if he might be sleeping, but his head was twisted grotesquely to one side, almost as if he had been hanged and rigor mortis had set his neck in such an angle.

But it was Billy who wore the most vivid mask of death. His eyes had creeped half open and his upper lip was pulled up, showing his teeth. The edge of his mouth and his cheeks were set in a grimace as if he were fighting against the pain of the bullets which had struck him. In life, Billy's features had been pleasant, almost handsome. Now they were ugly.

Grady passed on by, then went to the hotel to interview Morgan. Morgan's story substantiated Virgil's. They had not had time to compare notes, and, therefore, the fact that their stories were similar validated them as far as Grady was concerned.

He wondered what Sally's version would be. He was convinced that she wouldn't lie, but he knew that under her emotional strain she would have, no doubt, perceived things differently. Those differences in perception would have to be brought out on the witness stand. He was glad it would be C.V. who was going to cross examine her and not him.

The bodies lay on view for two whole days, during which time newspaper reporters came from Tucson and Phoenix to take pictures and write their stories of the great 'Gunfight at the O.K. Corral' as it was now being called. Of course, the gunfight didn't take place at the corral, and the only role the corral played was as an escape route for Ike. But 'Gunfight at the O.K. Corral' had a more pleasing alliteration than 'Gunfight at Fly's Photo Gallery,' or, more precisely, 'Gunfight in the yard between Fly's and the Harwood House.'

Every business in town shut down for the funeral.

The funeral procession was led by the town's brass band. The drums had been muffled with black bunting and they beat a low thump as the band played a funeral dirge. Behind the band two cowboys walked, carrying the same sign which had been displayed over the three coffins during their 'lying in state' in the window of the hardware store. Behind the two cowboys carrying the sign, came a hearse bearing Billy's coffin.

The hearse was a beautiful black and silver glass-sided vehicle costing over eight thousand dollars.

Behind the first hearse came the second, carrying the bodies of Tom and Frank McClaury. This hearse was nearly as elaborate as the first, lacking only some of the silver trimming.

Behind the second hearse came a three-seat phaeton. A cowboy, dressed in black, was driving the phaeton. Inside, Billy's mother and father sat on the front seat, riding backwards, and Sally and Sylvia on the back seat. Sally was crying, and dabbing at her eyes with a handkerchief.

Ike was riding a horse alongside the phaeton.

Behind the Clanton phaeton was another for the McClaury family, and behind that more than a dozen buggies, buckboards, traps, surreys and wagons. Behind those rode cowboys from both ranches, all of them wearing guns.

Grady went to the cemetery, both out of compassion for Billy, and because he hoped to see Sally.

There were three graves opened in the hard dry earth of Boothill. The funeral procession wound its way through the cemetery until it reached the gravesites, then the family was seated.

The Reverend Abner Crowel had been preaching in the West for over ten years, but he had never seen a crowd as large as the one gathered for this burial. He bristled with pride and preached his finest sermon at the graveside. It was entitled "The decision for Jesus." He was pleased to see that it was exceptionally well received, especially by the two young women at the graveside who wept real tears at his inspirational words.

Finally his sermon was over and the gravediggers began closing the graves.

It was not until that moment that Grady saw an opportunity to go over and speak to Sally.

"Sally?"

She looked up at him with eyes which were red-rimmed with her crying.

"Sally, I'm sorry about all this," he said. "I've tried to come to see you but Ike has posted guards. They won't let me through."

"Grady, are you defending Wyatt Earp?" Sally asked.

"Every man is entitled to a defense." Grady said.

"Are you defending him?" she asked again.

"Yes."

"How could you?"

'He hired our firm," Grady said.

"He murdered my brother."

"Sally, I know what Billy meant to you," he said. "But I have interviewed many people who say that it was a fair fight."

"A fair fight? There's no such thing as a fair fight between my brother and the Earps," Sally said. "Wyatt Earp is a professional gunslinger. He's a killer. Billy never hurt anyone in his life. He wasn't a gunslinger, and he never had a chance."

"Then it shouldn't have started." Grady said.

"That's what I'm trying to tell you," Sally said. "Billy came to town to get Ike—to take him home. He didn't come to fight. He was pushed into it. The Earps pushed my brothers and the McClaurys into the fight. All Billy wanted to do was go home."

"I'm sure it seemed that way to you, Sally, but there—"

"Seemed that way?" Sally said, interrupting Grady's reply. "I was there, Grady. I saw everything. I came to town with Billy. I know why we came to town and I know what he wanted. He wanted to get Ike and get peacefully out of town. But the Earps wouldn't let him. They pushed it into a fight and Billy was killed. I hope they hang Wyatt Earp."

"I've got to do everything within my power to see that he gets off," Grady said.

"I see," Sally said coldly.

"Sally, please, try to understand."

"I only understand one thing," she said.

"What's that?"

"I understand that I was a fool ever to think that I could love you. Come along, Sylvia. The company here has suddenly grown most undesirable."

"Sally—"

Sally didn't answer Grady, but turned and hurried on down the hill to the phaeton. She climbed in and rode away without once looking back.

A puff of wind came out of the desert and blew a cloud of dust across the graveyard, whistling through the sagebrush and around the tombstones. Grady looked back at the newly closed graves. The dirt had already been discolored by the sun so that

Billy's grave looked no newer or fresher than anyone else's. How quickly the earth out here covered up its scars, he thought. He only wished the people could do the same thing.

Chapter Fourteen

ON MONDAY, OCTOBER 31ST, which was Halloween Day, two men who were to have a role to play in the upcoming trial arrived on the afternoon train. One of the two men was J. Warren Bean, a prosecuting attorney known throughout the West, indeed throughout the United States, as the man who prosecuted cases in Judge Isaac Charles Parker's Federal Court at Fort Smith, Arkansas. Judge Parker's swift justice had resulted in so many hangings that he became known far and wide as the 'Hanging Judge.' Judge Parker's reputation rested somewhat on the successful prosecution of the cases which came before him, and that prosecution had been carried out by J. Warren Bean.

Warren Bean always dressed in tails and a stovepipe hat, and he carried a silver-headed cane. He wore a diamond stickpin in his cravat, and solid gold cufflinks, and a gold watch chain which stretched across the silk vest that did little to conceal his substantial girth. He had, like his mentor, Judge Parker, affected a Van Dyke beard. He kept his hair cut short, and neatly combed.

The other person to arrive was one who might have been an early arriving Halloween demon. His name was George

Maledon, and whenever he entered a town, mothers shuddered and pulled their children close to them.

Maledon was a very small, full bearded man who always carried a brace of hand-woven, well-oiled, expensive Kentucky hemp ropes with him. He was a professional hangman who had carried out more than fifty death sentences. He had been dubbed the 'prince of hangmen.'

The arrival of these two men, especially of George Maledon, created as big a stir in town as had the appearance of the celebrated songstress, Jenny Lind, some months earlier in Tombstone. Word of their arrival quickly reached the offices of Battenburg and Ford. When C.V. heard about it, he stood up and, without a word, walked over to a file drawer where he kept a bottle of whiskey, poured himself a glass, and drank it.

"C.V., what is it?" Grady asked.

"Ebersole," C.V. said.

"Who?"

"Ebersole. You remember my story about the client I defended who was hanged?"

"Oh, yes, up in Dodge, wasn't it? Under a Judge named Landis?"

"Yes," C.V. said. "Landis was the Judge." He paused for a moment, then took a deep breath and went on. "J. Warren Bean was the Prosecutor, and George Maledon was the executioner."

"Oh, C.V !" Bianca gasped.

Grady chuckled. "Don't worry about it," he said "This case is going to be heard by Judge Spicer. We've worked with Judge Spicer before, C.V.—you know he's a fair man."

C.V. rubbed the back of his hand across his mouth and smiled at Grady.

"Yeah," he said. "I know. It was just unpleasant to see that pair come in here, that's all."

"Look, it's obviously a case of self-defense. I don't see how anyone can make anything more out of it than that."

C.V. chuckled. "There are two old expressions which

were invented for our friend, J. Warren Bean," he said. "Bean can make a mountain out of a molehill, and a silk purse out of a sow's ear. Believe me, if there is the slightest chance to make this case, Bean is the man who can do it. And don't forget that he has Sally Clanton as a witness on his side.

"I see what you mean," Grady said. He smiled. "Well, I'm glad of one thing."

"What's that?"

"It's you trying this case and not me."

"Come on," C.V. said. "Let's walk down to the jail and visit Wyatt and Doc."

Though Sheriff Behan had arrested Wyatt and Doc, C.V. had already managed to get them transferred from the county jail, which was under Sheriff Behan's administration, to the city jail, Normally the city jail was controlled by Virgil Earp, but Virgil had been suspended from duty, so under the circumstances, Boston Corbett, the Federal Marshal, had been brought in to take charge of the prisoners until the trial.

When C.V. and Grady walked into the jail a short while later, they found Wyatt, Doc, Boston and another man sitting around a card table, playing poker.

"C.V.," Boston said, smiling at C.V. when he and Grady came into the jail. "Have you ever played poker with this man?"

"I learned not to a long time ago," C.V. said.

"I think he cheats," Boston said good naturedly. "I think we ought to put him in jail."

"I am in jail," Wyatt laughed.

"Oh, yes, so you are," Boston said. "Well, good enough for you. I fold."

Wyatt took the hand and raked in the pot, which consisted of a dozen or more matches. He looked at C.V. and smiled.

"How goes the fight for justice?" he asked.

"The opposition has brought in some heavy artillery," C.V. said. "J. Warren Bean."

"Yeah, I heard," Wyatt said. He reached up through the

bar and put his hand on C.V.'s shoulder. "C.V., if someone hired a couple of gunmen to shoot you down, like Billy the Kid and Bill Longley for example, who would you want fighting on your side?"

"For the life of me I can't think of anyone I'd rather have by my side than you," C.V. said.

Wyatt beamed. "I thank you for the compliment, and the vote of confidence," he said. "But in all modesty, I must say that you would be making a wise decision. I am an expert shootist. You, on the other hand, are an expert lawyer. So if they call in the big guns against me, I want you on my side. I have no fear of J. Warren Bean, or of George Maledon."

C.V. hadn't mentioned the hangman because he didn't want to upset Wyatt. He was surprised that Wyatt knew about him, and when Wyatt saw C.V.'s expression he laughed.

"Did you think I wouldn't know about Mr. Maledon?" he asked. "I've received reports on him, and on the progress of the instrument which is being built over on Toughnut Street."

"What instrument? What are you talking about?"

"Take a walk over there and see for yourself," Wyatt said. "It's on the corner of Toughnut at Fourth, in an empty lot belonging to Frank Stilwell."

"Stilwell? Behan's deputy?"

"The same," Wyatt said. He sat back down at the table and began shuffling the cards. "They tell me the workmanship is quite good," he said. "I'd hate to see it go to waste. Maybe there's someway I can get Behan, or Stilwell or Ike Clanton on it." Wyatt dealt out four hands then picked up his own. He smiled. "Ah. My luck is running good today."

C.V. left the jail and walked over to Toughnut and Allen. He knew the empty lot Wyatt was talking about. An itinerant preacher had held a campground meeting on that same lot a couple of months earlier. The structure on the lot now was a lot more ominous than the preacher's tent, though. C.V. was still a block away when he saw it.

It was a hangman's gallows.

There were a couple of dozen people standing around watching the construction. A large, hand- lettered sign stood in front of the gallows:

ON THIS GALLOWS, THE MASTER EXECUTIONER, GEORGE MALEDON, THE 'PRINCE OF HANGMEN' WILL HANG WYATT EARP, VIRGIL EARP, MORGAN EARP, AND DOC HOLLIDAY.

THESE FOUR MURDERERS WILL BE PROSECUTED BY J. WARREN BEAL AND LEGALLY SENT TO MEET THEIR MAKER.

ADMISSION IS FREE.

Ike Clanton was supervising the construction of the gallows. A ladder of thirteen steps led up to the floor, which was made of freshly cut, one-by-eight-inch planks. The 'tree' of the gallows was constructed of four-by-four timbers, three uprights, and one crosspiece at the top. There were places for two ropes on each side of the center brace, so that a total of four nooses, each made of 20-strand rope, one and a half inches in circumference, were hanging from the overhead crossbeam, now tied to sandbags. Four chairs had been placed invitingly on the twenty-foot square platform, with a name placard on each for Wyatt Earp, Virgil Earp, Morgan Earp, and Doc Holliday.

The platform looked solid, but C.V. could see that it had two ominous divisions which were supported by upright timbers. When those timbers were knocked out of place, the front part of the platform would swing down on hinges, and feet which had been standing there would be left dangling in mid-air, the falls broken only by a rope around the neck.

At this moment there were four one-hundred- pound weights on the platform, and Ike Clanton stepped back away from the edge.

"Okay, try it!" Ike shouted.

The two muscular men beneath the platform swung heavy hammers at the supporting posts. The posts were knocked away and the long, narrow trap fell open. The four weights dropped for a short distance, then were jerked up short by the rope. Several in the crowd cheered, and Ike held his hands over his head as if he were a prize fighter having just scored a knock-out win over his opponent.

Ike bounded down the steps to the congratulations of many in the crowd, then he saw C.V. and he came over to him.

"How do you like it?" he asked. "Mr. Maledon allowed as it was as slick as any gallows he's ever used. And he's used plenty."

"Clanton, why did you build this thing?" C.V. asked.

"As a matter of civic duty," Ike said. "You see, I've volunteered to foot all the expenses of the hangin'. I'm the one brought Maledon in here. I'm payin' him $250 per neck, plus all his expenses."

"You have no right to build this thing, or to bring in a hangman."

"This here lot belongs to Frank Stilwell," Ike said. "I'm rentin' it from Stilwell, 'n that makes me the proprietor. Now, accordin' to the law I got a right to build anythin' I want on my own private property, and I want to build a gallows."

"It's inflaming the passions of the people," C.V. said.

"You damn right it's inflamin' the passions of the people!" Clanton said. "That's what I was plannin' on doin'."

"I'll get a court order to have it taken down."

"That don't make any difference," Ike said triumphantly. "Ever'one's already seen it now anyway. And if I take it down. I'll leave it in pieces that can be put back together real easy. Besides, you can't get no court order to have Maledon run out of town, and ever'where he goes, people will see him 'n they'll know why he's here."

C.V. looked at the gallows and at the curious onlookers, many of whom were now, cautiously, venturing up the steps. He shook his head. Ike had won this round. He was right.

There was nothing C.V. could do about George Maledon. he was a private citizen with the right to go anywhere he pleased. And though he might be able to get a court order knocking down the gallows, the damage had already been done.

"All right." he said. "Leave it up. But don't be too sure it won't wind up being used in a way you didn't anticipate."

Ike laughed. "It'll be used right, don't you worry about that."

"Hey. Ike. you want me to change this here hinge?" one of the workmen called. "It's still hangin' up a bit."

"Yeah, change it. Make it real smooth," he said, drawing out the words, 'real smooth'.

C.V. left the gallows and the morbid crowd which surrounded it, and returned to his office. He was still angry when he went inside.

"What is it?" Grady asked. "What's wrong?" C.V. explained what Ike was doing, and how he was stirring up the population.

"You know, Grady, there are some people who are only too willing to believe that there's no difference between the men wearing the badge and those who aren't. If so, they'd be willing to hang Wyatt and the others, not because they think Wyatt was more responsible for the fight than the Clantons and the McClaury's, but because they are just sick and tired of justice being administered by the six-gun. We may be dealing with a phenomenon here that we don't even understand." He ran his hand through his hair. "If so, we are going to be in trouble."

"Yeah," Grady said. "But not as much trouble as the Earps and Doc Holliday."

"Doc Holliday," C.V. said. He sighed. "He's the real fly in the ointment."

"Why?" Bianca asked.

"Because," Grady answered for C.V. "Virgil, Wyatt and Morgan are all paid members of the Tombstone City Police Department. We can make a very strong case for them . . . they were just doing their duty. But Doc is a private citizen."

"I thought he was a permanent deputy," Bianca said.

"He holds that position only so he can wear firearms in the city limits," C.V. said. "He is not, officially, a member of the force. He's never drawn a cent from the city, not even for expenses."

"I don't want to sound insensitive here." Grady said. "But what about severable interest?"

"It won't work," C.V. said.

"What's severable interest?" Bianca asked. "And why won't it work?"

Grady added. "Severable interest means that we get the court to try them separately, and rule separately. That's what you do when the circumstances surrounding one defendant differ from those surrounding another. In this case, however, if Doc Holliday is found guilty then the Earps would be equally as guilty for allowing an unauthorized person to participate in the action. No, the best thing for us to do is to link Wyatt and Doc, and establish Doc as a bona fide member of the police force, acting in the line of duty."

"The fact that he confronted Ike Clanton in the Alhambra Cafe around midnight the night before isn't going to help," Grady said.

"No, it won't," C.V. said. "But the fact that it was Billy who was killed, and not Ike, will."

"C.V.. what are you saying?" Bianca asked. "Are you glad it was Billy instead of Ike?"

"No, of course not," C.V. said. "I always liked Billy, and the ironic thing is, if it had been Ike who was killed, I think Billy would have come around to being an upstanding citizen. But it wasn't Ike who was killed, and since that's the situation, we have to take advantage of it as best we can."

"How?" Bianca asked.

"I think I can answer that," Grady said. "It was well known that a great deal of animosity existed between Doc and Ike. If Ike had been killed. Bean could have made his case by saying that Doc had wanted to kill him all along, anyway."

"Right," C.V. said. "But it wasn't Ike who was killed, it was Billy. And if Doc didn't exactly like Billy, at least they had never had words."

"I see," Bianca said. "So that means that Doc took part in the battle because he felt an obligation to. and not because he wanted to."

"We hope. But even there we have some problems," C.V. said. He pointed to a plotting Grady had made of the scene. He'd drawn a map of the block which was bordered on the south by Fremont Street, the north by Allen Street, the east by Third Street and the west by Fourth Street. He had drawn in the Papago Cash Store, Bauer's Meat Market, Fly's Photograph Gallery and boarding house, with the photo studio behind it, and Harwood House. He had figures drawn of all the combatants, too. Billy Clanton was lying against the side of the house, Virgil was no more than six feet right in front of him. Wyatt was standing just in the front of the Gallery, Morgan was in the dirt to Wyatt's right, and Doc was in the dirt just in front of Morgan. Frank McClaury was lying dead just to the right of Doc Holliday and Tom McClaury was dead alongside the buckboard which was occupied by Sally, who was the closest, nonparticipating eyewitness. Ike Clanton was drawn in all the way back at a Mexican Dance Hall, on Allen Street, a block away from the action.

"As you can see," C.V. said. "We have plotted every bullet which was fired. The Clantons and the McClaurys fired seventeen shots, hitting with only three. The Earps and Doc Holliday also fired seventeen shots, but they scored with eleven. But for all of it, Doc didn't shoot Billy. Doc shot Tom, and he put a bullet in Frank. He also—and this is the most damning part—took a shot at Ike. But he didn't shoot Billy. Billy was shot by Wyatt and Morgan."

"There aren't any easy answers, are there?" Grady said.

At that moment someone knocked on the door and Bianca went to answer it. It was a young boy.

"A fella gimme a dime to bring this to you," he said, handing a message to Bianca.

"Thank you," Bianca said, smiling pleasantly at him. She gave the message to C.V.. and C.V. opened it. He smiled.

"Well, maybe something is going to come easy for us," he said.

"What?"

"This is from Mr. N.H. Clanton. He wants to meet us to work out a compromise agreement on the Santa Anna Land."

"When?"

"Now," C.V. said. "This afternoon."

"Well come on, let's go."

"No," C.V. said. He stroked his chin as he studied the note. "It's odd, but for some reason he asks that you not come. He wants just Bianca and me.

"Oh," Grady said, crestfallen. "I think I know why."

"Why?"

"It's Sally," Grady said. "She doesn't want to see me."

"Yes, of course," C.V. said. "That must be it."

"I'm sorry, Grady," Bianca said. "Really I am. Maybe when all this dies down, maybe then Sally will realize how much she loves you and she'll be willing to put everything else aside."

"Sure she will," C.V. said. "After all, she doesn't blame you for Billy's death."

"No, but she blames me for defending the man who killed him."

"She'll get over it eventually," C.V. promised.

"C.V., don't you think it's a little strange that after all these years of fighting Clanton, he has finally agreed to talk? And now, right after his son was killed?" Bianca asked.

"No, not necessarily," C.V. said. "I'm sure that Billy's getting killed has taken all the fight out of him. It's actually quite a normal reaction. I hate to take advantage of such a situation, but if he is willing to negotiate, I think we should go hear what he has to say. Grady, my lad, you hold down the fort."

C.V. rented a buggy and he and Bianca started west toward Clanton's ranch.

It was a pleasant ride, late enough in October that the desert heat wasn't devastating, though it was still quite warm. The buggy was well sprung, and rolled along quite easily on the wagon road.

"C.V., if the land is returned to us, I'm going to give it to my husband's younger brother," Bianca said.

"What?" C.V. asked, looking at her in surprise.

"Are you serious? You've been fighting it all this time and you intend to give it away?"

"Would you be willing to live in the hacienda on the ranch?"

"Bianca, I'm . . . I'm not the ranching type," C.V. demurred. "I would be worthless on a ranch."

"I know it," Bianca said, laughing. "That's why I intend to give it away. If you won't live there with me. I've no intention of living there alone."

"Well, if you are really serious about this," C.V. said, "we should be able to work out a compromise which is satisfactory to you, your brother-in-law, and Clanton."

Suddenly a rifle shot rang out from the rocks halfway up a hill alongside the road, and the horse, which had been trotting along at an easy gait, shuddered, and dropped in his harness. C.V. saw blood spilling from the horse's head, spewing out like a fountain to turn the dirt crimson. He started to stand up when another shot rang out, and the bullet smashed into the front of the buggy, then careened off with an echoing whine.

"Just stay where you are, Mr. Lawyer," a voice called down.

"C.V., who is it? Highwaymen?"

"I doubt it," C.V. said. "They know I'm a lawyer, I have a feeling it's something else entirely."

Two men raised up from behind the rock and started down

the hill. C.V. looked toward them, but he didn't know either one of them. One was a small Mexican man, swarthy skin, dark hair and dark eyes. The other was a big man, with red hair and a red beard.

"Pretty good shootin', don't you think?" the big redheaded man asked. He smiled when he reached the road. "My name's Red Bear," he said. He laughed, unpleasantly. "Well, it ain't my actual name, but it's what the injuns call me, 'n it suits me. This here's Pancho, or some such name. It don't matter none, you don't need to know. All you gotta know is you're gonna do what we say."

"What do you want?" C.V. asked. "We aren't carrying any cash."

"Didn't figure you was or I'd'a already took it," Red Bear said. "All I want is for the two of you to come along with us. We're gonna keep you locked up for a while."

"Locked up?" Bianca said. "Why?"

"Just 'til after the trial's over," Red Bear said. "The fella I'm workin' for seems to think you're a good lawyer. He don't want you gettin' the Earps off. so he's gonna hold you here 'til after the trial."

"That won't change a thing," C.V. said. "My partner will try the case."

"Yeah, I know. I asked the fella that hired me to do this iffen he wanted me to take care of your partner too 'n he said no. He was afraid that if both you lawyers got took out of the picture, why the judge'd just let the case go. He figures ol' Bean has enough smarts to beat your boy."

"You're talking about Ike Clanton, of course," C.V..said.

"Yeah, that's who I'm talkin' about. If I'd'a met up with someone like him a long time ago, I'd'a never took to ridin' with the damn injuns in the first place." Red Bear waved the barrel of his rifle menacingly. "Come on, let's go."

"When we don't get back to town, my partner will come looking for us," C. V. said.

"Yeah, I reckon he will," Red Bear said. "'N I reckon he'll

find this here dead horse, then he'll know for sure somethin's happened to you. Then he'll be willin' to listen to reason."

"Listen to reason? What sort of reason?" C.V. asked. "What are you talking about?"

"It's simple enough," Red Bear said. "All your partner's gotta do is agree not to defend Earp and Holliday too good. If Earp 'n Holliday are found guilty, Ike'll send word to me 'n we'll let you two go. Iffen Earp 'n Holliday are found innocent, why then I reckon he'll have to send the undertaker out after you two." Red Bear looked at Bianca. "Tell you what, though, afore I kill this here woman, I aims to have a little pleasure with her. It's been a long time since I had me anythin' but a injun woman."

"Why you filthy mouthed—" C.V. said, starting toward Red Bear. He didn't make it half way to him when the other outlaw, the silent one, slammed him over the head with his rifle. C.V. went out like a light.

Grady didn't get too worried when C.V. and Bianca didn't come back that night. But he got very worried the next day when he couldn't find them. This was the last day before the trial, and there was still too much to be done. Grady knew that C.V. wouldn't stay away unless he was being detained by something beyond his control.

C.V. and Bianca still hadn't returned by two o'clock in the afternoon, and Grady was about to go looking for them, when the liveryman at the corral came to see him.

"Do you have any idea where Mr. Battenburg is?"

"No," Grady answered, "I don't. Why?"

"Someone brought in the buggy he rented yesterday. They said the horse was dead in the harness, shot through the head."

"What? What about C.V. and Bianca? Did he say anything about them?"

"Never said nothin' 'bout anythin', except my horse," the liveryman said. "When you find Mr. Battenburg, you tell him there's gonna have to be some accountin' for that animal. I can't go rentin' horses to people and lettin' 'em get shot. I'd go outta business."

Grady thanked the liveryman for the message, and assured him that some accounting would be done for the horse in due time. Right now he was more interested in seeing to the safety of C.V. and Bianca.

Grady hurried down to the marshal's office where he found Boston Corbett. He told Boston about the liveryman's message, and he and Boston rode out toward Clanton's Ranch. They found sign where the horse had been shot, and footprints to indicate that C.V. and Bianca had left the buggy and been joined by two more men. After that the footprints went into the rock and couldn't be read.

"Come on," Grady said. "We're going out to the Clanton Ranch, and this time we aren't going to be turned away."

Grady and Boston rode another mile toward the ranch. They were met by the usual armed guard, but this time Grady was ready for him. When the guard came up to stop them, he was surprised to find that Grady already had his pistol out and pointed at him.

"Hold on here!" the guard said. "What are you doing?"

"I'm going in to talk to the Clantons," Grady said.

"I got orders to stop anyone who tries," the guard said, though, realizing that he was now at a disadvantage, he didn't say the words very menacingly.

"You won't stop me," Grady said easily.

"No. I reckon I won't," the guard said.

"Give me your guns," Grady said. "I'll leave them with the Clantons."

The guard handed his rifle to Grady, then he pulled out his pistol and handed it over as well.

"You got a spare in the saddlebag?" Boston asked.

"No, I ain't got nothin' there," the guard insisted.

"Mind if I check?"

"All right, take it," the guard said. He took off the bag and tossed it over. "I got me another gun in there, but it ain't loaded."

Warriors of the Code

"You can pick this up too," Grady said.

Grady and Boston slapped their heels against the flanks of their horses, and started for the main house at a gait. A moment later they pulled up out front of the house, and they were met by N.H. Clanton, who came out onto the front porch holding a rifle.

"I got a guard posted down the road to keep people away," Clanton said gruffly. "Now git."

"Mr. Clanton, we have to talk to you," Grady said.

"I ain't in a talkin' mood."

"Clanton, you might get one of us with that rifle," Boston said. "And then again, you might not. But I guarantee you, we'll get you. Now, why don't you put it down and we'll talk?"

Sally came out of the front door then, and she, too, was carrying a gun.

"Now the odds are a little more even," Sally said.

"Sally!" Grady said, and the word tore like a cry from his throat. "My God, Sally, has it come to this?"

Sally looked at Grady for a long moment, then Grady saw tears sliding down her cheeks.

"Put your gun down, daughter," her father said. "Let's hear what these fools have to say."

"Mr. Clanton, did you see Bianca and my partner yesterday?"

"Did I see 'em yesterday? Now, why should I have seen 'em?"

"Because you sent them a message, asking them to come talk to you."

"Mr., I don't know what you been drinkin'," Clanton said. "But I never sent no such message, and I never saw anybody yesterday. Wouldn't see you today if that fool cowboy I got out on the road would do his job."

"Sally? Have you seen them? Do you know anything about the message?"

"No," Sally said.

"They were set up," Boston said quietly.

"Yes, it looks that way," Grady answered. "The question is, why?" '

"Mr. Ford, what's all this about?" Sally asked. Her cool use of the words 'Mr. Ford' rather than Grady, cut to the quick. How could something which had been so beautiful have soured so?

Grady sighed. "Yesterday afternoon we got a message which was supposed to have been from your father. The message invited C.V. and Bianca out here to talk about the lawsuit. The message indicated that we might be able to work out a deal."

"What kind of a deal?" Clanton asked.

"That's what we were going to talk about," Grady said.

Clanton rubbed his chin and studied Grady for a moment.

"You're the fella who filed a claim to get some money back on the mules, aren't you?"

"Yes, sir," Grady said.

"I got it," Clanton said. "Got a bankdraft in the mail last week."

"I'm glad."

"Tell you what," Clanton said. "I didn't send no message about makin' a deal on the land. Don't know where you got the idea. But Sally tells me there might be a way I can keep a way open to the water."

"Yes," Grady said. "We would work something like that out."

"I might be willin' to talk," Clanton said. "Afterward."

"Afterward?"

"After the trial's over 'n the Earps are brung to justice for murderin' my boy."

"Mr. Clanton, you aren't going to make your deal contingent upon a guilty verdict, are you?"

"Don't have to," Clanton said. "They're guilty, they'll be found guilty. Then we'll talk. Until then, stay the hell off my property."

Grady looked at Sally.

"Sally?"

Sally didn't answer.

"Sally, it can't end like this," he said. "We had too much to let it die like this."

"Please," Sally sobbed. She turned and started to go back inside. "Please, Grady, just . . . just go away!"

"Come on, Grady," Boston said gently.

Grady turned his horse and rode away with Boston, though with every fiber in his soul he wanted to stay and plead with Sally to come back to him, to make things as they once were.

Chapter Fifteen

"OYEZ, OYEZ, OYEZ, the Fourth Circuit Court of the Territory of Arizona is now in session, the Honorable Judge Wells Spicer presiding. All rise!" Sheriff Behan intoned. Everyone in the courtroom rose as the judge emerged from his chambers and walked over to the bench.

Sally was in the first row of the gallery, and Sylvia was with her. Sitting in the same row with Sally was her brother Ike and Billy Claibourne, both of whom had already been identified as witnesses for the prosecution. Also in the first row of the gallery, but sitting on the opposite side of the courtroom, were Virgil and Morgan Earp, each of whom wore the marks of the recent fight. They would be witnesses for the defense.

Grady was at the defendant's table with Wyatt and Doc Holliday. C.V. and Bianca were still missing, and Grady felt an emptiness in his soul as he thought of them. Where were they? Were they still alive? Were they in danger? This would be a difficult enough case to try by itself. It became nearly impossible when he was also burdened with worry over the fate of his friends. Because of that, this morning he had submitted a petition to Judge Spicer, asking that the hearing be delayed until such time as C.V. could be found. So far the judge had made no response to the motion.

Judge Spicer took his seat.

"Be seated," the sheriff announced. There was a rustle of clothes and a squeak of boots and shoes as the spectators got themselves settled. The court was packed. Admission had been granted on a first come, first seated basis, and some people had been outside the courtroom since before dawn.

The press was there. There were representatives from THE NUGGET, which was Tombstone's anti- Earp newspaper, as well as from THE EPITAPH, which, if not a pro-Earp newspaper, was at least more objective. There were also reporters and artists present from the big papers in Tucson and Phoenix, and one from as far away as the ST. LOUIS POST-DISPATCH. The artists were busy sketching the principals as the case began.

Judge Spicer removed his wire-rimmed glasses and polished them industriously for a moment, holding them up to the light of the window and staring through the lenses, then polishing them even more vigorously. During this ritual of cleaning and polishing there was total silence in the court. Finally. Judge Spicer deemed his glasses clean enough, or perhaps he just considered the mood in the court somber enough, because he put his glasses back on, hooking them very carefully over one ear at a time. Then he fixed a long, studied stare upon the courtroom, and cleared his throat.

"Ladies and gentlemen, I'm not unaware of the intense public interest in this case. But I want it understood right now that this kind of public interest will not be allowed to interfere with the process of justice. If there is the slightest incident or disturbance in this courtroom which, in my opinion, interferes with the judicial process, I will clear the court and conduct the remainder of the trial in closed session."

Judge Spicer looked down at his desk while he let the full impact of his statement penetrate. He picked up a piece of paper, examined it for a moment, then gazed out toward the lawyers' tables. To the judge's right was the defense table with Grady, Wyatt and Doc. To his left sat the prosecuting attorney, J. Warren Bean, who was decked out as if he were attending a night at the opera.

At a small table near the prosecution sat the court stenographer, a small, thin man of indeterminate age, with very thick glasses which so enlarged his eyes that it made him look almost deformed.

"Mr. Ford," Judge Spicer said. "I've studied your motion that this hearing be postponed until such time as C.V. Battenburg is found. Are you declaring yourself incompetent to defend your clients, sir?"

"No, Your Honor," Grady replied. "But Mr. Earp and Doctor Holliday secured our firm in the expectation of having Mr. Battenburg argue their cases. I believe it would do a disservice to them to start the trial without Mr. Battenburg."

"Do you know where Mr. Battenburg is?"

"No, Your Honor," Grady admitted. "He and Mrs. Santa Anna drove out of town to answer what they thought was an invitation to discuss another case, and they haven't come back. Their horse was found dead in the traces, shot in the head."

"And you suspect foul play."

"I'm afraid I do, Your Honor."

Judge Spicer cleared his throat. "Mr. Ford, as much as it pains me to say this, I feel that we much face the possibility that Mr. Battenburg will be unable to return. Therefore it isn't feasible to postpone this case on the premise that he will return. Reluctantly, I must deny your motion. You will defend Mr. Earp and Doctor Holliday."

"Yes, Your Honor," Grady said. He turned in his seat and looked over toward Ike Clanton. Ike was smiling broadly at the judge's decision.

"The Territory of Arizona versus Wyatt Earp and John Holliday," Judge Spicer said. "Is the prosecution ready?"

J. Warren Bean stood, put one hand inside his silk vest, then looked over toward the jury.

"Ready, Your Honor," he said in a deep, resonant voice."

"Is the defense ready?"

"Yes, Your Honor," Grady responded, half rising from his chair. This was the biggest case of his life, and he was up against the most famous and effective prosecutor in America. And he was facing him alone, because C.V. Battenburg, a man whom the word 'friend' was insufficient to describe, was missing, perhaps dead. He had not felt such a degree of panic since that awful day on the plains of Kansas, when a band of renegade Indians had attacked his father and mother's wagon.

C.V. and Bianca were bound, hand and foot. They were just inside an old, abandoned mine shaft, sitting against the wall of the mine. Red Bear and Pancho had cooked a rabbit, and Red Bear was eating half of it, oblivious of the pieces of meat and the grease which tangled and matted the hair of his beard.

Yesterday, C.V. and Bianca had been given a plate full of beans. They hadn't eaten anything today. Red Beard looked over at them.

"Iffen you're hungry, I'll let you clean off what's left on these bones," he said, laughing evilly.

C.V. strained at the ropes but they were too tight. His blood boiled with impotent rage. The only thing he had to be thankful for was the fact that, so far at least, he hadn't touched Bianca.

Ike Clanton was the prosecution's second witness, after Billy Claibourne. Under Bean's questioning, Ike told the story that he had come into town to collect money which was owed to him by Mr. Bauer, of Bauer's Meat Market. When he arrived in town he met Tom and Frank McClaury, who also had some money due them from Bauer's, so they decided to celebrate their good fortune.

"And how did you celebrate your good fortune?" Bean asked.

"We had a few drinks," Ike said. "At around midnight I tried to have dinner, but . . ."

"Wait a minute," Bean said, holding his finger up in the air. He was standing just in front of the jury rail, looking into the faces of the jurymen as Ike gave his testimony. Now he turned slowly back toward his witness. "Did you say you tried to have dinner?"

"Yes, sir," Ike said.

"What prevented you?"

"Doc Holliday," Ike said. "He came into the lunch room of the Alhambra, and told me to 'get heeled, or get out'."

"Get heeled, or get out?"

"Yes, sir."

"What does that mean?"

"He challenged me to a gun fight. I explained to him that I wasn't armed. He grew very angry. I think he wanted to kill me right there."

"Did you think about going to the law, to protest this threat?" Bean asked.

"Ha!" Ike said. "The law was there."

"The law was there?"

"Wyatt and Virgil Earp were both there at the time," Ike said.

"And what did they do?"

"Wyatt told me I should go home and go to bed."

The testimony continued. Ike told about his brother arriving to 'share breakfast' with him before walking down to collect their money and return home. He told how they were attacked by the Earps on the way to the market, hauled off to court and fined. Then, when they were ready to leave, the Earps and Doc Holliday dogged them, actually blocking their way to the meat market.

"When it finally reached the point to where I knew gunfire was about to break out, I rushed up to Wyatt Earp, and attempted to put my body between his gun and my brother, to protect my brother if possible, while making one last effort to prevent gunplay."

"What did you say to Wyatt?"

"I said, 'Don't do any shooting, we don't want a fight'."

"What did Mr. Earp do?"

"He reached down and pulled my gun out of my holster with one hand, while clubbing me on the head with his gun. Immediately after that the gunfire erupted. Doc fired his shotgun at me, first, and missed. The next part . . . " Ike started, then he stopped. "The next part is hard for me to say." Bean had a habit of wandering all around the courtroom area while he was questioning, and now he was on the opposite side from the jury, standing just in front of the railing which separated the front row of the gallery from the lawyers' bay area. He looked at Ike, and with the compassion of a priest granting absolution, asked, "What happened next, Ike?"

"I was half senseless from the blow to my head," Ike said. "I don't remember doing it, but I must have run. When I came back to my senses, I was standing on the front porch of Rosita's Place, over on Allen Street. I don't know how I got there."

"You don't know how you got there?" Bean asked. "Tell me. do you think the fact that you were unarmed, clubbed in the head, and were fired on at point blank range by a known killer might have had anything to do with it?"

"Objection!" Grady called.

"Sustained," Judge Spicer replied. Spicer glared at Bean. "Please refrain from any more such theatrics," the judge ordered.

"Yes, Your Honor. Now, Ike, you say the Earps pushed this fight. Why do you think they did so?"

"Mr. Ford?" the judge interrupted at that moment.

Grady looked toward him. "Yes, Your Honor?"

"Aren't you going to object to counsel asking for a conclusion from the witness?"

"No objections, Your Honor. I'm willing to let the witness answer this line of questions."

Judge Spicer took off his glasses and polished them as he looked at Grady.

"Mr. Ford, I'm not sure what tactic you are using here. I'll allow the questions to proceed, subject to my own objections. If I feel that you are inadequately representing your clients' best interests, however, I'll declare a mistrial and hold you in contempt of court."

"I understand. Your Honor," Grady said. Grady knew where the questioning was going, and he was prepared for it.

"Witness may answer the question," Judge Spicer said.

"I'll tell you exactly why the Earps wanted a showdown," Ike said. "Me 'n my brother, and the McClaury boys had been marked for death by the Earps and Doc Holliday, because we knew they were the ones who pulled the Wells Fargo holdup last March. And we knew it was Doc Holliday who killed the stage driver, Bud Philpot." There was a gasp from the gallery, but under Judge Spicer's stem glare, there was no demonstration. Seats were too difficult to come by in this trial, and no one wanted to risk being thrown out.

"How did you know all this?" Bean continued.

"I know all this because Wyatt Earp offered me the full $6,000 reward if I would turn in three of my riders, and claim they were the culprits. At that time, he confided that it had been him and Virgil and Doc Holliday who done the robbery. I refused to go along with his treachery, so Wyatt made up his mind that I had to die. That was why he pushed the fight at the O.K. Corral."

"Thank you, Ike. I know some of this testimony was painful to you, and some was dangerous. But we must explore every avenue if justice is to be served." Bean turned toward Grady. "Your witness," he said.

"No questions, Your Honor."

"Very well," Judge Spicer said. "Prosecution may call his next witness."

"Grady!" Wyatt hissed. "The son of a bitch is lyin through his teeth!"

"I know he is," Grady replied. "And if I questioned him, he will just get that much more of an opportunity to poison the jury with his lies."

The next witness was Sheriff Johnny Behan. Under questioning Behan testified that he had attempted to disarm the cowboys in order to head off the gunbattle which he was sure was about to erupt.

"And were you successful?" Bean asked.

"No, they demurred," Behan said.

"What happened next?"

"The Earps marched down toward the boys, even though I shouted at them to stay away and leave the boys alone, that they were about to go home and this would all blow over. I heard Wyatt say to someone, 'you sons of bitches have been looking for a fight and now you can have it.' Then somebody, Doc Holliday I believe it was, blasted away at Billy Clanton with a nickel-plated pistol even as the boy pleaded, 'don't shoot me. I don't want to fight.' After that, it was all over in a matter of seconds, and when the smoke cleared away both the McClaury boys and Billy lay dead."

"Thank you, Sheriff. Mr. Ford, your witness."

"No questions," Grady said.

This was the second witness Grady had refused to question, and the people in the gallery reacted to it by wondering among themselves what kind of defense tactic Grady was following. Judge Spicer was also concerned.

"Mr. Ford, please bear in mind, sir, that I am monitoring your tactics very carefully."

"I am aware, Your Honor," Grady replied. Judge Spicer looked at the big clock on the wall. It was nearly noon. He picked up the gavel. "This court will recess until one o'clock this afternoon."

Grady took advantage of the recess to talk to Boston Corbett. They had lunch together in The Grotto. Boston had spent the entire morning looking for C.V. and Bianca, so far, without success. Nevertheless, he gave Grady a complete report of how things were going.

"How is the trial progressing?" Boston asked. "So far

only Claibourne, Clanton and Behan have testified," Grady said. "They said pretty much what I thought they would say. This afternoon Bean will put Sally on the stand."

"I've seen Bean operate before," Boston said. "He's a slick one, all right."

"He plays the jury, the judge, even the gallery, with all the virtuosity of a Shakespearean thespian," Grady said. "I never thought I would see the equal to C.V., but Bean may be. Oh, what a magnificent battle it would be if C.V. were here to take on Bean."

"You'll do all right, Grady," Boston said. "I know you will."

"I can't match him in oratory, I know that," Grady said. "My strongest weapon in this fight will be the truth."

"Truth always has been the strongest weapon," Boston said.

Just before they finished their meal, a boy brought a message to Grady. Grady thanked him, and took the letter out of the envelope. As he read the letter, his cheeks grew red with anger.

"What is it?" Boston asked. "What does the letter say?"

"It says that if I ever want to see C.V. and Bianca alive, I'll see to it that Wyatt and Doc are found guilty."

"Who's it from?"

"It isn't signed, but I'll lay you odds as to who it's from," Grady said.

"Ike?"

"It has to be."

"Grady, show this letter to the judge. He'll throw the case out of court."

"And C.V. and Bianca will be killed," Grady said.

"What are you saying? Grady, you aren't going to go along with this, are you?"

"No, of course not," Grady said. "But I'm not going to tell the judge about it either. That way, Ike may think I'm at least considering it. That could buy more time for C.V. and Bianca, and maybe you could find them."

"If they are anywhere within a hundred miles of this place, I'll find them," Boston said. "You can count on it."

"I am counting on it," Grady said. He finished the last of his coffee. "It's time to get back to work."

Sally was the first witness called that afternoon. She made a powerful witness for the prosecution, as she told how she and Billy had come to town, together, to get Ike and take him back home. She told of their conversation on the way in, and how, that very day, Billy planned to call on Sylvia. Every word she spoke about Billy showed him to be a young, ambitious rancher who was concerned for the future.

"Did Billy, at any time, mention that he was going to 'get the Earps', or 'settle a score with the Earps'?" Bean asked.

"No," Sally said.

"Did Billy in any way provoke the Earps when he came into town?"

"No," Sally said. "He went into the Alhambra to get Ike, and when he came out he gave me a sign that he had talked Ike into coming back home with us. They had started down to the corral to get Ike's horse, when Wyatt and Virgil Earp came out of the alley by the Alhambra and hit them over the head."

Under Bean's questioning, Sally continued her story, finally ending with her holding Billy's head in her lap as her brother died in her arms. Sally began crying then, and Bean, graciously, and advantageously, allowed her to cry. Finally, when she had wiped away her tears, Bean turned to Grady.

"As you have not questioned either of the other witnesses, may I assume that you will grant this young lady the right to her sorrow and not question her either?"

"I do have questions for this witness," Grady said.

The gallery, which had gasped in surprise when he refused to cross examine Ike and Sheriff Behan, now gasped again at his decision to question Sally. She, after all, was the one who was the most innocent, the one who showed the most genuine pain over what had happened.

Grady stood up and walked, not to the witness chair, but to the jury. "Before I cross examine this witness, I feel I owe this court an explanation as to why I passed on the first three, and decided to question this one."

"Objection, Your Honor," Bean said. "His reasons are immaterial to the proceedings."

"Objection overruled," Judge Spicer said. "I'd like to know the reason for his behavior."

"Your Honor, gentlemen of the jury, I believe Billy Glaiboume, Ike Clanton and Sheriff Behan lied on the witness stand. I feel that had I cross examined them, they would only have had the opportunity to repeat their lies and thus intensify the damage they did. This witness, on the other hand," Grady pointed to Sally. "This witness is telling the truth. I feel that if the correct questions are asked, we will be able to use the truth of her answers, not to prosecute, but to defend my clients. I am, therefore, willing to construct my case around her answers."

Grady looked toward Sally, who was meeting his eyes with a questioning gaze. And yet, behind the question in her eyes, Grady saw that she was willing to trust him. He was thrilled by that, for on that trust, he felt, there would be a basis for the reconstruction of their love.

"Sally," Grady started, then he stopped. "May I call you Sally?" he asked gently. He thought of the last time they had made love, when, her name had emerged from his throat in praise of the rapture they were sharing. He felt a quick flash of heat, and he had to squeeze his hands into a fist to make the thought go away.

"I suppose so," Sally answered quietly.

"Sally, we have heard you tell how you and Billy came into town to collect your brother Ike. Why did you do this? Why didn't you wait for Ike to come home on his own accord?"

"Billy was . . ." Sally started, then she stopped and looked over at Ike. "Billy was afraid to leave Ike in town any longer," she said.

"Why?"

"He was afraid that Ike would get into trouble."

"Has he been in trouble before?"

The gallery laughed, and Judge Spicer banged his gavel. They quieted.

"Yes," Sally admitted. "He seems to have a propensity for trouble."

"Why, do you think?"

"He drinks a great deal. When he drinks too much, he does things that he shouldn't."

"Objection, Your Honor, that question called for a conclusion on the part of the witness," Bean interrupted.

"Sustained. The jury will disregard the last question and response."

"Very well," Grady said. "Sally, I believe you when you say that you and Billy came to town to get Ike and take him back home. I'm convinced that Billy was an innocent victim of circumstances who happened to be in the wrong place at the wrong time. Things like that happen sometimes. People are killed by runaway wagons, or in train wrecks, or by a bolt of lightning from the blue. But conceding Billy's innocence does not admit guilt on the part of the Earps and Doc Holliday. Now, we are coming to the most critical part of the entire trial. It will be a painful part for you, because you must relive an experience which, I know, was horrible." Grady took a deep breath. "Sally, as accurately as you possibly can make it, recreate the gunfight for us, shot for shot."

"Your Honor, is this necessary?" Bean asked. "We've already had two accounts of the battle."

"Your Honor, I want a shot by shot account," Grady said. "My clients are on trial for murder. There were thirty-four shots fired during that exchange. The way they were fired is critical to my case."

"You may proceed," Judge Spicer said.

Sally ran her hand through her hair. "When the shooting

started . . . "

"Sally, wait a minute," Grady said. "Let's start before that. What words were spoken when the Earps and the cowboys confronted each other?"

"Virgil called out for my brothers and the McClaurys to throw up their hands."

And did they?"

"Your Honor, Ike Clanton has already testified that they did throw up their hands," Bean said. "We're going over the same ground."

"The witness may answer," Judge Bean said. "Did your brothers throw up their hands, Sally?"

"No," Sally admitted.

"What did happen?"

"Billy and Frank cocked their pistols. I know, I could hear it very clearly." She shuddered. "It was a sound which cut through to my very soul."

"Did the Earps have their guns drawn?"

"No. Wait, Doc did. He was carrying a shotgun."

"What happened next?"

"Virgil spoke again. He said, 'Hold, I don't mean that. I've come to disarm you'."

"What happened next?"

"Tom McClaury had a pistol stuck down in his waistband. He yelled something, some sort of curseword, and he pulled his pistol. After that, things happened so fast."

"Try."

"Suddenly everyone had guns in their hands. I don't know who got their gun out first ... it all happened at about the same time. Everyone . . . everyone except Ike."

"What did Ike do?"

"Ike ran toward Wyatt Earp, and he . . . he," Sally looked toward Ike, who was now looking toward the floor in shame. "He begged Wyatt Earp not to shoot him. He said he wasn't shooting."

"What did Wyatt do?"

"Mr. Earp pushed him away. He told my brother, 'This Fight's commenced. Get to fighting or get out.'"

"Did Wyatt hit your brother on the head with his pistol?"

"No," Sally said. "At that moment the shooting had already started, and Wyatt Earp shot Frank in the stomach."

"Did Doc fire point blank at your brother?"

" I . . . I don't know," Sally admitted. "I really don't know. I know Doc is the one who shot Tom, but not before Tom shot Morgan Earp in the shoulder. Billy got hit about then, and he went down. I was concentrating more on Billy then than anyone else. Billy hit Virgil Earp in the leg, then Morgan Earp hit Billy in the chest and Virgil Earp hit him in the stomach."

"Did any of Wyatt's bullets find their mark?"

"Yes. He shot Tom and Frank. Doc and Morgan Earp also shot Tom and Frank. Tom staggered over to my buckboard before he died."

"Tom and Frank were killed instantly?"

"Yes."

"What about Billy?"

"No. He was the last one to die," Sally said. "After Tom and Frank had gone down, the Earps turned their attention back to Billy, but when they saw he was no danger to them, they held their fire."

"Thank you, Sally," Grady said. "I know this has been difficult for you."

Grady walked over and sat down at the table. He had taken a calculated gamble in what he had just done. He hoped it would pay off.

Grady decided not to call Wyatt or Doc to the witness stand. Their version of the fight pretty much coincided with the version given by Sally, and he believed it would strengthen his case if he let her story stand undiluted. Because he had no witnesses, the case moved to summation.

Bean was eloquent in his summation. His deep voice

rumbled like thunder in the mountains, sometimes soft and distant, sometimes crashing and immediate. Even his weakest points sounded damning under the skill of his oratory. There were some points however, which were particularly powerful indictments.

"Why did Virgil and Wyatt Earp hit Ike and Billy over the head when they came out of the cafe? Is having an innocent breakfast a crime in this city?" Bean asked. "Or was it merely one more in the long string of misdeeds perpetrated by the Earps, and designed to force the Clantons into a battle?"

Bean paused for a long moment, then with his silver tongue and golden words he went on.

"I submit to you gentlemen of the jury, that every man has his breaking point. The weakest and the most cowardly among us can be pushed to a point at which we will turn and fight. The McClaurys and the Clantons were not weak and not cowardly. But they were foolish. They were foolish to let professional gunfighters goad them into drawing against them. Consider this, gentlemen. The total number of men killed by the Earps and Doc Holliday is estimated at over twenty, not counting this latest episode. Before this battle, twenty men had already fallen before their blazing guns. Now, by contrast, how many had the Clantons and the McClaurys killed? For Billy, Frank and Tom, the answer is zero. Ike, who had been deputized by Sheriff Behan, was involved in the shooting death of one desperado, but you can hardly match that with the experience of the Earps and Doc Holliday. Perhaps that is why Ike, who was the oldest and most mature of all the cowboys, made one last, desperate effort to head off the fight. We know of course, that he was unsuccessful. And the final, most damning evidence of all, gentlemen of the jury, is the final score. The cowboys, frightened, desperate men, fighting to preserve their lives, fired seventeen rounds. Only three of their shots found their mark, and none of the three were killing shots."

Again Bean paused for effect. He was a master at such

pauses.

"The Earps and Doc Holliday, on the other hand, fired an equal number of shots, seventeen, and eleven found their mark. Eleven of seventeen shots hit their targets and, listen to this. Ten of those shots, gentlemen ... ten of them . . . were killing shots. Frank was hit in the head, abdomen, and twice in the heart. Tom was nearly torn in two by a shotgun blast, and Billy was hit six times, with only one of those, the one which hit him in his gun wrist and effectively took him out of action, not being a killing shot. Contrast this with the unskilled firing of frightened, desperate men. This is cool, professional gunplay. This, gentlemen, is murder."

Bean took one more masterful pause before he sat down, purposely drawing it out so Grady couldn't start his own summation too quickly.

Now it was Grady's time.

Bean was skilled, yes, but Grady was no slouch. In effect, he had been studying the law since he was twelve years old. In the very early days when he was following C.V. from town to town, he often had to watch the trials from the very back of the room, but even then he had been studying, watching, waiting for his own hour upon the stage. That hour was now.

Grady walked over to the jury rail and looked at the jurors.

"The question you are asked to decide is a simple one," he said. "Did Wyatt Earp and Doc Holliday kill Billy Clanton and the McClaurys because of some bloodlust, or were they driven to it? I submit that they were driven to it, and as substantiation for that contention, I ask only that you recall the words of Sally Clanton. Sally, who suffered the most, told in sweet, pained words the story as only she could tell it. Only Sally could tell it because she was the closest non-participating witness . . . and she is not capable of lying. Sally is a witness for the prosecution, Sally was hurt by the tragedy of the event, but out of her mouth came the words which will free my clients, because out of her mouth came the truth."

Grady walked away from the jury box and looked at Sally.

Sally was crying quietly. In this act, Grady had borrowed a page from Bean's book, in that he had created a dramatic pause.

"Consider this," he went on. "By Sally's admission, the last thing Virgil said before the shooting started was; 'Hold, I don't mean that.' He said that when Billy and Frank cocked their pistols, that ominous sound which sent a chill to Sally's soul. What is the significance of that statement by Virgil? It is significant because it proves, that in that last second before the fight, Virgil still was not committed to gunplay. He was not committed to gunplay until it was forced on him by Tom McClaury, who, by Sally Clanton's own testimony, went for his gun first."

Grady knew he was scoring points now, because he could see the reaction in the faces of the jurors. Some of them were even nodding in agreement.

"Now, consider Ike Clanton's last act before the fighting began. He ran toward Wyatt. Just what he said to Wyatt, and what Wyatt did may be in question, but there is one thing which is not in question. Wyatt did not kill Ike. He could have. If, as Ike claims, the Earps instigated this entire thing just to kill the Clantons and the McClaurys, why didn't Wyatt kill Earp then? In the heat of the battle it probably wouldn't have caused any more stir than what didn't happen. But the fact remains that Wyatt didn't kill Ike, and neither did Doc. You heard the distinguished prosecutor regale us with tales of the skill of my clients. Would a person of such skill, firing a shotgun at point-blank range, miss, if he intended to kill? The answer, gentlemen, is no. Ike wasn't killed, because he was no threat, and Wyatt, Virgil, Morgan, and Doc were acting not from blood lust, but in self-defense. Finally, from Sally Clanton's own words, when Frank and Tom lay dead, the Earps and Doc Holliday didn't shoot Billy again because he represented no danger. Wyatt and Doc were officers charged with the duty of arresting and disarming brave and determined men who were experts in the use of firearms, as quick as thought and as certain as death, and who had previously declared their intentions not to be arrested nor disarmed. When you consider the condition of lawlessness and disregard for human life which exists in this country, the fear and feeling of insecurity that has existed; the supposed relevance of bad, desperate and reckless men who have been a terror to the country and have kept away capital and enterprise, and considering the many threats which were publicly made against the Earps, you can attach no criminality to their act. There is only one decision to be rendered, gentlemen, and that is not guilty."

The jury deliberated for twenty minutes. While they were out Ike came over to speak to Grady.

"If you want to see your friends again, you better hope the jury comes back with a verdict of guilty."

"So, it was you," Grady said.

Ike smiled. "Was there ever any doubt?"

"If anything has happened to C.V. and Bianca . . . " Grady started, but Ike interrupted him.

"Nothin's happened yet. It's up to you to see that nothin' does happen." Ike laughed, evilly, then walked away. Sally came over to Grady then.

"Grady," she said quietly. "I'm sorry about everything. I was badly hurt when Billy was killed. I wanted to strike back. I don't hold the Earps blameless, but neither do I hold them solely to blame. I will accept whatever decision the jury renders. What I'm more interested in now is what decision you are going to render about me."

"What do you mean?" Grady asked, scarcely daring to hope.

"Would you be willing to start again? Could we go back to where we were and pick up the pieces?"

Grady smiled at her. "Pick up the pieces of what?" he asked. "My heart never broke ... I never fell out of love with you, Sally. If it's possible, I love you now more than I ever did."

"The jury's comin' back!" someone shouted. "The jury's comin' back!"

Because Grady and Sally considered it inappropriate to kiss here, in the courtroom, they merely squeezed each other's hand, then Sally hurried back to her seat while they awaited the verdict.

The jury filed in, then sat down, trying not to give away the decision by the expressions on their faces. Judge Spicer returned to the court, then called it to order.

"Mr. Foreman, have you reached a verdict?"

"We have, your Honor."

"Would the defendants and their counsel please stand?"

Grady, Wyatt and Doc stood up. Behind them, in the gallery, Grady could hear the collective pause of breath while they waited.

"What is your verdict?"

The foreman looked right at Grady, Wyatt and Doc.

"We find the defendants Wyatt Earp and John Holliday ... not guilty," the foreman said.

"Good job, Grady!" Morgan shouted from the gallery, then the court exploded into shouts, some of joy, some of anger.

"Ford!" Ike shouted.

Grady looked over at Ike.

"You've seen the last of your friends!"

Chapter Sixteen

"WHAT WAS ALL THAT ABOUT?" Wyatt asked Grady after Ike left the courtroom.

"Ike has C.V. and Bianca held prisoner somewhere," Grady explained. "He was holding them to ensure . . . "

"I think I know," Wyatt said. "He wanted to make sure he didn't miss out on an invite to my necktie party, right?"

"Yes."

"We've got to stop him now, then," Wyatt said. "If he gets to them, he might carry through on his threat."

"I know," Grady said. "But so far we haven't been able to find them. I've got Boston outside the courthouse. He's going to follow Ike."

"That'll still be risky," Wyatt said.

"It's our only chance."

"No, it isn't," Sally said. Sally had been standing back several feet, ostensibly out of the conversation, though it was obvious that she was listening to what was being said.

"What?" Grady asked. "Sally, do you know where C.V. and Bianca are?"

"I didn't know until now that Ike was responsible for their disappearance," Sally said. "But if he is the one responsible, then I know where they must be."

"Where?"

"Ike tried to mine some silver once," Sally said.

"Yes, I remember," Grady said. "Your father mentioned it when I went with Boston to recover those mules."

"My guess is he has them stashed away in that old silver mine," Sally said. "Marshal Earp, if you can find some way to prevent my brother from going there, arrest him and hold him on some charge for a few hours, I could lead you to the mine."

"Why would you do that?" Wyatt asked suspiciously.

"To save Ike's life," Sally said simply. "If you follow him there, you'll kill him, won't you?"

"I won't lie to you ma'am," Wyatt said. "I won't be going there to kill him, but if he stands in the way, I'll have to."

"Marshal, you know and I know he'll stand in the way," Sally said. "Arrest him."

"On what charge?" Wyatt asked.

"Come now, Marshal. What charge?" Sally fixed Wyatt with a cynical smile. "Since when did that become so important to you?"

Wyatt responded with a little laugh. "Yeah," he said. "I guess you're right. All right, I'll find somethin' to pull your brother in on."

"Come on, Sally," Grady said. "Whoever has C.V. and Bianca might start getting antsy."

It had taken Grady and Sally an hour of hard riding to reach this point, which was only ten miles out of town, but they were nearly to the top of Apache Peak, a mountain which was over 7600 feet high. They got off their horses to give them a much needed breather, then walked out to an overlook. Far below them, the San Pedro river resembled a green snake stretched out across the yellow desert floor. The green was from the vegetation which grew alongside the riverbank. The river itself was a small, brown line scratched through the middle of the green.

"How much further is it?" Grady asked. "It'll be dark in an hour and a half."

It was cool up here, and Grady imagined that at this altitude, and this late in the year, it was probably very cold at night. He hoped C.V. and Bianca had not suffered unduly from the cold.

"Not much further," Sally said. She pointed to a high, obelisk-shaped rock. "It's just on the other side of that rock."

"Which way does the trail approach?"

"This way," Sally said, pointing.

"Then I'm going in the other way. They'll be watching the trail."

"You won't be able to ride," Sally warned. "And there's one stretch that you can't make on foot."

"If C.V. is in there, I'll get to him if I have to walk on the side like a fly," Grady said. He checked his pistol, then put it back in the holster.

"You stay here," he said. He pointed to a rock. "If anyone comes down that trail but me, C.V. or Bianca. . . ." he let the sentence hang there, but Sally picked up on his meaning.

"If they get this far, Grady, they won't get any further," she said. She pulled a rifle from the saddle sheath.

Grady started to go, but Sally reached out for him. They kissed, a long, slow, hot kiss which held within it a poignant farewell if things went wrong, a promise for the future if things went well. Grady smiled at her, then started working his way around the side of the mountain to the mineshaft opening.

It was very hard going. Grady had been at it for half an hour and he could still see Sally, watching him anxiously. He was now clinging to the side of the mountain, moving only when he could find the tiniest handhold, the smallest crevice for a foot. Behind him was nothing but air, and if he missed a hand or a foothold, he had a drop of over a mile to the rocks below.

Sweat was pouring into Grady's eyes. It was funny. Just half an hour ago he had thought it was cool, and had even worried as to whether or not C.V. and Bianca had managed to stay warm.

Grady stopped worrying about C.V. and Bianca now, and started worrying about himself. He had almost reached an impasse. He had progressed four fifths of the way around the rock, but for the last five minutes he had been unable to go on, because he hadn't found another foothold.

Reluctantly, Grady decided to start back. He would have to approach the mine opening by the trail. It would mean he would risk being seen, but his alternative was to fall to a certain death from this rock.

Grady reached for the handhold he had surrendered five minutes earlier, the first step in retracing his path. He had a good handhold, then he moved his foot across. This time the small, slate outcropping which had supported his weight earlier failed, and with a sickening sensation in his stomach, Grady felt himself falling. He threw himself against the side scraping and tearing at his flesh. He flailed against the wall with his hands, and after a drop of some fifteen feet, found a sturdy juniper tree. The tree supported his weight and he hung there for a moment, looking down between his feet at the desert floor, far below. He saw the slate outcropping which had broken under his weight, still in free fall. Almost ten seconds later he saw the little puff of dust from where it impacted.

Grady looked to his right. About four feet away from him there was a narrow shelf. If he could gain that shelf he would be all right. He took a deep breath, then swung his feet to the right and up. He caught the ledge with the heel of his boot, then, slowly, he worked himself up, pushing away from the juniper tree until his knees were also on the ledge. Finally he let go of the tree and worked himself up slowly until, at last, he was on the ledge.

After that it got easy. The ledge showed signs of having been a trail at one time, possibly a trail which had existed until erosion took part of it away. Grady found that he could even walk upright. After a moment the nauseating fear which had overtaken him earlier was gone, and he strolled as easily

Warriors of the Code

along the trail as if he were walking down the board sidewalks of Tombstone. A few minutes later he smelled a campfire, and he knew he was close. He drew his pistol and walked very quietly.

"I make it no more'n half an hour till dark," Grady heard someone saying. "If he ain't back by dark, we'll just kill 'em 'n be done with it. We'll kill the man first, 'n then have us a little fun with the woman. You'd like that, wouldn't you Pancho?"

There was no answer to the question, and Grady wondered if whoever was talking was talking to himself, or possibly to a horse. He knew that mountain men, men who lived long periods of time all by themselves, often talked to themselves just to hear a voice. It became such an ingrained habit in them that even when someone else was around they continued to do it.

"When that Apache cut out your tongue, he sure didn't do me no favor," the voice said. "One of these days I'm gonna get spooked by your bein' so quiet all the time, 'n I'm just gonna have to shoot you."

Grady eased his way closer until he was behind a small rock outcropping. He had his gun in his hand as he looked over the top of the rock. From here he could see two men around a small fire. Behind them, the mouth of a mine. One of the men was sitting down. He was a small, wirey-looking Mexican. The other man was standing with his back to Grady. He was a big man, as big as Boston Corbett. There was a fire going, and the big man walked over to the fire. He held his hands over it to warm himself, and when a puff of wind blew smoke into his face, he walked around to the other side of the fire so that he was facing Grady.

Grady gasped aloud. This was the same man who had led the renegade Indians in the attack which had killed his mother and father. That had been many years ago, but the face was so imprinted in Grady's mind that he would never forget it. If he lived for one hundred years, the face would still be fresh.

"What the hell was that?" the big, redheaded man said. He pulled his pistol and looked toward the rock.

Grady picked up a stone and threw it. When it hit, the redheaded man and the Mexican turned toward the sound. That gave Grady the opportunity to step out from behind the rock. He stepped into the open with his gun in his hand.

"Drop your guns," he commanded.

Both men turned toward him. Inexplicably, the redheaded man smiled.

"Boy, how the hell did you get there?" he asked. "I done scouted that way out pretty good. There ain't no way a mountain goat could come from that way."

"Where are C.V. and Bianca?"

"Oh, they're back in the mine," the big man said. "They can't come out right now, they're tied up." He laughed at his joke.

"You," Grady said to the Mexican. "Drop your gun and go in there and untie them."

"Don't do it, Pancho," the big man said. "Let's just kill this little son of a bitch 'n get it over with."

"You forget, I'm holding a gun on you," Grady said.

"There's two of us," the big man said. "While you're shootin' at one of us, the other'n will be shootin' you. And I gotta tell you now, I don't think I can be stopped by one bullet. I've eaten more bullets than you've shot away in your lifetime, pup. When the smoke clears away, you'll be lyin' there dead, 'n I'll ride away."

"No," Grady said. "I watched you ride away once. I don't intend to watch a second time."

The redheaded man looked puzzled.

"Do I know you, boy?"

"No," Grady said. "But I know you."

"You know old Red Bear?"

"Not by name," Grady said. "But I watched you and that bunch of savages you were with kill my mother and father."

"Which mama and daddy was that, boy? I've killed lots

of mamas and daddies."

"We were in a single wagon in Kansas."

Red Bear suddenly grinned.

"About fourteen or fifteen years ago. Yeah, I remember you, boy. You know, that was real dumb of your ol' man to be travellin' out there, all alone. And without 'ny money too, as I recall. All we got for our troubles was a little grub. But what are you complainin' for? I let you live didn't I? What were you then? Thirteen, fourteen years old?"

"I was twelve," Grady said.

"Well, 'n look at you now. I should'a killed you then, saved the trouble of having to go through it now."

"You've got a gun in your hand, mister," Grady said menacingly. "Drop it or use it, right now."

Red Beard started up with his gun hand, but at the first twitch of his arm, Grady squeezed his trigger.

Red Beard was wrong on two counts. He had said that while Grady was shooting at one of them, the other would be shooting Grady. The Mexican, however, showed quickly that he had no taste for action, and as soon as Brady's gun roared, he threw his own gun down and his hands up.

The other thing Red Beard was wrong about was the number of bullets it would take to kill him. He said he couldn't be killed by one bullet. Grady's bullet hit Red Beard right between the eyes. One bullet had been enough.

"C.V.!" Grady called. "C.V.! Are you all right?"

"Grady! We're in here!"

One week later, Sally was standing in front of the mirror in the bedroom of her house. A heavy set Mexican woman was helping her get dressed. The noise of a celebration from outside floated in and a child's squeal of delight told them that another pinata had been broken.

Sally moved over to the window and looked outside. The people were celebrating a wedding ceremony. This was the second wedding ceremony in as many days. Yesterday, Bianca had become Mrs. C.V. Battenburg. Today, Sally was becoming Mrs. Grady Ford.

"Maria, do you think the people out there are upset that there isn't enough room to invite everyone inside for the ceremony?"

"Do they sound upset?" Maria replied. "Listen to the music and the laughter. They're very happy for you."

"I wish Ike could be happy for me," Sally said. Ike had been in town, drunk and sullen, ever since the trial. The news that his sister was marrying Grady Ford had made his disposition even worse.

"I do not wish to speak ill of your brother, senorita, but I do not think he can be happy about anything."

"I know Billy would have been happy. I just wish Ike would come around."

"You cannot live your life for your brother, senorita," Maria said. "Senor Billy tried to, and it got him killed."

"Yes," Sally said. She sighed. "Yes, I know."

Sally returned to the mirror to look at herself. She smiled. "This is the last time I will see myself as a single woman," she said.

"Senor Ford is a good man. You will be very happy, I know."

"Oh, I know I will." She looked around her bedroom. "I'm going to miss this room," she said. "I'm going to miss this ranch." She hugged herself. "But Maria, I'm so happy that there's no room for sadness that I'm leaving. Is that terribly wrong of me?"

"No," Maria said. "This room, this ranch, these are the things of your childhood and your childhood will be with you forever. Now you become a woman, and you start a new life. It is good to start a new life in a new place'"

"Los Angeles," Sally said. She laughed. "What a funny name for a town. A town with such a name can never become much. Why Grady and C.V. want to go there I'll never know."

There was a knock on the bedroom door, and when Maria

opened it, Bianca stood there, beaming.

"Good morning, Mrs. Battenburg," Sally said, laughing.

"Good morning, Miss Clanton," Bianca replied. "It is about time for you to become Mrs. Ford. Are you ready?"

"Yes."

In a moment, Sally's life would change forever. Every step she took now was putting distance between her and the violent past, and bringing her closer to a new future. It was all she could do to keep from running.

Robert Vaughan

A look at Hearts Divided (The Founders Book 5) by Robert Vaughan

Arriving in St. Louis to search for his missing brother, Danny O'Lee meets a lovely but mysterious young girl named Liberty Wells who has known his brother and perhaps been his lover before they were parted by the bitter slavery question. Danny is led to Quantrill and his guerrillas, among them Frank and Jesse James, who are ravaging anti-slavery Kansas. Next, he meets and is converted to the Union cause by a beautiful black abolitionist.

Finally, after having his hairbreadth adventures, Danny O'Lee finds his beloved brother—fighting on the other side—at the bloody Battle of Shiloh, a turning point in the little known Civil War in the West.

There, a hero is born, a villain unmasked and a loved is renewed, while the Union finds a general in an obscure, cigar-smoking, whiskey-drinking sphinx of a man names U.S. Grant.

About the Author

Robert Vaughan sold his first book when he was 19. That was 57 years and nearly 500 books ago. He wrote the novelization for the mini series *Andersonville*. Vaughan wrote, produced, and appeared in the History Channel documentary Vietnam Homecoming. His books have hit the NYT bestseller list seven times. He has won the Spur Award, the PORGIE Award (Best Paperback Original), the Western Fictioneers Lifetime Achievement Award, received the Readwest President's Award for Excellence in Western Fiction, is a member of the American Writers Hall of Fame and is a Pulitzer Prize nominee. Vaughn is also a retired army officer, helicopter pilot with three tours in Vietnam. And received the Distinguished Flying Cross, the Purple Heart, The Bronze Star with three oak leaf clusters, the Air Medal for valor with 35 oak leaf clusters, the Army Commendation Medal, the Meritorious Service Medal, and the Vietnamese Cross of Gallantry.

Find more great titles by Robert Vaughan and Wolfpack Publishing at http://wolfpackpublishing.com/robert-vaughan/

Robert Vaughan

Made in the USA
Middletown, DE
17 August 2023